ONE INCREDIBLE JOURNEY

From City to Farm

Enjoy ¨

Wendi Hartman

Wendi Hartman

Blessings,

Patricia Lewis

eGenCo

eGenCo
Chambersburg, Pennsylvania

Email: info@egen.co
Website: www.egen.co

facebook.com/egenbooks

twitter.com/egen_co

youtube.com/egenpub

pinterest.com/eGenDMP

instagram.com/egen.co

Cover illustration by Bill Davis
Interior illustrations by Bill Davis and Sharon Henley

Library of Congress Cataloging-in-Publication Data

Library of Congress Control Number: 2020920410

ISBN: 978-1-68019-017-5   Paperback
         978-1-68019-018-2   eBook
         978-1-68019-019-9   eBook

Printed in the United States of America

DEDICATION

I dedicate this book to my Heavenly father and my earthly father. I have always known that my Heavenly father had a special plan for me. There was a reason that He had my time on earth begin on Epiphany, January 6th. There was also a reason that I weighed 3 pounds, 3 ounces and was, as my favorite truckie put it, hatched at 0331.

I also dedicate this book to my earthly father, Lieutenant Frederick Benjiman Creps Hartman. He was the one who first introduced me to Jesus. It is also because of him that I enjoy studying history, decorating my home with antiques, serving others, and using the creative gifts God blessed me with to make the world a better place. I also inherited his personality. My favorite truckie answered his last alarm on January 17, 2020. Though he is no longer physically here, in some way, he is part of my life every single day. Folks, I encourage you to spend time with those you care about and love because you never know when you will have to say, "See ya later."

Blessings,

Wendi Hartman

A NOTE FROM THE AUTHOR

I live in Pennsylvania with Mike, my husband of twenty-seven years, and two four-legged meowing children, Miss Holly and Miss Molly. They own our home, and Mike and I just live there. I am the daughter of a career firefighter and Pennsylvania farm girl. From watching my dad serve our community and helping out on my mother's family farm, I learned the value of hard work and caring for others. I completed my undergraduate degree in elementary education, at Messiah University (back when it was Messiah College) and then returned there thirty years later to complete a master's certificate in social entrepreneurship. Now, I'm looking forward to a seminary education journey. My diverse background has helped me minister to a wide variety of individuals and will continue to do so.

To me, it is important to live one's faith daily and be an encouragement to others. God has given me a mission to Happily Offer People Encouragement (HOPE) by Walking with Women on their life journeys. I use writing, puppetry, Snack-n-Chats, balloon art, and many other avenues to minister to others. As a result of my many interests, I am becoming known as Wendi Hartman – The Renaissance Writer. To learn more about my ministries, visit my website at wendiwrites.com.

I started my writing adventure in 2006. At the time, I had a medical issue that gave me insomnia, so I found myself writing between the hours of 11 p.m. and 1 a.m. I used my background to write stories about what I know. Over the course of several months I wrote three middle-grade books for children ages 9 to 12. These writings will be published in my next book.

I wrote Part 1 of this book, "The Amish Impact," after my husband and I lost our home in 2009 as a result of personal financial reversals and a serious car accident in 2010. Since we were down to one vehicle, he would drop me off at work hours before I had to clock in. So, to pass the time, I sat in the breakroom and wrote. Then, in 2013, God provided us with another home and told me to keep writing. Therefore, that is what I did. I followed God's lead and have been blessed in many ways by doing so.

I would like to encourage you to find that gift God has blessed you with, your passion, and go use it. Follow your dream. Yes, you may be criticized and judged for doing so. However, I can tell you from personal experience that you will never be truly happy until you are doing what God has called you to do. Therefore, I Happily Offer People (YOU) Encouragement to follow where He is leading you.

Blessings,

Wendi Hartman

TABLE OF CONTENTS

PART 1

THE AMISH IMPACT

CHAPTER 1
LEAVING BOSTON

Eleven-year-old Elizabeth Hopewell's eyes ran down the page, trying to take in each word. Her friend Ann, a package of pretzels in her hand, sat down beside her under the tree in front of their school, but Elizabeth barely looked up from her book.

"Hello? Earth to Elizabeth!" Ann waved her hand in front of Elizabeth's face. Elizabeth jolted back to reality.

"Oh, I'm sorry, Ann. I didn't mean to ignore you. This book about the Amish culture is really interesting. My grandparents actually live near them in Pennsylvania. Are you feeling any better?"

Ann shrugged. "I'm not feeling as bad as I was on Saturday. So I guess you could say I am." She shuffled the pretzels in her package and held them out to Elizabeth. "Want one?"

"Sure." Elizabeth reached into the bag and pulled out a pretzel. "You know. These are really good."

Ann smiled. "Yeah, the taste of gluten free foods has improved the last few years."

"Have a great summer!" a snotty voice said behind the girls.

"You too, Samantha," replied Elizabeth as she watched her walk past them.

Samantha turned around and gave Elizabeth a disapproving look as she got into her mother's car. Elizabeth waved to her as they drove past.

"How do you manage to be nice to her when she is so mean to everyone?" Ann asked.

"My dad has often told me that those who are hurting are usually mean to others," said Elizabeth. "And my parents always say to treat others the way you want to be treated. So, that's what I try to do with Samantha."

Just then, her twelve-year-old brother Eli came walking toward them with his buddy Josh. "Hey, Elizabeth! What did you guys do for the last day?" Eli said.

"Oh, the usual stuff, snacks, a movie, and sharing what we're planning to do this summer. What about you?"

"The same thing," said Eli. "Well, we better start walking home."

As they started towards home Eli and Josh talked about the soccer game from the movie their class had watched.

As Ann and Elizabeth walked together Ann asked, "So have you written any more stories?"

"I just finished writing one last night," replied Elizabeth. "When I was supposed to be sleeping!"

They both laughed in unison. "Will you let me read it this summer?" asked Ann. "I really loved your last two."

"Sure!" said Elizabeth.

When the group arrived at Eli and Elizabeth's home, they said goodbye to their friends and started walking towards the open garage door. About halfway up their driveway, Elizabeth turned and waved to her friend Ann one last time as she and Josh turned the corner.

When they opened the door, they saw their parents sitting in the living room, heads bent over their hands. Their father, Jacob, looked up at them, his eyes sober and his brow knitted with concern.

Eli and Elizabeth couldn't help feeling worried. Dad wasn't supposed to be home this early. Something wasn't right.

"Sit down, kids," Jacob said, his voice strained. He gestured to the adjacent love seat.

Eli and Elizabeth sat quietly and braced themselves. Their mother, Mary, sniffed, her eyes red-rimmed and teary.

Jacob cleared his throat. "Kids, I have some big news. Last week, my boss called me to say the agency had to make some large budget cuts. They can't afford to keep me on staff anymore. I'm losing my job."

Eli looked stunned as Elizabeth gasped. "Daddy!" she burst out. She ran to him, sat in his lap and gave him a hug.

"Everything's going to be okay, honey," Jacob assured her, hugging her back.

"Dad…can you get another job?" Eli stammered.

Jacob sighed deeply. "I spent all last week looking for jobs, son. There are no suitable positions available. A lot of social workers are out of work at the moment. It's just…a difficult time."

"But…what are you going to do?" Elizabeth whispered.

"Well," Jacob said, glancing at Mary and then back at the kids. "We talked on the phone with Grandma and Grandpa today."

"Grandma and Grandpa?" Eli asked amazed.

"Grandpa told me that the local counseling center needs a part-time social worker. One of their neighbors, Mr. Hersh, has a house on his farm, where he would let us stay if I helped him with farm work for a while. His kids have all grown up and moved out on their own, so he could really use the extra help."

Elizabeth's eyes widened in shock. "You mean…we're moving to Pennsylvania?"

Jacob nodded and Mary took a deep breath. "You both know I've been longing to retire from the public-school system so I could homeschool you," she said slowly. "Moving to Pennsylvania is really the perfect opportunity to do that, and the timing couldn't be better. I'm so sorry it means taking you away from your friends though, honey." She squeezed Elizabeth's knee reassuringly. "I promise we'll do what we can to stay in touch with them."

"We're all going to miss Boston," Jacob said. "And we will try to come back and visit when we can. We've done and shared so much here—we've made lots of memories. But Mom and I have looked at all our options and we've agreed that it won't work to stay here anymore. But we know new friends, adventures, and memories are waiting for us in Pennsylvania."

Eli and Elizabeth sat silent and stunned, trying to take in this world-shattering news. Leave Boston?! They had grown up in this city. How could they say goodbye to their best friends, the Central Library, the Boston Commons, their favorite restaurants and museums? From what they remembered of their few summer trips to Grandma and Grandpa's country home, there weren't many of those places in rural Pennsylvania. Sure, those week-long visits had been fun—they had both loved playing with their grandparents' dogs and kittens, and once even had gotten to feed a newborn calf with a bottle. But living there? That was hard to believe.

Glancing first at his sister and then back at his concerned parents, Eli quietly asked the hard question: "So, when do we have to leave?"

Their father sighed again. "At the end of the month. Friday is my last day. Then we'll have a couple weeks to pack up the house and say goodbye to our friends and favorite spots."

"Oh, thank goodness!" exclaimed Elizabeth.

"We wouldn't leave without letting you say goodbye, honey," Jacob assured her. "Mom and I want to make this move as easy on everyone as possible. If we all work and stick together, we're going to make it just fine, okay? Think you two can do that?" He looked hopefully at his children.

After a pause, Eli nodded, "I'll try, Dad."

"Me too," Elizabeth chimed in quietly.

"Excellent." Jacob smiled at them. "Well, we have a lot to get done to get ready for this new adventure…starting tomorrow. The end of the month will be here in no time. Why don't you guys wash up and get ready for dinner? It'll be ready in a few minutes."

"Okay, Dad," Eli said. He looked over at Elizabeth. She nodded, confirming what he was thinking: *Let's get upstairs where we can talk about this.* They hugged their parents, zipped upstairs, washed their hands, and hurried to Elizabeth's walk-in closet.

They sat down cross-legged on the floor. "What are we going to do?" Elizabeth whispered. "I don't want to move!"

"Me either," Eli said, his brow furrowed. "There has to be something we can do."

After a moment of intense concentration, Elizabeth said, "What if we convinced Mom to wait just one more year to homeschool us. Then she could keep working...at least until Dad finds another job."

"Yeah!" Eli said. "I don't want to leave my friends. The other thing is, Mom and Dad could sell the house. If we move back to a smaller house like our old one, then maybe we would have enough money to stay in Boston."

"I liked our old house." Elizabeth smiled.

"How about this," Eli suggested, "You talk to Mom about not homeschooling next year and I'll ask Dad about the house idea."

"Okay," Elizabeth nodded. "Oh, I hope this works!"

"Me too!"

"What if..." Elizabeth's voice faltered. "What if it doesn't? What if we really have to go live in Pennsylvania?"

Eli's face fell. "I guess...I guess we can just pretend that we're on vacation for a while. I mean, Mom and Dad won't make us stay there forever if we hate it, right?"

"I don't think so," Elizabeth said.

"But let's see if we can find a way to stay first."

"Yeah," Elizabeth said. She threw her arms around her brother. With a sigh, Eli hugged her back, then put a finger to his lips and silently snuck out of the closet and back downstairs for dinner.

The next day, Eli and Elizabeth both tried to find the right moment to talk with their parents, but it never arose. While their father finished out the final days at his job, their mother tackled putting their house up for sale and delegating the kids with a seemingly endless list of tasks to get it packed and spotless. Each day was filled from morning to evening with putting their belongings in boxes, designating items to throw or give away, and deep cleaning every available surface. Free time was slotted with final goodbyes to friends or visits to their favorite places around Boston.

When Elizabeth broke the news to Ann, Ann's face crumpled. "Oh, Elizabeth," she said, throwing her arms around Elizabeth. "I'm going to miss you."

"I'll miss you, too," Elizabeth said. As she pulled away, she said, "If you ever go into the hospital again, please tell me. I want to help you in any way I can."

"Okay," said Ann. "Thanks for being there for me."

Eli and Elizabeth kept trying to find the proper moment to talk to their parents. Finally, on Saturday Jacob asked Eli to help him clean out the garage. Eli set to work untangling a mass of electrical cords while Jacob gathered up tools. After a few minutes, Eli braved the issue. "Dad, what if we got a smaller house like we used to have? Couldn't we stay in Boston then?"

Jacob straightened up, his arms full of wrenches and hammers. "I'm sorry, son," he said. "Mom and I thought about that, but houses in Massachusetts are very expensive right now—even the small ones. We have people in Pennsylvania who are willing to help us, and unfortunately, we just simply don't have that type of support here. It's not that people here don't care; it's just they don't deal with problems the same way as people do where Grandpa and Grandma live."

"Why is that, Dad?" Eli asked.

Jacob snapped his tool box shut. "It's just different in the city. It's easier to help one another in some ways and harder in others. You will find that the people in Grandma and Grandpa's community help each other a lot. Life is slower and simpler there and folks have the time to help one another."

"Slower and simpler..." Eli repeated as he wrapped the coils of an extension cord around his arm.

"Yes." Jacob said, giving his son a knowing smile.

"Does that mean...*boring*?" Eli ventured, flushing as he confessed this secret fear. "I mean, what are we going to do there? It's fun to play with the animals for a week at Grandma and Grandpa's, but what else are we going to do?"

Jacob laughed. "Don't worry, son. It will be different, but I'm pretty sure you won't be bored. I grew up there, remember? And I had plenty of adventures at Grandma and Grandpa's. You know, one time, I chased a calf that escaped its pen. I had to get it back somehow, so I chased it all through the pasture. But it was a Sunday, and we had just gotten back from church. So I chased it and came back, covered from head to toe in mud. Your grandmother shook her head and smiled when she saw my clothes and said, 'So much for good Sunday clothes.'"

Eli laughed heartily at the thought of his dad covered in mud.

Meanwhile, Mary and Elizabeth washed window frames and baseboards in the living room.

"Mom, may I ask you something?" Elizabeth said timidly.

"Sure, honey," Mary replied, scrubbing away at a stubborn scuff mark.

"Well, I talked with Eli, and we were just wondering…what if we put off homeschooling for a year? That way you could teach until Dad gets a job and we wouldn't have to move."

Mary looked over at Elizabeth, her face softening. "Oh, sweetie," she sighed. "I know you want to stay." She put her cleaning rag down, walked over to Elizabeth and drew her into her arms. "But I've already put in my resignation. I've dreamed of coming home to teach you for years," she said, looking into her daughter's face. "Your father and I both agree that it's time, and I think it will be a lot of fun to start in Pennsylvania. I'm already looking forward to all the things we can do together there that we can't do here."

"Really?" Elizabeth said, surprised. "Like what?"

"Well…" Mary began, stroking her hair. "We'll be able to have a garden. Maybe some chickens. You may learn how to milk a cow."

Elizabeth couldn't help growing curious. *Maybe it won't be so bad after all,* she thought.

By the last day of the month, the moving truck was fully packed and the house was spotless. At midnight, the Hopewells bundled into their SUV. Jacob's friend, "Mr. Bob," as he was known to Elizabeth and Eli, was scheduled to follow them the next day with the moving van. Elizabeth and Eli pressed their faces to the window to take their last look at their beloved home. Elizabeth couldn't help shedding tears as it disappeared from view. "Goodbye, house…Goodbye Boston," she whispered.

When they reached the highway, everyone except for Jacob, who was driving, snuggled in for a long nap. Hours later, they stopped in New Jersey for an early breakfast, then pushed on into Pennsylvania. Now wide awake, Eli and Elizabeth again pressed their faces to the windows to take in the sights of their new state. The vibrant green hills rolled on forever, it seemed. After a few minutes of hearing the two of them read off every sign they could see, their mother spoke up. "Hey, let's play the Alphabet game!"

"Yes! Allentown!" Eli announced, wasting no time.

"Bethlehem!" Elizabeth cried out.

After a few rounds of the game, Jacob interrupted and asked, "Hey, we're getting near Harrisburg. Do you want to see where I went to college? We could make a quick visit to the campus—just drive through."

Neither Eli or Elizabeth knew what to say. Their dad had never really told them much about his college days. After a moment, Eli said, "Sure, Dad, if you want to show us."

"Great!" Jacob replied. "The exit is just a few miles ahead." Minutes later he took an exit off the expressway. Soon, they saw a huge sign marking the entrance of Messiah University. "This is it," Jacob said, turning into the campus drive.

Eli and Elizabeth soaked up the sights of the grand brick and cement buildings. Stately old trees stood over green lawns as students swarmed beneath them on the sidewalks.

"Hey, there's my old dorm!" Jacob said, pointing to one of the buildings. "And there's Boyer, where I spent most of my time—the social work department is in there." As he drove slowly along, he explained each of the school buildings as they passed. Last of all, he drove them over a red covered bridge leading to the athletic fields. "This is Yellow Breeches Creek," he said. "When British soldiers crossed it in the Revolutionary War days, their white breeches turned yellow from all the limestone in the water. That's how it got its name."

"Cool," said Eli, scanning the fields ahead. Suddenly he noticed a young woman with a small white circle of fabric on her head sitting by the creek, reading a book. "Hey Dad, what is that lady wearing on her head?" he asked.

Jacob looked to see where Eli was pointing. "She's wearing a prayer covering[1], son. Some of the church women down here wear them."

"Like Grandma Hopewell," said Elizabeth, reminding her brother.

"Oh, yeah," Eli nodded.

"That's right," replied her father. "It's part of the Plain church culture."

"Will we be going to a Plain church now?" asked Eli curiously.

Jacob didn't answer right away. He sighed and said, "I don't know yet, son. But we'll certainly be getting to know some of the

---

1   A small, usually white head covering commonly worn by women in Plain churches. In Amish society, it's known as a Knapp.

Plain people more including Grandma and Grandpa. Though, as you'll find out soon enough, not everyone lives like Grandma and Grandpa. Their church members have electricity and cars, but some Plain people do not."

"Like the Amish," said Elizabeth. "Grandma told me that one time."

"Right again, Elizabeth," said her father, smiling.

"Wait!" Elizabeth burst out. "Does this mean I'm going to have to wear a skirt all the time? Yuck!"

"No, no," replied Jacob. He glanced over at Mary, pausing for her to comment. But she shook her head, so Jacob continued. "Most women do wear skirts where we're going. But we're not going to force any kind of radical changes on you guys just so you can fit in. We're just introducing you a little more to Grandpa and Grandma's way of life, and…" He caught their eyes in the rearview mirror. "You'll undoubtedly be learning about the beliefs and practices of the Plain people. I expect you to be respectful, kind, and understanding towards them as I would expect you to be to anyone else. Okay?"

"Yes, sir," they both replied softly, looking down.

"Don't worry, kids, you're not in trouble. I'm simply trying to prepare you. I'm sure you're going to do just fine adjusting to everything." He smiled into the rearview mirror. "Now, let's head to Grandpa and Grandma's house. I'm ready to get out of this car."

The Hopewells were quiet as they departed from Messiah and navigated back to the highway. After a few minutes of cruising along past townships and forest, Elizabeth asked, "Dad?"

"Yes, honey?"

"If Grandma and Grandpa are Plain people, doesn't that mean you grew up in a Plain church too?"

Her father hesitated, then nodded. "Your mother and I both grew up in Plain churches, Elizabeth."

"So...why did you leave?"

"Well..." Jacob began. "It's a long story... But I promise you both that we will tell you that story soon. Deal?"

Eli and Elizabeth looked at each other, eyes wide, thoughts racing. Why had their parents never told them about this? What did it mean? Instinctively, Elizabeth scooted closer to her brother. Everything in their world was changing, but at least they had each other.

"Deal, Dad," she said softly.

CHAPTER 2
SETTLING IN

"There it is!" Eli announced as the stone-end barn came into view. He pointed to the limestone house, rail-fenced yard, and well-groomed flowerbeds. To his and Elizabeth's surprise, however, their father did not slow down as they approached the gravel driveway, but continued past it.

"Dad, where are we going? Aren't we going to stop and say hi to Grandma and Grandpa?" asked Eli.

"We'll be seeing Grandma and Grandpa very soon," replied Jacob. "I just want to get to where we're going first. When I get out of this car, I want to stay out of it."

After driving a few hundred feet further, he turned at a mailbox that read "Hersh." Ahead, they saw a large brick house and a white, wooden-sided barn, both surrounded by green, perfectly trimmed lawns. About fifty yards from the brick house stood a small, two-story, weatherboard house with peeling white paint.

"This is it, kids. This is Mr. Hersh's farm, and that's the house he's renting to us. Our new home."

"Are we going to fit in there?" Eli said with a disbelieving laugh. The house appeared to be about half the size of their house in Boston.

"We'll fit just fine, son," Jacob said. "Mr. Hersh is doing us a great kindness by letting us stay here in exchange for me helping him with his farm work. Between that and working part-time at the local counseling center, I think we'll be able to make ends meet. So let's be thankful, okay?" Just as he parked the SUV, a man appeared from behind the brick house. "There's Mr. Hersh now," Jacob said, pointing. "Time to meet our new landlord."

As the Hopewells emerged from the car, Mr. Hersh greeted them. "Welcome! You made it." He extended a hand to shake Jacob's, then held up his other hand, from which dangled a key. "To your new home," he explained, surveying Eli and Elizabeth with a smile. "What a fine-looking family you have, Jacob. I hope you find the little house cozy and comfortable. I'm so glad you can use it. I wasn't sure what I would do with it after Mother passed since my children are all married and have places of their own. The paint is a little worn, but I believe you'll find the inside acceptable. The church ladies had a work frolic[2] here yesterday so you wouldn't have to clean up after such a long drive. They dusted, washed windows, wiped down door frames, and cleaned the floors."

"Wow," Eli said. "That's really nice of them!" Neither he nor Elizabeth could believe that a group of women who didn't even know them would come and clean for them.

"Oh, Mr. Hersh, please tell them thank you for me," said Mary.

---

2   An event where a group of men or women get together to work on a particular project.

"You can thank them yourself when you see them—I'm sure it will be sooner than later." Mr. Hersh beamed at her. "Now Jacob, if you don't mind, I need to get back to a project I'm in the middle of. I'll let you get settled in. You can always come find me if you need anything."

"That's fine, Mr. Hersh," Jacob nodded. "Thank you again, sir."

"My pleasure. I'll see you and your family this evening," Mr. Hersh declared. "It is my understanding that we're all invited to your parents' home for supper."

Jacob smiled and raised an eyebrow at his children, as if to say, "I told you so." Then, he said to Mr. Hersh, "I haven't had a chance to speak with my parents yet. Do you know what time?"

"I've been told six o'clock."

"All right," Jacob said. "We will see you then." He nodded to Eli and Elizabeth.

On cue, Eli said politely, "It's nice to meet you, Mr. Hersh."

"Thank you for letting us stay here," Elizabeth added.

"You're most welcome," Mr. Hersh said, then turned and strode back toward the back of the house again.

Jacob grinned at his children. "Are you two ready to see your new home?"

"I guess," Eli said, shrugging.

"I am, Dad," Elizabeth said.

"I think you'll be pleasantly surprised," their father assured them as they began trudging over to the little house. Instead of walking to the front door, he led them around to the side of the house, where they saw another door. He fit the key Mr. Hersh had given him into the lock, pushed the door open, and stood aside to let Mary and the kids enter.

Elizabeth gasped with delight. They had stepped into a sparkling-clean kitchen with green blinds on the windows and hardwood floors partly covered with colorful braided rugs. "It looks like something out of a magazine!" exclaimed Elizabeth.

Full of curiosity, Eli and Elizabeth began to explore, opening cupboards, peeking behind doors, and drawing open all the window-blinds. Sunlight soon spilled into the kitchen, front room, bathroom, and a tiny guestroom at the back of the house. Next they clambered upstairs. The second story contained two small bedrooms, a larger master bedroom, and another bathroom, all spotless, light and airy. The kids giggled when they saw the claw-foot tub in the bathroom.

"How about you have the front bedroom and I have the back bedroom, Elizabeth," Eli suggested.

"That's what I was thinking," Elizabeth said. "The closet in the front bedroom looks big enough for when we need to meet."

"Cool," Eli nodded. "Let's go check out the yard!"

"Yes!" said Elizabeth.

"Well, what do you think?" their father asked as they came down the stairs.

"I love it, Daddy! We picked out our rooms!" Elizabeth clapped her hands.

"Wonderful!" Jacob said, laughing.

"What about you, Eli?" Mary smiled at her son.

"Well, it *is* the smallest house I've ever been in..." he began. "But...I like it. Where are we going to do school?"

"I'm not quite sure yet," Mary replied, considering the front room and the kitchen. "Maybe we'll turn that little guest bedroom into our schoolroom."

"May we go see the yard, Mom?" asked Elizabeth.

"Let's bring in our things from the car first, honey," said her mother. "And I think it would be good to shower and change before dinner at Grandma and Grandpa's."

"Okay." The kids sighed in unison, slightly disappointed, and headed for the door.

Eli and Elizabeth each hauled their suitcases and backpacks up to their new bedrooms. Their mother had packed a few hangers so they could hang up some of their clothes in their new closets. They also laid out their sleeping bags, which they had brought for the night, as the moving van wouldn't bring their beds till the following morning. By 5:30, they had showered, changed, and climbed back into the now-empty SUV to drive to their grandparents' home for supper.

Grandma and Grandpa Hopewell met them at the door with shining faces, open arms, and a round of hearty compliments about how grown-up Eli and Elizabeth had become. "And now you've come to live here so we can watch you grow up in person!" Grandma exclaimed.

Eli and Elizabeth gladly followed their grandparents into the familiar house. A wave of mouth-watering scents wafted over them from the kitchen.

"What did you make for dinner, Grandma?" Eli asked in awe.

"It smells amazing!" Elizabeth chimed in.

"You'll see soon enough." Grandma laughed. "I've made some of my favorites for you tonight."

Soon Mr. and Mrs. Hersh arrived, and the eight of them gathered around the heavily laden dining table. Eli reached for one of the serving spoons, ready to dig in. Jacob cleared his throat across the table, catching Eli's attention. He shook his head at Eli, mouthing, "Wait till we pray." Grandpa gave a prayer of thanks, and then he and Grandma filled Eli's and Elizabeth's plates with fried chicken, mashed potatoes, dried corn[3], ham with green beans, pepper slaw, chow-chow[4], red beets with eggs, applesauce, cottage cheese, homemade apple butter, and homemade bread.

Eli and Elizabeth dug into the feast with gusto. Having the whole family together again felt like Thanksgiving or Christmas. With evenings filled with ballet rehearsal and band practice, sitting down to a family meal was a rare event in the Hopewell home. Also, prayer before a meal was not practiced in their home—it was something Eli and Elizabeth had only experienced when they visited their grandparents. They

---

3   Air dried sweet corn. It's a favorite in Pennsylvania because of its sweet, nutty flavor.

4   A popular vegetable relish canned in a syrup of water, vinegar, and sugar, and often made with green beans, yellow beans, kidney beans, carrots, cauliflower, onions, and other vegetables.

savored Grandma's expert cooking and listened intently to the adults as they narrated recent happenings in their lives and communities.

Just when Eli and Elizabeth thought they couldn't eat another bite, Grandma announced, "Time for dessert! Mary and Rose, will you help me bring it in from the kitchen?"

The three ladies returned from the kitchen with an angel food cake decorated with fresh strawberries, a shoofly pie, a plate of chocolate chip cookies, and a carton of vanilla ice cream. After setting them on the table, Grandma said, "Just one more thing." She disappeared again into the kitchen and returned a moment later with a plate of enormous chocolate sandwich cookies filled with white icing. "Whoopie pies[5]!" she announced.

Eli and Elizabeth had never heard of such a hilariously named dessert, and couldn't help giggling. They each reached for a whoopie pie and immediately rewarded their smiling grandmother with groans of approval.

"Well, my dear, you've outdone yourself as usual," Grandpa declared as everyone sat back in their chairs, full to the brim with excellent food and conversation. "This was more of a Sunday dinner than Sunday night supper, though," he teased.

"It's a special occasion, Samuel," Grandma said firmly, looking affectionately at the four Hopewells. "Our family has arrived safely, and I couldn't be more thankful you are all here. We had to celebrate." Getting to her feet, she said, "Now if my

---

5 A cake-like sandwich cookie filled with sweet cream. The cookie is most often chocolate-flavored, but may also come in red velvet, shoo-fly pie, vanilla, or pumpkin flavors, as well as others. The filling is usually vanilla-flavored, but may also come in chocolate or peanut butter flavors.

oh-so-grownup granddaughter and grandson will help me clear the table and wash up, I will wrap up the rest of those whoopie pies to send home with you. Why doesn't everyone else head into the living room and pick out some games to play?"

"Are you sure you don't need help, Rebecca?" asked Mrs. Hersh.

"We'll be just fine," Grandma assured her. "You and Mary get to know each other. After all, you're neighbors now. Go on now, go sit and relax. I insist," she declared firmly, waving her hands in a shooing motion.

As the adults rose and wandered to the living room, Eli and Elizabeth carefully stacked the dirty plates and utensils, carried them to the kitchen, and finished clearing the last of the serving dishes. Grandma showed them how to cover the leftovers and put them in the fridge.

"You two are so helpful," commented Grandma. "I think I can handle the rest of the dishes. You should go join the game."

"Thanks, Grandma," they said in turn, each giving her a quick hug around the waist. Exiting the kitchen, they found the others seated around a small table playing UNO.

"Just in time," Grandpa called to them. "We're about to start a game of dominoes. Would you like to join us?"

Eli and Elizabeth found empty seats and watched with interest as their father played the winning hand at UNO. Mr. Hersh swept up the cards and stacked them neatly as Grandpa placed a box of dominoes on the table. He then explained to Eli and Elizabeth that they played the dominoes like cards in a card game. After a few rounds, they started to get the hang of things, but not before their father had taken the lead. Jacob won the domino game decisively.

"Well done, Jacob, congratulations," Mr. Hersh commended. "And seeing as it's 8:30, I think it's time for us to get home to bed. I look forward to seeing you in the morning, Jacob. Samuel, many thanks to you and Rebecca for the excellent meal."

"Oh, thank you for joining us," Grandpa replied.

"We should get going, too," Mary announced. "Our moving van is supposed to arrive first thing in the morning, and I know two helpers who are going to need their rest." She winked at Eli and Elizabeth, who rose reluctantly to leave.

"And you can't expect those helpers to work without feeding them," Grandma said as she entered the room with a large basket, beaming. "I fixed up some of the leftovers for you."

"Thank you, Grandma!" Eli and Elizabeth each said.

As the Hopewells drove back to their new house, Eli spoke up. "Dad, why didn't we ever pray before meals in Boston?"

After a moment, Jacob replied, "That's part of that long story I mentioned earlier, son."

"Is that why we've never met Mom's family too?" Elizabeth ventured in a small voice.

At that moment, Jacob parked and the four of them wordlessly got out and trooped into the dark kitchen. Jacob flipped the light switch and looked down at his children. "How about this?" he began slowly. "Tomorrow night, after dinner, your mother and I will answer all of your questions. It will be a special time, just for us."

"Jacob…" Mary said.

"It's time, Mary," Jacob said, his voice gentle but firm. "Now I want you two to head upstairs. Mr. Bob's coming with the truck at 8 a.m."

"Yes, sir," they said, and without another word climbed the stairs to their new bedrooms.

Instead of going to his room, however, Eli followed Elizabeth into hers. "Do you want to talk?" Eli whispered to her.

"Not tonight," Elizabeth said, yawning. "Let's talk tomorrow after we hear Mom and Dad's story."

"Okay," Eli agreed. "Are you scared? I mean, they've been keeping it a secret our whole lives. It must be something big."

"Yeah…" Elizabeth pondered this. "I'm a little nervous. But they must have had a good reason for waiting to tell us. I'm sure it will be okay."

"I hope so," Eli shook his head. "At least we like the house. And whoopie pies."

Elizabeth grinned back at him. "Those were so good. I hope Grandma makes them for us every week."

"Yeah, there are definitely some good things about being closer to them," Eli nodded dramatically, then turned to go. "Sweet dreams, sis."

"Goodnight, Eli."

CHAPTER 3
THE STORY

Eli and Elizabeth were taking their empty breakfast plates to the kitchen when they heard the beeping of a large truck backing into the driveway.

"Mom, Mr. Bob is here!" Elizabeth called. She and Eli left their plates in the sink and hurried out the kitchen door. As they came around the house, they saw their father's friend striding toward them and their mother closing the front door behind her.

"Good morning, Mary! Morning, kids!" Bob greeted them.

"Morning, Mr. Bob!" Eli and Elizabeth returned.

"We're so glad you made it, Bob," said Mary, opening her arms to give him a hug. "How was your trip? Can we feed you some breakfast?"

"Oh, it was fine." He grinned. "And I stopped to get something to eat just a bit ago. I'm ready to get this truck unloaded if you are. What do you two say to that?" Bob clapped his hands and looked expectantly at Eli and Elizabeth.

Eli nodded. "We're ready."

"Great!" Mr. Bob turned and strode back to the truck, Eli and Elizabeth on his heels.

Mary propped open the front door and then joined them at the truck. She and Elizabeth carried the smaller boxes and items into the house, while Mr. Bob and Eli shouldered the larger boxes and pieces of furniture. Despite having driven all night, Mr. Bob's infectious energy and humor were undimmed, and his steady stream of jokes, stories, and praise for Eli and Elizabeth as they tackled each load made the work fly by. After two and a half hours, with a few breaks, they had emptied the truck.

"All right, Eli, how about we set up the bed frames and mattresses upstairs?" Mr. Bob asked.

"Okay, Mr. Bob," Eli replied. He was thoroughly enjoying the chance to do all these manly jobs.

"We'll get some lunch ready," Mary announced. "Just wait till you try my mother-in-law's leftovers, Bob."

"Oh boy," Mr. Bob grinned. "We better build those beds as fast as we can."

While Mr. Bob and Eli worked upstairs, Mary and Elizabeth found some boxes marked "KITCHEN" and unpacked enough dishes, serving plates, and utensils to set the dining table for four and put out Grandma's delicious leftovers. By the time Mr. Bob and Eli came downstairs at noon, the meal was ready.

"Yes!" Eli exclaimed at the sight of the food. "I'm starving!"

"We've all worked up a good appetite," Mary laughed. "I think Grandma knew we'd need all these leftovers today."

"You're going to love what we have for dessert, Mr. Bob!" Elizabeth declared. "Whoopie pies!"

Mr. Bob laughed. "I've heard of those, but never had one. Sounds like quite the treat!" Sure enough, after lavishing compliments on every dish, Mr. Bob announced that the whoopie pies were truly superb. "I think I'll be coming to visit you often," he joked. As the four of them stood to clear the table, the kitchen door opened.

"Jacob!" Mr. Bob exclaimed. "I was just thinking about trying to find you before I took off."

Jacob heartily embraced his friend. "I'm so sorry I couldn't help you unload this morning," he said. "Mr. Hersh needed me to start work right away. But he told me I could take lunch to come see you before you headed back. I can't thank you enough for helping us."

"No problem at all, and it was my pleasure," Bob said. "We got that truck unloaded in no time."

"Wonderful," Jacob said gratefully. "I hope you and Mary were alright carrying the big stuff in."

"Actually, this strong young man helped me carry all the furniture," Bob said, thumping Eli on the shoulder. "We even built the beds."

"Well done, Eli!" Jacob beamed with pride. "Thank you, son."

"It was fun, Dad," said Eli. "You should see how big my muscles got." He laughed and flexed his arms.

"Here's some lunch, Jacob." Mary placed a loaded plate on the table next to Bob. "You and Bob can catch up before you have to leave. Eli, Elizabeth, I'd like us to get started unpacking some of these boxes."

Mary assigned Eli the task of stacking books in the bookcases in the living room, while she and Elizabeth continued unloading the kitchen boxes and putting dishes, cutlery, and cooking items in the drawers and cupboards. They paused twenty minutes later when Jacob and Mr. Bob both stood to leave. The four Hopewells each hugged Mr. Bob and thanked him for all his help, inviting him to visit again soon.

"Oh, I will," he promised. "You have a great little place here and I'm sure you'll be having all sorts of adventures. I bet you won't ever want to come back to Boston!"

"I'll walk you out to the truck," Jacob offered, before Eli and Elizabeth could respond. They stood and watched from the front window as Mr. Bob and their father strolled to the now-empty truck, waving vigorously when he turned to wave goodbye to them. A few moments later, the truck pulled out of the driveway and disappeared from view. Eli put his arm around Elizabeth as they silently bid farewell to Mr. Bob—to Boston and their old life.

Before they could feel too sad, however, their mother called them back to their tasks. "Let's see how much we can get done before dinner, okay?" she said.

Eli and Elizabeth returned to their projects and were soon engrossed in turning their new little house into a home. By four o'clock, they had finished setting up the kitchen and bookcases, made the beds upstairs, and unpacked their clothes into their dressers. After applauding them for all their hard work, Mary told them to take showers and then rest for a while in their rooms while she made supper.

A freshly showered and dressed Eli found his sister napping on her bed. "Elizabeth, I'm done in the bathroom," he whispered. "You can shower now."

Her eyelids fluttered open. "Okay," she whispered, yawning. "I'm so tired."

"Hey, what if Mom and Dad forget to tell us the story tonight?" Eli asked.

Elizabeth sat up, rubbing her eyes. "Oh yeah," she said. "I almost forgot about that."

"I haven't," Eli confessed. "I've been thinking about it all day. But we've all been so busy, and I won't be surprised if Mom and Dad forget to bring it up."

Elizabeth slid off the bed. "So what do you think we should do?"

"We could have a signal to ask them," whispered Eli. "Like a wink or a code word. Or maybe a hand signal like in baseball?" He experimented with different gestures.

Elizabeth laughed. "They'll definitely know we're up to something if you do that. I think we should wink."

"Aw," Eli gave in, ceasing the gestures in feigned disappointment. "Okay, it's a plan. Better get in the shower soon—it's almost supper time."

At 5:30, Eli and Elizabeth heard the front door open and their father's voice boom, "Something smells mighty good in here!" They skipped down the stairs in time to see Jacob giving Mary a quick kiss on the lips.

"This place looks wonderful," Jacob said, surveying the table set with their own plates and silverware. "Already feels like home."

"Wait till you see the upstairs, Daddy," Elizabeth said, beaming. "Our bedrooms are all set up!"

"I'm going to go see right now." Jacob made his way around the dining table and patted his children's heads as he headed to the stairs. "I need to wash up."

A few minutes later, Jacob joined Mary, Eli, and Elizabeth at the table. "Great job on the bedrooms," he said, smiling broadly. "And I have to say those beds looked pretty tempting, though not as tempting as this feast. We've all worked hard today, haven't we?" Everyone nodded, returning Jacob's smile. Something about sitting around their table in their new home was making every Hopewell feel happy.

"Dad, can we say a prayer before we eat…like Grandpa did last night?" Eli asked.

"*May* we say a prayer," corrected his mother gently. "I believe we're all capable of praying."

"Fine, Dad, *may* we say a prayer before we eat?" Eli said.

Jacob took a deep breath. "Eli, it's been a long time since I've done that. But how about this: You could say a prayer out loud if you would like, or we could all bow our heads and have a silent prayer like the Amish do. Then we can all talk to God in our own way."

Eli considered this. "I don't think I'm ready to pray out loud yet either," he admitted. "Let's do a silent prayer."

Each family member bowed their heads for a few moments. When everyone had finished, Jacob declared, "Amen. Let's eat!"

As they dug into the last of Grandma's leftovers and Mary's macaroni and cheese—a family favorite—Jacob regaled the family with all the details of his first day of farm work with Mr. Hersh, which he had enjoyed much more than he'd expected. "There's lots to be done around here," he said. "I'm sure we'll all end up helping out with different projects. But it will be fun."

Eli and Elizabeth took turns telling their father about their morning with Mr. Bob, repeating as many of his jokes and funny stories as they could remember. By the end of the meal they were all laughing heartily.

When Mary stood to clear the table, Eli caught Elizabeth's eye and winked. She winked quickly back and darted her eyes toward their parents.

Eli nodded and blurted out, "Hey, Mom, Dad...are you still going to tell us the story tonight like you said?"

Mary froze, plates in hand, and locked eyes with her husband, who nodded. "Of course, son," he said quietly. "I think we're still up for it...though we could always wait till tomorrow if we're all too tired. It has been a pretty long day."

"We're not too tired," Elizabeth blurted out. Eli nodded in agreement.

"Let's clear the table first," Mary said. "I don't want to be distracted by all the dirty dishes."

"Sounds good," Jacob agreed.

"May we make some popcorn?" Elizabeth asked.

"Good idea, Elizabeth," her father said, smiling. "Nothing like something to munch on to take the edge off of a serious conversation."

Ten minutes later, the Hopewells took their seats again at the dining table and scooped popcorn from a big bowl in the middle of the table into smaller bowls.

"All right," Jacob began, after finishing a handful of popcorn. "The story. Before we start, I want to say that there is no way we are going to get through everything tonight. I'm sure you both will have lots of questions to ask us, but if we can't answer them right away, we will try to do so in the days ahead, okay?"

Eli and Elizabeth both nodded, trying to restrain their anticipation.

"We promise that we'll answer as honestly as we can," their father continued. "However, this story has some parts that are still tough for your mother and me to talk about, so we may reach a point where we need a break. If we say it's time for a break, please honor that request and don't continue to push us for more explanations and information. Okay? Is that fair enough?"

"Yes, sir," they said.

"Okay then, how about this—where would you like me to start?"

Surprised, the kids looked at each other, and this time, Elizabeth took the lead. "Well...could you tell us why we've never met Mom's family?"

"Oh boy," Jacob said, shaking his head with a sad smile. "Mary?" Grief filled their mother's eyes as a tear trickled down her cheek. Jacob asked, "Should I start, honey? You can stop me anytime."

Mary nodded "Go ahead, Jacob," she said hoarsely, wiping her eyes with a napkin.

Jacob patted Mary's shoulder and turned back to the kids. "Mom grew up in a different Plain society than I did, kids. Her family didn't have electricity. She didn't have a car."

"Wait!" said Elizabeth, comprehension dawning. "Are you saying that Mom grew up Amish?"

"Yes, that's exactly what I'm saying."

"Wow." Elizabeth's brow furrowed as she pondered this. "I guess that explains why we don't have any pictures of them. Grandma told me the Amish don't believe in having their picture taken."

Jacob nodded. "It's true. Mom grew up Old Order Amish. The Old Order Amish have a unique way of life. They live by a set of rules known as the Ordnung. The Ordnung spells out how they are to live in separation from the world—'in the world but not of it,' as they say—and protect their character. For example, the Ordnung states that a person should work hard, and that a woman is to be submissive to her husband and should wear certain clothes. Old Order Amish also don't buy insurance, have electricity or phones in their homes, or own cars. They don't have phones in their homes because they don't want the distraction. Some church districts allow their members to have bicycles and cell phones; others don't."

"Wow," said Eli, trying to comprehend life with no electricity.

Suddenly, a disturbing thought occurred to Elizabeth. "Dad… Um…"

"Go ahead, sweetheart."

"Well, I read a book from the library, and it was about an Amish girl who was…*shunned*. Is that what happened to you, Mom?"

"No, sweetie," Mary responded, sniffing. "It wasn't that…"

"What's 'shunned'?" Eli asked, confused.

"It's when…" Elizabeth began, "Well, when an Amish person decides not to follow the rules, the Ordnung," she enunciated the word carefully, hoping she said it right, "then everyone has to stay away from that person and have nothing to do with them. Right, Dad?"

"Goodness, Elizabeth," Jacob shook his head and smiled wryly. "You know a lot more than you've let on. You're right. Young people in the Amish community all get the chance to take classes and decide whether or not they want to join the church and live by the Ordnung for life. If they later decide to leave the community, the Order, after they're baptized and become a church member, they are shunned. That means those in the community are not allowed to eat at the same table with them, do business with them, or even talk to them. Only if the person comes back and repents in front of the community during the church meeting can he or she be welcomed back."

"Whoa," Eli gulped.

"But like I said, that's not what happened to Mom," Jacob continued. "Mom decided not to join the church. So even though she left her community, her family could remain in contact with her if they chose. Your mother still gets letters from her mother—your grandmother—from time to time. But…" Jacob reached for Mary's hand and held it in his. "When Mom decided to leave, her family, especially her dad, were very upset. Not only did they want her to stay in the Order…they had their heart set on her marrying the bishop's—the leader of the community's—son."

"What?" Eli exclaimed.

"But instead, she left, married me, earned her teaching degree, and had you two," Jacob said, squeezing Mary's hand. "She took a very different path than everyone had planned for her."

Elizabeth sat wide-eyed, her mouth hanging open.

"But what about you, Dad?" Eli asked. "You decided to leave your church too, didn't you? Were Grandpa and Grandma upset with you?"

Jacob shook his head. "They would have been happy for me to join the church, son, but they supported my choice. By the way, Grandma and Grandpa are Brethren, not Amish. There are many similarities between the two cultures, but as I'm sure you've noticed, Grandma and Grandpa have a car, a phone, and electricity. They go to church in a building every week, whereas the Amish take turns hosting church in their homes every other week. And some of the Brethren women can wear print fabric like Grandma's dresses, depending on what 'group' they belong to, while the Amish women wear plain colored dresses. There's plenty more to learn about the cultures and divisions or subcultures, but we'll have time for all that."

"So…is that why you didn't join the church, Dad?" Eli asked. "Because you didn't want to follow all the rules?"

"Well, it's pretty complicated, but in part, yes. Your mother and I actually agree with a lot of the church's beliefs. I just could never embrace the idea that the rules were more important than what's in your heart—that the only way to serve God is to go to church every week and wear a prayer bonnet."

Mary cleared her throat. "That's something we're going to study together," she said quietly. "We'll have the chance to look at religious beliefs and practices now that we're homeschooling. I want you to learn all about the Amish, Mennonites, Brethren, as well as the Shakers and Quakers."

Her husband nodded in agreement. "We both received many gifts growing up as we did. But I ultimately felt that I could help more people if I left this community. Boston was a great place for us to use our training and give you two the kind of experiences we wanted you to have. However, when my job fell through, we decided to take it as a sign that maybe we could also share some other experiences—experiences we had growing up—with you. Of course, in order to do that, we have to face our past, which comes with some challenges." He looked at Mary, who gave him a watery smile.

"It's worth it," Mary assured them.

"But Mom…" Elizabeth said, her voice dropping to a near whisper. "Will we ever meet your family?"

"I…" Mary's voice faltered. "I don't know, Elizabeth. I can't tell you how much I wish things could be different. But…I've been estranged from everyone but my mother for nearly fifteen years. Two years ago she wrote and told me..." Tears brimmed in her eyes once more. "She told me that my father had passed away. I hadn't heard a word from him since he told me how angry and disappointed he was in my decisions. My siblings still haven't forgiven me. It's all still very painful."

Elizabeth and Eli stood up. They stepped around the table and put their arms around their mother, who began to sob. Jacob pressed several fresh napkins into her hand. After a few moments, she wiped her eyes, blew her nose, and patted her children's arms. They released her, but remained at her side.

"Thank you," she said, looking up into each of their faces in turn. "Seeing you every day reminds me how worth it was for me to follow my heart, even though my family didn't understand. I have you and your father, and I'm so blessed. You're my family now." She stood to hug Eli and Elizabeth, and soon Jacob joined in the embraces, drawing the whole family into a tight huddle.

"I think that's enough for tonight," Jacob said finally. "We need to head to our oh-so-comfortable beds and enjoy a nice long rest after all of today's labors."

"Here, here," Mary agreed, still sniffing. "What a day."

"Thank you for telling us the story," said Eli. "It's definitely a lot to think about...but we've been dying to know."

"Yeah," Elizabeth agreed. "I have so many questions. But there's always tomorrow."

"Oh, here we go," her father teased. "I knew once we opened this can of worms we'd be in for a long interrogation."

"It's okay, Daddy," Elizabeth promised. "We won't be annoying. Just...persistent." She grinned at Eli, who smiled back. Without another word, they climbed the stairs, brushed their teeth, and headed for their bedrooms, hearts and heads full of all they had heard.

CHAPTER 4
RECONCILIATION

The scents of bacon, pancakes, and coffee greeted Eli and Elizabeth when they woke the next morning. They hurriedly washed and dressed, then clambered downstairs to the breakfast table, where they saw their father just standing to leave.

"Hey, sleepyheads!" he said. "How about a hug before I go find Mr. Hersh?"

They ran over to him and took turns getting swept up in Jacob's bear hug. "I'll see you all this evening for dinner." He pecked Mary on the cheek and strode out the kitchen door.

Eli and Elizabeth wasted no time filling their plates and digging into a stack of pancakes.

Mary joined them at the table with her cup of coffee. "You two look well rested," she said, smiling. "I hope you're ready for a full day. We need to run some errands in town and then try to get more unpacking done this afternoon."

"Okay, Mom," Eli said between bites.

"Hey, Mom…I forgot to ask you something last night," Elizabeth said.

"Yes, Elizabeth?".

"How did you and Dad meet?"

A slight color came into their mother's cheeks, but her smile remained. "We met at a farmer's market, where I worked scooping ice cream. Your father had a weekend job near the market and he started coming over during his lunch breaks to get a milkshake or an ice cream cone. He was very polite...and also very funny. He always made me laugh. After a few weekends he introduced himself and asked for my name. With my mother and sisters watching us we never had more than a few moments to talk, but then one week he slipped me a note..."

"A love note?" Elizabeth blurted out.

"Not yet." Mary shook her head with a laugh. "It simply said that he would really like to get to know me. But I read that note at every spare minute that whole week."

"So what did you do?" Eli asked, equally rapt with curiosity.

"Well, first I had to work out a place where I could meet him without attracting attention. I did have *some* freedom as I was having my Rumspringa."

"Rum...what?" Eli tilted his head.

"The running around years, Eli—that's when an Amish young person gets to learn about both the church and the outside world. At the end, they decide whether to join the church or go live among the English—everyone not in the Plain society."

"Oh," Eli nodded. "So they wouldn't mind you meeting someone like Dad then?"

"Well...sort of—as long as I was safe. I found a place where we could meet after work the next weekend, told my mother that I needed to stay behind and would come home with friends, and wrote a note to your father telling him where to meet me. I gave him the note the next weekend when he came for ice cream at lunch. After closing up the ice cream booth, I went to the spot we'd arranged and there he was, waiting for me."

"Cool," Elizabeth said. "So what did you do?"

"We just went for a walk and talked. He told me about his family and his home and I did the same. He was very funny as always. But then he got serious and told me that he had a dream to help the people outside his Brethren community. He wanted to make a real difference in some way, though he was torn over leaving the church he grew up in. I think that was when I started to fall in love with him. I couldn't believe that someone his age could already have such a strong vision of what he wanted to do, even if it meant sacrificing so much. I was drawn to his courage. You see, I too had dreamed of helping the wider community. I didn't want to be confined to helping or teaching just one group of people. Yet, I didn't see how it was possible for my dream to come true, until I met your dad. I came back from that walk just glowing. It was like a new world had opened up for me." She beamed, as if the glow had never left her face from that meeting.

"Wow," said Elizabeth, enchanted. "So then what?"

"Well, everything was lovely for a few months. We kept exchanging notes and tried to meet on whatever weekends we could. We began speaking about the future. He told me he loved me and wanted to marry me, and I said the same to him. So he decided to approach my father and ask for his blessing. That's when things got hard." She winced. "I was devastated by my father's anger and refusal to bless our union. I hope you never have to experience being torn in two like that. It was just…heartbreaking. But I was in love. I couldn't let your dad go and he didn't want to let me go. Finally, he wrote me a letter asking if I was willing to elope. I thought and prayed about it for days, and at last I wrote him and told him that I would. We set a date for a few months ahead, so we could both work and save money to move to Harrisburg, as your father had been accepted at Messiah, though back then, it was Messiah College. Everything went as planned. It was hard to leave our families, but we both felt it was worth it to have each other and our dreams. And then you two." She smiled fondly at them.

"I'm glad you eloped," Eli declared. "Or I wouldn't be here."

"Or me," Elizabeth chimed in.

"Exactly." Mary nodded energetically as she stood and began stacking dishes to take to the sink. "And who else would help me get everything done today if I didn't have you? We'd better get going if we're going to tackle all the items on my list."

"Mom, may I ask one more thing?" Elizabeth ventured, following her mother with her own dishes.

"Sure, honey."

"Does your mom…our grandmother…know that we've come to Pennsylvania?"

Her mother sighed. "I wrote her a letter right before we left Boston telling her our plans, dear. But I haven't heard back from her yet."

"Oh," Elizabeth said.

"I think we'll stop at Grandma and Grandpa's before we head to town," said Mary. "They may need us to pick up some things for them."

Half an hour later, they pulled into Grandma and Grandpa's driveway. "You two wait here in the car," their mother instructed, unbuckling her seatbelt. "I'm just going to run in and ask them for a list of what they need from town. We'll get a chance to stay and visit when we drop off their supplies, okay?"

"Okay," they said.

Mary disappeared into the house and returned ten minutes later with a list of items. In town, they first stopped at the library, where they signed up for library cards and, per their mother's instruction, each checked out a book having something to do with Pennsylvania. Elizabeth checked out a book on the Amish people, and Eli checked out a book on Pennsylvanian birds. They then drove to the bank and sat in the car reading their new books while their mother went inside to open a new account. Thirty minutes later, they drove to the grocery store and then to the feed store, where they found the various types of birdseed and suet Grandpa had requested on his list. After helping to unload their groceries at home, they returned to Grandma and Grandpa's.

Grandpa came out to meet them at the car. "All right!" he said, rubbing his hands and surveying the bags of seed and suet they had brought. "Would you two like to help me carry these out to my birdfeeders?"

"Sure, Grandpa," Eli said, putting a bag of seed under each arm.

Elizabeth picked up the bag with packets of suet. "Where are your birdfeeders?"

"Follow me," said Grandpa, picking up the last seed bag. "Feel free to join us, Mary. The Sanctuary is looking especially lovely this summer."

"You go on ahead, Samuel," Mary said. "I'll take these groceries in to Rebecca first and catch up with you in a bit."

"The Sanctuary? What's that?" Elizabeth asked, hurrying alongside Grandpa.

"You'll see," said Grandpa, grinning. He led them past the house and across the back lawn. There, huge trees shaded an expansive brick patio furnished with lawn chairs. A brass fire pit stood in the middle. Bird feeders of all types hung from tree branches or stood on poles, and birds of every hue chirped and flew between them. Two squirrels sat at one feeder, eating what appeared to be peanuts. Lush bushes and flower beds surrounded the patio, and to the right, just beyond a low, gated fence, was a pond, bordered on the far side by a forest.

"This is awesome, Grandpa!" Eli said.

Grandpa laughed. "I'm glad you like it. This is the Sanctuary. We added it since your last visit. Now you see why we need so much birdseed."

As Grandpa showed Eli and Elizabeth how to fill the feeders with either suet or seed, he explained which birds they attracted and identified any and all they could see around them. He pointed out cardinals, yellow finches, martins, and house wrens. As they worked, a flock of geese landed on the pond, followed moments later by two mallard ducks.

"There are turtles and fish in that pond, too," Grandpa told them. "And deer and wild turkey live in that forest. Sometimes a bear even comes down from the mountain to visit."

"Whoa," gasped Elizabeth. "I'm not sure I want to meet a bear."

"Don't worry," said Grandpa. "They're pretty shy about coming all the way up here."

After they had stored the feed bags, they sat down in the lawn chairs to enjoy the symphony of various birds flitting around the feeders.

"Why do you have this place, Grandpa?" Eli asked. "Just because you like birds?"

"For the birds and for your Grandma and me to share it with those we love," he replied. "And last summer, we had special children come and visit us. Some were ill, others had bad life experiences, some lived in bad neighborhoods, and some simply needed to escape for a while. They loved to come out to the Sanctuary to think and pray."

"Did they stay the night with you?" asked Elizabeth.

"A few did," said Grandpa. "Grandma and I are getting a little old for overnight guests so most of them came for day trips with their families. It is a way for us to show other people God's love."

"Cool!" said Elizabeth. "You were ministering to people like a missionary, without leaving home."

"Exactly," replied Grandpa.

"Oh Samuel, this is marvelous," Mary said behind them. She and Grandma had both come to find them.

Elizabeth ran to her mother. "It's like *The Secret Garden*, Mom!"

"It is, darling," Mary agreed, squeezing Elizabeth and admiring the scene. "But I'm afraid we can't stay and enjoy it right now. We need to get home and get more unpacking done before dinner."

"Yes ma'am," the kids said, slightly crestfallen.

"May we come back here tomorrow, Grandpa?" Eli asked.

"I think we should plan a picnic here—Sunday, after church," Grandma suggested brightly. "How does that sound? And if we can talk Grandpa into starting the fire pit, we can have s'mores for dessert!"

"Mom, may we come Sunday, please?" Eli and Elizabeth begged together.

"I'll have to talk to your father, but I'm sure it will be okay. Thanks so much for the kind invitation."

They all turned and walked back to the house and car. Suddenly, Grandma hurried ahead of them toward the house, saying, "I forgot something, Mary—I'll just be a second." She disappeared into the house, then reemerged moments later carrying a wrapped pie plate. "Strawberry pie!" she proclaimed. "Just what you need after a hard day of unpacking boxes."

"Yum!" said Eli.

"Oh Rebecca, you're too sweet," Mary thanked her, taking the pie. "Jacob will be over the moon."

"Oh, I know. That man and his sweet tooth." She beamed knowingly at her daughter-in-law.

"We'll let you know about Sunday," Mary added, getting in the SUV.

"Wonderful. Thanks again for picking up those supplies for us. And thanks for helping me with the bird feeders, you two." Grandpa waved to Eli and Elizabeth.

"You're welcome, Grandpa!" they called back, waving.

Mary, Eli, and Elizabeth worked all afternoon unpacking boxes in every room of the house and hanging curtains on the windows and pictures on the walls. Finally, Mary announced that it was time to prepare supper. While Eli and Elizabeth set the table, her mother fried ham and apples in a cast iron skillet, put potatoes to bake in the oven, and set a pan of green beans to simmer in ham broth on the back burner. When Jacob walked through the door, Eli and Elizabeth had just placed the last dishes on the table.

"Oh boy!" he boomed. "My stomach has been growling for the last hour."

Over dinner, Elizabeth and Eli told their father about their trip to town and the Sanctuary, and Grandma and Grandpa's picnic invitation, which he agreed sounded like the perfect way to spend a Sunday afternoon. He groaned with pleasure when Mary brought out Grandma's strawberry pie for dessert. After they each had devoured a large slice, he said, "Let's sit on the front porch for a bit tonight. It's too pretty of an evening to be stuck inside."

Eli and Elizabeth exchanged looks. Sit on what? The front steps? But they stood and followed their father out through the front door. To their surprise, there at the bottom of the steps stood four brand new, gleaming rocking chairs.

"They have our names on them!" Eli exclaimed. He and Elizabeth rushed forward to examine the custom-made chairs. Sure enough, each rocking chair bore one of the four Hopewells' names, painted skillfully in white.

"Come on kids, help me get these on the porch," Jacob said, lifting one of the chairs and carrying it up the steps.

"Jacob, where did these come from?" Mary asked. "I didn't hear anyone here today."

Jacob smiled. "They came while we were eating dinner. Someone wanted to give us a housewarming gift. They asked if I would like a picnic table or rockers, I thought rockers would be easier to store during the winter. I offered to pay for them, but they declined. They said that they were just glad we had come home."

"Hey, Mom, there's an envelope on the back of your chair," Eli said.

Jacob reached over and pulled it off. "It's addressed to you, dear." He handed the envelope to Mary.

Mary gasped. "Mamm[6]..." Trembling slightly, she opened the envelope and drew out a short note. Tears welled in her eyes. "*Walk around to the side of the house,*" she whispered. Immediately, she hurried down the steps and around the corner, Eli, Elizabeth, and Jacob following close behind her. Not far from the kitchen door, they saw a small wooden table with another note on it.

---

6   Mother.

Mary snatched the note up and read it. "Oh, Mamm," she murmured, her voice breaking as tears now spilled down her cheeks. She handed the note to Jacob, who read:

My Dearest Mary,

A family cannot have rocking chairs on their porch without something to set their drinks on.

Blessings,

Mamm

"Well," he said slowly. "It appears our parents have been in communication. It was Grandma and Grandpa who gave us the rocking chairs. They must have told Emma."

"Who's Emma?" Elizabeth asked.

"She's your mom's mom, honey," her father answered. "Your Mammi[7] Esh. Here, I'll take this table up on the porch. Elizabeth, would you fetch your mother some tissues, please?"

Elizabeth promptly ran ahead into the house. By the time she returned with a handful of tissues, her father had brought the little table up on the porch and placed it in the middle of the rocking chairs. Elizabeth handed her mother the tissues and the four Hopewells sat down in their rockers.

Before she plopped in her chair, Elizabeth studied its seat. "Hey, Dad," she said. "What's this written on my chair?"

---

7 Grandmother.

Jacob looked over at the rocker. "Oh, Grandma's friend Patricia Lewis writes acrostic poems. I suppose she offered up her giftings to grace our chairs."

Eli sprang up from his chair to inspect the poem on his chair. He read his poem aloud:

HEAL
H e
E liminates
A ll
L ies.

"Huh," he said. "That's cool. What does yours say, Elizabeth?"

"Mine says,

FRIEND
F orgiver
R esponder
I nspirer
E difier
N otifier
D efender."

She smiled as she took in the words. "Read yours, Dad!"

Jacob read off his poem:

CHANGE
C ircumstances
H appening
A llowing
N ew
G od
E ncounters

"Hmm…Very interesting…" He turned to Mary. "What does yours say, love?"

Her voice grew soft as she read her poem.

GRACE
G od
R eaching
A cross
C ircumstances *and*
E vents

She smiled as she wrapped an arm around her husband, another happy tear coming to her eye.

After his mother had wiped her eyes and blown her nose, Eli asked, "So…does this mean we're going to meet Grandma…er… Mammi Esh?"

"I don't know, Eli." She shook her head. "I would like you to. We'll just have to wait and see. I will at least send her a card to thank her for this table."

"It's quite a beautiful piece of craftsmanship, isn't it," Jacob said. "And I think we should put it to use. Eli, why don't you get the UNO cards? I'm going to beat you all."

"Sure you will," Eli retorted, jumping up to find the cards. As it turned out, both he and his father won a round each before Jacob announced that it was time for bed.

As Eli and Elizabeth climbed the stairs to their bedrooms, Eli whispered, "Closet." His sister nodded. Ten minutes later, Eli snuck silently into Elizabeth's room and they tiptoed to their meeting place.

"Grandma and Grandpa know Mom's mom!" Eli whispered. "I wonder if they could help us meet her."

"Maybe…" Elizabeth's eyes widened with an idea. "What if they invited her to the picnic on Sunday?"

"Perfect!" Eli agreed.

"But how can we get over there to ask them if they will?" Elizabeth pondered.

"I've got it," said Eli, snapping his fingers. "When we were at the Sanctuary, I thought it would be really cool to take some pictures of all the birds and squirrels and other wildlife with my birthday camera. I haven't used it in a while. Mom loves it when we do projects—remember when I took all those pictures for my Boston Tea Party history report?"

"Yeah," Elizabeth nodded. "If we're learning anything, Mom is usually into it. It's worth a try."

"We'll find a way somehow," Eli said with determination. He stood to leave. "Goodnight, sis."

"Night, Eli."

The following morning at the breakfast table, Eli asked nonchalantly, "Mom, may I go over to Grandma and Grandpa's for a little bit? I was thinking it would be fun to take a few pictures of the birds in the Sanctuary. I want to send some back to my friends in Boston."

Mary looked up from the pan of scrambled eggs. "We need to set up the schoolroom today. You could just as easily take them when we go over for the picnic."

"I know," said Eli. "But there might be too many people around."

"And may I go too?" Elizabeth added. "I can help Grandma in her garden while Eli takes his pictures."

Mary considered her children for a moment, squinting slightly. It sounded like they were up to something. "All right. I think that sounds like a lovely way to spend your morning. We can work on the schoolroom this afternoon. I know it's not far, but please stay together as you walk over. And I want you home by lunch time. Deal?"

"Deal!" they agreed.

After they washed their breakfast dishes and Eli had fetched his camera from his bedroom, he and Elizabeth skipped through the kitchen door. "See you at lunch, Mom!" Eli said.

"Okay, be careful! Have fun!"

They tramped up to their grandparents' back door and knocked. Grandma opened the door with a delighted smile. "Well, look here, Samuel! We have company. Come on in, children. We're just finishing breakfast. May I get you something?"

"Oh no, thank you," said Elizabeth. "We just ate."

Just then, Eli spied what Grandpa was finishing and his eyes widened.

Grandpa smiled. "Rebecca, I think you might be able to talk Eli into half of an apple dumpling."

"Would you like a dumpling, Eli?" asked Grandma.

"Yes, please." Eli quickly took a seat beside Grandpa.

"Elizabeth, would you like the other half?"

Blushing, Elizabeth nodded, moving to another seat. "Yes, ma'am."

Without another word, Grandma sliced one of the flaky dumplings in half, deftly served it up on to two plates and set them before her grandchildren. A moment later, she handed them each a fork. "Enjoy!"

"I think you might spoil us," Elizabeth said matter-of-factly after finishing her first bite. "Whoopie pies and strawberry pie and now these!"

"Fine with me," Eli stated firmly before inhaling another bite of dumpling.

Sitting back in his chair with a grin, Grandpa asked, "So how did I get so lucky to have a visit from my beautiful granddaughter and handsome grandson this morning?"

Elizabeth blushed again. "Well, Grandpa, I thought I could help Grandma in her garden, and Eli was hoping to take some pictures out in the Sanctuary."

"I see," Grandpa's eyebrows rose.

"And..." Eli began. "We were also hoping that maybe you could help us with something." He launched into the story of the previous night. "Dad said that you must be in contact with Mammi Esh because she knew about the rocking chairs."

"It's true, Eli," Grandpa admitted. "She wrote to us about arranging a housewarming gift. We told her we were planning to give you the rocking chairs, so she had the table delivered with her note and instructions for where to leave it for your mother."

"Well...so...do you think you could help us meet her?" Elizabeth pleaded. "Mom says she really wants us to, but I think she doesn't know what to do. Eli and I thought maybe you could invite her to come to our picnic on Sunday. But we don't want to cause problems..." She trailed off.

Grandma and Grandpa were quiet for a moment. Eli and Elizabeth looked anxiously up at each of them, and saw that their eyes were shining.

"You two are something," Grandpa said, shaking his head. "I'm proud to have grandchildren who care so much about others. As it happens...your grandmother and I have already invited your Mammi Esh and two of your mother's sisters—your aunts Rachel and Abigail—to the picnic. It seems great minds think alike. So if either of your parents become upset, you can say it was our idea."

"Really?" Eli's face lit up.

"Really. But I think we should let it be a surprise, don't you?"

"Yes! Thank you, Grandpa!" Elizabeth cried.

Overwhelmed with excitement, Eli and Elizabeth both hurried to hug their grandparents.

"Okay, you two, let's get to work," Grandpa declared. "Eli, you go take your pictures, but stay on the bricks. Do not open the fence—I mean it."

"Yes, sir," replied Eli.

"Elizabeth, you can help me pick green beans, tomatoes, squash, and cucumbers," Grandma invited. "I'm sure that I will have enough to send some home with you."

"Okay, Grandma!" Elizabeth said.

A few hours later, Eli and Elizabeth trooped home, each carrying a full sack of vegetables from Grandma's garden. To their relief, their mother did not ask any probing questions about their activities beyond gardening and photography. Nor did she the rest of the week, though she did comment once that Eli and Elizabeth seemed especially excited about the upcoming picnic.

Finally, Sunday morning came. The family had decided to go to church with Grandma and Grandpa Hopewell before the picnic. Elizabeth and her mother agreed to wear dresses, and Jacob and Eli were both wearing white shirts and black pants. When they arrived at church, the parking lot was filled with dark-colored cars. Men in black pants and white shirts and women in dresses or skirts and blouses made their way into the church. Some of the men wore hats and some women had prayer bonnets. Elizabeth and Eli now understood why their parents had them dress the way they did.

"There's Grandpa and Grandma!" Elizabeth whispered as they entered the building, pointing discreetly. Grandpa waved at them from the front of the room and gestured to indicate that he had saved seats for them. Jacob greeted a few people he recognized as they made their way over.

Suddenly, Mary stopped in her tracks and gripped her husband's arm. "Jacob..."

Jacob, Eli, and Elizabeth all whipped their heads to see where Mary was staring, dumbstruck. Three women—one older and two closer to Mary's age—stood just behind Grandma and Grandpa Hopewell. The family resemblance was undeniable. These ladies had to be Mammi Esh and Mary's sisters, Abigail and Rachel. Eli and Elizabeth huddled close to their parents, their hearts pounding. They had no idea their Amish relatives were coming to church!

"Jacob...I can't," Mary choked.

"Mary," he murmured. "They're crying too. I can see it. You can do this."

Slowly, arm in arm with her husband, Mary walked toward her mother and sisters. As they approached, the sisters left their places and walked quickly to meet Mary, embracing her with flowing tears. After they released her, Mary turned to her mother, who opened her arms and held her tightly for a long time.

"*Denki*[8] for the gift, Mamm," said Mary, sniffing.

"You're welcome," her mother said. "I hope it was all right for us to come. Samuel and Rebecca invited us to your picnic this afternoon."

"Of course," Mary managed with a teary smile.

"Jacob, it is good to see you."

"Thank you, Emma. I'm glad to see you as well."

"And these are your two youngsters, *ya*[9]?"

"Ya," Mary nodded, placing a hand each on her daughter and son. "This is Elizabeth, and this is Eli."

8   Thank you.
9   Yes

"I'm happy to meet you, Eli and Elizabeth. I am your grandmother, Emma. My other grandchildren call me Mammi or Mammi Esh, so please do the same." She gestured to her two other daughters, who both smiled at them. "This is your Aunt Rachel and your Aunt Abigail. Your *Dawdi*[10] Hopewell picked us up last evening so we could come and spend today with you."

"It's nice to meet you," Elizabeth and Eli said together, a little shyly.

"Let's sit down," Jacob urged. "We'll have plenty of time to talk after the meeting."

With that, the four Hopewells, Grandma Rebecca, Grandpa Samuel, Mammi Esh, Aunt Rachel, and Aunt Abigail took their seats—filling an entire row.

When the pastor stood to give the message, he announced that there were a number of visitors this morning. "Jacob, we are very glad to have you and your family as part of our community. And Mary, we knew your family was coming to join you today. We are very happy that we could be part of your reunion. In light of this glorious day, I have changed my sermon topic. Today I would like to speak briefly about faith, hope, and love."

After the service, Mary's mother and sisters departed with Grandma and Grandpa Hopewell and Jacob's family headed to their car.

"Do you want to go home and change before we head to the picnic?" Jacob asked.

---

10   Grandfather

"No," said Elizabeth. "All the other ladies will be in their dresses."

"Yeah, I'm fine in my clothes too, Dad," Eli seconded.

"Then let's head straight to Grandma and Grandpa's."

When they pulled in the drive, Jacob saw his mother carrying a large dish of fruit toward the patio area at the pond. Mary's mother and two sisters followed close behind, each carrying dishes.

"This is going to be some picnic," Jacob observed.

Grandpa met them as they exited the car, carrying a huge jug of iced lemonade. "This is going to be some picnic!"

"That's what Dad just said!" Elizabeth laughed.

"Great minds think alike, remember?" Grandpa teased.

"We've brought the s'mores supplies," said Eli, hefting the bag beside him.

"Good, good," Grandpa clapped a hand on Eli's shoulder. "Let's walk down to the Sanctuary. I think lunch is ready."

When they reached the patio, they saw two picnic tables set for nine practically groaning under dishes mounded with sandwich fixings, chow-chow, fruit salads, potato salads, and much more.

Mary gasped. "Oh my, Rebecca, you went to too much work!"

"Nonsense!" replied Grandma. "I enjoyed doing it. Besides, I had help." She smiled and nodding her head towards Mammi Esh, Aunt Abigail, and Aunt Rachel, who all smiled back at them.

The family sat at the picnic tables and bowed their heads in prayer, but to Eli and Elizabeth's surprise, no one prayed. After a few moments, Grandpa cleared his throat and everyone began talking and passing dishes.

It seemed to the children that Mammi Esh was more interested in getting to know them than catching up with their mother. She asked them many questions about growing up in Boston, what their schools and friends were like, where they had traveled, and more.

Finally, Eli worked up the courage to ask Mammi Esh a question. "What is your house like, Grandma?"

Mammi Esh smiled, obviously pleased. "Well…it would be much easier to show you my house than to tell you about it, Eli. I would love it if you would come and visit me sometime. What do you say, Mary? I have a beautiful guesthouse available."

Mary looked stunned. "Mamm…that's very kind. But I'm not sure the children are ready to come and visit the People by themselves just yet." She paused, then asked, "What if I drove them down to spend a night or two?"

"That would be fine if you're willing, Mary," Mammi Esh said.

"Jacob," Mary turned to her husband. "Can you do without us for a night or two?"

"I'll be fine as long as you're fine," he assured her. "You should go."

"Okay…" Mary turned back to her mother. "When should we come?

"What about tonight?"

CHAPTER 5

AN AMISH FARM

"Tonight!" Eli and Elizabeth both gasped in surprise.

"Someone needs to drive Abigail, Rachel, and me home," Mammi Esh said. "You could take us, Mary, and come back Tuesday morning."

"I guess that could work..." Mary hesitated. "Jacob?"

"Fine with me," he nodded. "And it looks like Eli and Elizabeth like the idea." He grinned at the two of them as they bounced in their seats.

"I'd like to go, Mom." Elizabeth said.

"Me too," added Eli.

"Well then..." Mary smiled at the hopeful faces all around her. "I guess that settles it. Tonight it is."

"Wonderful!" Mammi Esh beamed at them. "Your Uncle Elam and Aunt Ruth will be glad to meet you too, Eli and Elizabeth. And your four little cousins—soon to be five."

Mary's face lit up. "Ruth is expecting another *bobbli*[11]?"

"Ya," Aunt Abigail nodded.

"I've been longing to meet their little boys," Mary breathed, tears springing to her eyes.

"And they you," Mammi Esh replied warmly.

Mary fought back a sob. "We'll...we'll need to pack," she managed.

"Please don't feel the need to bring any special clothes on our account," Mammi Esh said.

"Oh, Mamm." Mary reached across the table and grasped her mother's hands. "Thank you. I...it will be good to see home again."

A tear trickled from the corner of Mammi Esh's eye. "I wish your *daed*[12] could have seen and talked with your two beautiful children," she said, her voice trembling. "Oh well, at least we can make the most of the time we have."

Grandpa, who had been busy lighting the fire pit, spoke up. "Here, here! How about we get those s'mores cooked up so you can embark on this historic visit?"

"Samuel..." Grandma reproached.

"What? I'm ready for dessert."

"S'mores!" Elizabeth and Eli jumped up from the table to join Grandpa, who held out two skewers. They eagerly took them and speared two marshmallows each on the end.

---

11 Baby
12 Dad

"I'm making one for you, Mammi Esh," announced Eli.

"And these are for Aunt Rachel and Aunt Abigail!" Elizabeth called.

"You two." Jacob shook his head as he joined them at the fire pit and picked up a skewer. "I guess that means I'll have to make yours."

Soon, everyone had joined in the s'more-making, laughing as they grew sticky from the messy but delectable little sandwiches. When they had finished, Grandma directed them to carry the picnic food back to the house and wrap up the leftovers, most of which she forced Jacob to take—"to help tide you over while Mary is away." After loading his leftovers and family in the SUV, Jacob promised Mammi Esh that Mary, Eli, and Elizabeth would return to pick them up after packing some overnight things.

As they drove back home, Eli asked Jacob, "Why didn't we pray over dinner this time?"

"What do you mean?" Jacob said. "Of course we did...Oh!" He realized where their confusion lay. "The Amish pray over their meals silently. Grandpa did that out of respect for Mammi Esh and your aunts."

"But how does everyone know when the prayer's over?" Elizabeth asked.

Mary cleared her throat to demonstrate. "That's how." She smiled at them in the rearview mirror.

Half an hour later, Mary drove back into Grandma and Grandpa's driveway, the three ladies climbed in, and the group was on their way.

For the entirety of the drive, Mammi Esh, Aunt Abigail and Aunt Rachel continued to ask Eli and Elizabeth about their friends, schools, and life in Boston. It seemed only a few minutes had passed before Mammi Esh declared, "Here we are!"

Mary pulled into a farm lane. Ahead, Eli and Elizabeth saw a charming little house with a sign that read *Emma's Bed and Breakfast*. Fifty yards further, they saw a larger two-story farmhouse, painted white.

"You have a bed and breakfast, Mamm?" Mary asked.

"A great deal has changed since your father passed," Mammi Esh replied as they all climbed out of the car. "This is where you and the children will be staying."

Eli and Elizabeth trotted to the back of the SUV and put on their backpacks. Eli also grabbed his mother's overnight bag.

"I have a few things to take care of before bed," Mammi Esh said. "So if you don't mind, Abigail, I will let you show them to their rooms?"

"Yes, of course, Mamm."

"Thank you. I imagine you'll want to turn in soon," Mammi Esh said to her daughter and grandchildren. Eli stifled a yawn and smiled sheepishly.

"I guess that's a yes, Mamm." Mary smiled. "Are you sure you don't want us to help with anything?"

"Oh no, of course not. You're my guests. Please come and find me or Abigail or Rachel if you need anything to make you more comfortable. Otherwise, sleep well and I'll see you at eight o'clock for breakfast."

"Thank you, Mammi Esh," Elizabeth said, hugging her.

"We're so happy you're all finally here," Mammi Esh said, then set off toward the farmhouse.

"All right, let's get you to your rooms." Aunt Abigail clapped her hands. "Follow me."

Mary, Elizabeth, and Eli set off after Aunt Abigail. They noticed several handcrafted rockers, which looked suspiciously like their chairs, on the wooden porch of the guest house as they approached the front door. Just inside the cozy entryway stood a long sideboard with a few old-fashioned coffee pots, cups, cream, and sugar ready for guests. Passing this, they saw a sitting room with several comfortable-looking tan armchairs surrounding a low, round coffee table atop a round green and tan braided rug. The floor was spotless. On the back wall was a gas fireplace, above which hung a large painting depicting a barn-raising. Everything was crisp and beautiful.

Abigail led Mary, Eli, and Elizabeth straight ahead and up a short flight of stairs to a long hallway with doors on each side. Between each door, small, colorful quilts hung on the cream walls. Abigail stopped at the second door on her left. "This will be your room, sister."

Mary entered the room, followed by Eli and Elizabeth. All three Hopewells murmured in admiration. The beautiful hardwood floors were accented by blue and cream braided rugs. A handmade quilt of variegated blue shades covered the queen-sized bed. On either side of the bed stood a simple nightstand—one had a gas-powered light on it and the other, a windup alarm clock. Opposite to the bed was a simple chest of drawers and a rocking chair with a blue seat cushion. A metal luggage rack and a low chifforobe for hang-up clothes stood on either side of a door, through which was a small bathroom. Eli deposited his mother's bag on the metal rack.

"It's beautiful," Mary whispered. "Are you sure you won't allow me to pay you for this?"

"*Nee*[13]," replied Abigail. "You and the children are staying as her guests. But she did think it might be okay for Eli and Elizabeth to share a room, as they aren't teenagers. Will that be all right?"

"Oh yes," Mary assured her, raising an eyebrow at Eli and Elizabeth. "They will get along and respect one another very well."

Eli and Elizabeth eyed one another suspiciously. "I will if you will," Elizabeth teased.

"I will if *you* will," Eli retorted.

Aunt Abigail laughed. "Follow me, then," she said, and led Eli and Elizabeth down the hall to the next room.

Everything in this room looked like their mother's, but the color scheme was antique red. Two faceless dolls lay on the bed, a boy and a girl. They placed their backpacks on the metal rack beside the bathroom door.

"I'm sure Mamm has a big day planned for you all tomorrow," Aunt Abigail told them. "So rest well. *Gut Nacht*[14]."

---

13   No
14   Good night.

"Gut Nacht, Aunt Abigail," Elizabeth replied, enunciating carefully. "Denki."

Just then, Mary appeared in their doorway. Aunt Abigail asked, "Mary, have you been teaching the children the People's language?"

"Nee," replied Mary. "I think Elizabeth has picked it up by reading books about the People."

Elizabeth nodded shyly.

"Very good," Aunt Abigail said. "Gut nacht, Eli and Elizabeth, and you too, sister." She gave Mary a hug and turned to go.

"*Ich werde*[15]," Mary said as Abigail departed. "*Gleichfalls*[16]." Then she turned to her children. "Let's get ready for bed, shall we? I'll show you how to set those alarm clocks for seven. That should give us enough time to get up for breakfast."

Eli and Elizabeth each took turns in the bathroom changing into their pajamas and brushing their teeth, then padded out to the big, red-quilted bed, where Mary met them to kiss them goodnight.

"Hey Mom, may I say a prayer?" Elizabeth asked. "It's been such a big day."

Tears welled again in Mary's eyes, as they had countless times that day. "It has been a momentous day," she agreed. "God has been very good to us. I'm overwhelmed to be here and to feel welcome after so many years. Yes, please say a prayer."

---

15   I will.
16   You, too.

Elizabeth and Eli both took their mother's hands and they all closed their eyes. "Dear God," Elizabeth prayed. "Thank you for making a way for Mom to see her family again and for bringing us safely here to Mammi Esh's. Please help us as we get to know our Amish family members, and keep Dad safe and happy while we're gone. Amen."

"Amen," Eli and Mary echoed.

"All right, my dears," Mary said, giving each of them a quick kiss on the forehead.

"You've already been very sensitive and respectful with Mammi Esh and your aunts. You may experience some things that you don't understand, but I want you to know that you can ask me any questions you like about the People and I will explain. Okay?"

"Okay, Mom," they both said.

"Love you. Good night."

"Goodnight," said Eli, yawning.

"Gut nacht, Mamm." Elizabeth grinned.

"Gut nacht, Elizabeth." Mary squeezed her arm affectionately. She went toward the door.

"Mom?"

"Yes, Elizabeth?"

"Why don't these dolls have faces?"

Mary came to Elizabeth's side. Elizabeth held out the girl doll to her. Mary knelt by the bed and took the doll.

"The Amish believe that capturing a human likeness—like a photo or a doll like this—goes against the Bible," Mary explained. "In the book of Exodus, there's a list of rules called the Ten Commandments, and in one of those commandments, it says not to make graven images because it would be making something that could be worshipped besides God, and God is the one who deserves all our worship. Nothing else can have it. That's why Amish dolls don't have faces."

Elizabeth took this all in, then nodded. "I guess I get it," she said.

Mary smiled, wished her children good night once more, and went to bed.

The next morning, Eli and Elizabeth were up well before their alarm clock went off. They quietly dressed and tiptoed downstairs and out to the front porch.

"Hey look," Eli pointed. "A porch swing!"

They went straight for it and sat down, breathing a sigh of delight. The sun spread its light across the rich, green fields. Cows mooed in the distance. Soon, a horse and enclosed buggy appeared up the lane. The man driving the buggy waved as he passed, and the children waved back, watching as he drove around the barn. A few minutes later, the man reappeared on foot and entered what appeared to be a large shed.

"Hey, kids." Eli and Elizabeth turned to see their mother standing in the front door. "Are you ready to go and get some breakfast?" she asked.

"Yes!" Eli and Elizabeth both jumped to their feet.

"I think Mammi Esh will be waiting for us in the main farmhouse," Mary said. "Now you'll finally get to see the house where I grew up."

As they approached the big farmhouse, Mammi Esh walked out on the porch. "Come this way," she called. "Abigail and Rachel are already in the dining room."

The Hopewells followed Mammi Esh into the dining room, where a huge dining table bore dishes of scrambled eggs, sausage, bacon, fresh fruit, French toast, milk, juice, and coffee. Everything looked and smelled mouth-wateringly good, and the group quickly sat down around the table. After a silent prayer, they began to pass the dishes.

"Eli, Elizabeth," Mammi Esh said after a few minutes. "I was hoping you might like to help us feed the calves and gather the eggs after breakfast."

"Okay, Mammi Esh," Eli said. Elizabeth nodded, washing her French toast down with orange juice.

"Wonderful. After that, I think we should all go for a buggy ride. I have a few things to deliver to one of the local businesses— a quilt, some pillows, and a few dolls."

"Cool!" Elizabeth exclaimed. "Did you make all those things, Mammi Esh?"

"Abigail, Rachel, and I made them, dear." Mammi Esh smiled at her. "We thought about having our own gift shop, but we have our hands full enough with the bed and breakfast. So we just make a few items each week and sell them at a local shop."

"Aw," Elizabeth said suddenly, as though disappointed.

"What's wrong, child?" asked her grandmother.

"I wish I would have thought to bring some of my allowance with me," she said. "I've wanted an Amish doll for a while now. I would have bought one of yours. That would have been really special."

Her grandmother smiled. "Okay, I'll make you a deal. If you help feed calves and collect eggs this morning and tomorrow morning, I'll let you have one. What do you say?"

"Deal!" cried Elizabeth, bouncing in her seat.

"I have a question, Mammi Esh," said Eli.

"Yes, Eli?"

"Elizabeth and I were sitting on the porch for a bit this morning and we saw a man come up the drive. He parked his buggy and then went into a little building. What's he doing in there?"

"Oh, that's your Uncle Elam. He has a leather shop in that building. Would you like to see it?"

"Yes, I would," replied Eli.

"Well then, how about this? Abigail, why don't you show Elizabeth how to collect eggs and feed the calves, and Rachel, you can take Eli to ask Elam to show him the shop?"

"All right," replied Abigail.

Soon, everyone had cleaned their plates. Abigail stood and picked up the dish of eggs, as if to clear the table.

"Mary and I can take care of it, Abigail," Mammi Esh told her. "You and Rachel get going with the *kinner*[17]."

"All right, Mamm," Aunt Abigail agreed. "Elizabeth, let's start with the milk house."

"Okay," said Elizabeth, hurrying to follow her. "Have fun with Uncle Elam, Eli," she called to her brother.

"Have fun with the calves," he said, laughing as he and Aunt Rachel departed for the front door.

Aunt Abigail led Elizabeth out the back door of the farmhouse and across the lawn to a small stone building. Abigail opened the door and gestured for Elizabeth to step inside. The room was cool and smelled of fresh milk. Rows of stacked metal milk cans stood against the nearest wall, and on the opposite wall were two shelves—one lined with what appeared to be oversized plastic baby bottles, and the other carrying an assortment of funnels, pails, and odd utensils. On the wall to their left was a low faucet with hot and cold taps. Beside it stood a wide metal rack with two heavy rubber buckets on it, and a five-gallon plastic bucket. Beside the rack was a large plastic trash can.

Elizabeth remembered a trip she and her family had taken a few years ago to a dairy farm not far from Boston. It was in the middle of a state park with various Native American sites, and their mom wanted them to take in some Massachusetts history. After they wandered some of the trails, they took a tour of the farm, which boasted the state's first robotic milking system. She looked around for Abigail's milking machine, but saw nothing.

"Aunt Abigail," Elizabeth asked. "Where's your milking machine?"

---

17   Children

"Oh, we don't have one, dear," Aunt Abigail said. "We do all our milking by hand."

"But why?" Then Elizabeth remembered the clocks. "It's because of the electricity, isn't it?"

Aunt Abigail smiled. "That's right."

"What's the big deal about electricity? Is it that bad?" Elizabeth blushed after realizing what she said. "I'm sorry, Aunt Abigail. I didn't mean to…"

Aunt Abigail chuckled. "Not to worry, child. See, it's not that we think electricity is bad. The Bible calls us to be in the world, but not of the world. We've set ourselves apart, and this is one of the ways we show that to the world."

The idea pricked Elizabeth's curiosity. What did that mean, *be in the world but not of it?* And what else did the Bible say?

"Now," Abigail said, breaking into Elizabeth's thoughts. "The first thing we need to do is to fill this plastic bucket with warm water," Abigail instructed. "It needs to be hot enough to dissolve the milk replacer, but not too hot to hurt the calves."

"Okay," replied Elizabeth, a bit unsure. But she leaned in to watch as Aunt Abigail adjusted the taps with one hand and felt the water pouring into the bucket with the other.

"That's the right temperature," said Aunt Abigail. When the bucket was full, she set it on the floor. Next, she opened the trash can, revealing the bag of milk replacer. She handed Elizabeth a cup from the container. "Please scoop out eight full cups of milk replacer into the bucket. Then grab that wire whisk from the shelf and mix everything together."

While Elizabeth measured, poured, and whisked the milk replacer, Abigail gathered six of the plastic milk bottles and a spouted measuring cup. She carefully filled the bottles with the warm liquid, placing three in a rubber bucket.

"Here, you carry this bucket," Abigail said, handing it to her. "And I'll carry the other one."

"Okay," said Elizabeth, grabbing the bucket handle and lifting it. Thankfully, the bucket did not feel too heavy.

"Now, follow me," said Aunt Abigail.

Aunt Abigail and Elizabeth carefully walked together back out through the milk house door and headed left for the cow barn. They rounded the back corner of the barn, where a row of calf hutches stood arranged in a semi-circle.

"Most farmers have their hutches in a straight line," Aunt Abigail remarked. "I like mine like this." She and Elizabeth carried their buckets down the line, stopping to hang a milk bottle in the first six of the ten hutches. Elizabeth couldn't help giggling as she watched the calves slurp down their milk bottles in a wide-eyed frenzy.

"They're hungry!" she declared. In moments, it seemed, the calves had finished their milk.

"Yes, they eat fast," Aunt Abigail agreed. When the calves were finished, they collected the bottles, returned to the milk house, and mixed a second batch of milk replacer for the last four calves. Once all the calves were fed, Elizabeth retrieved the milk bottles and placed them in the buckets, which Abigail was holding out to her. "Now we'll go and wash the bottles, and I'll show you how we store them to dry," Abigail said, Elizabeth on her heels. "We don't want our calves getting sick."

Back in the milk house, Abigail and Elizabeth washed the bottles and tops and lined them up to dry.

"That went quickly with your help," Abigail said, smiling at Elizabeth. "Now for the chicken house."

"Okay." Elizabeth fell into step beside Aunt Abigail. The chicken house, which was on the other side of the barn, was a small wooden shed with an attached wire-and-wood pen, in which ten or so chickens milled around. Abigail opened the door and motioned for Elizabeth to hurry in without letting any chickens out. Elizabeth stepped quickly through the door and into the small room, causing one chicken to flap away from her with a little squawk. A row of nesting boxes lined the right-hand wall, covered by a wooden lid. Abigail raised the lid to reveal the boxes, which had a few chickens in them. The back wall of the nesting boxes was open, allowing the chickens to pass in and out from the outdoor pen.

Abigail took a basket down from a hook beside the door and handed it to Elizabeth. "Hold this, please. I'll gather some eggs first and then you can try it."

Elizabeth watched, fascinated, as her aunt reached in to each box, pulled out eggs of various shapes and hues, and placed them in the basket. She was glad to see that the nesting hens all retreated as Abigail drew near to their boxes. At the last box, Abigail took the basket. "Now it's your turn," she said. Elizabeth uncovered four smooth eggs, all still warm, and placed them carefully in the basket.

Abigail put the egg basket down. Scooping two metal cups of chicken feed from a canister in the corner, she handed one to Elizabeth, and led her back outside.

"Just empty the seed in the trough, like this." Aunt Abigail poured the seed into the trough. The chickens swooped down on their breakfast, pecking furiously at the trough. Elizabeth emptied her cup, laughing as even more chickens stalked over and joined the feast.

After filling the chicken's bowls with water, Abigail said, "All right, let's get those eggs up to the kitchen." She disappeared inside the henhouse for a moment, then reappeared with the egg basket. Just as they started to leave, a rooster crowed loudly just behind Elizabeth, who jumped.

Abigail laughed. "He's just saying, '*Gut*[18] morning.' Good thing I had the egg basket, eh?"

"Ya." Elizabeth blushed.

"But now, if you don't mind, I'd like you to take these up to Mamm at the farmhouse. I need to go back to the guest house and change the bed linens. Can you manage?"

Elizabeth nodded, taking the basket from Aunt Abigail. "Thanks for showing me the calves and the chickens."

"You're most welcome," Aunt Abigail said, tweaking Elizabeth's hair before striding away back to the guest house.

Elizabeth set off for the farmhouse. As she mounted the porch steps, the front door swung open and Mammi Esh appeared. "How did things go?" she asked.

---

18 Good

"Pretty well, I think," replied Elizabeth. "The rooster made me jump."

Mammi Esh grinned and reached for the egg basket. "I'm sure you were a great help to Abigail. Come, I'll put these in the kitchen and we can get ready to go to town."

As they entered the kitchen, Aunt Rachel appeared behind them, alone.

"Where's Eli?" Mammi Esh asked.

"He's staying with Elam. He decided that he doesn't want to go to town with a bunch of girls after all." Rachel grinned and shook her head.

Mammi Esh's brows knitted with concern. "But I wanted him to have a chance to ride in the buggy."

"Oh, he'll have a chance for a buggy ride. Elam is going to take him to his home for lunch."

"Oh my," replied Mammi Esh, surprised. "Do you think Ruth will be all right with that?"

"Elam doesn't think it will be a problem," Rachel said. "She has four boys. What's one more?"

Mammi Esh smiled. "Well, I would like to help. We'll leave for town when you get back." She fetched a basket from a nearby counter, draped a dishtowel in it, and filled it with various goodies from around the kitchen—a pie, some cookies and whoopie pies, a can of chow-chow, and a can of peaches. Rachel hung the basket on her arm and whisked out the door.

"What about Aunt Abigail?" asked Elizabeth. "Will she come to town with us?"

"She'll be staying here and preparing the evening meal," Mammi Esh replied. "We have more guests coming to spend the night."

"Oh..." Elizabeth pondered this news.

"What is it, child?" Mammi Esh inquired.

Elizabeth hesitated. "Well...I know you want to take me on a buggy ride...and I really want to do that. But would it be possible for me to stay and help Aunt Abigail?" The words tumbled out in a rush. "I loved doing chores with her this morning and I want to learn more about cooking."

Before Mammi Esh could respond, Abigail and Mary walked into the kitchen. "The beds are all made, Mamm," Abigail said brightly. "Mary helped me. I'm going to start gathering everything for tonight's meal."

"Elizabeth has just told me that she would like to stay and help you, Abigail," Mammi Esh disclosed with a half-smile.

"Oh." Abigail's face lit up with delight. "I would enjoy that, Elizabeth."

"Really?" Elizabeth was elated.

"Are you kidding? I can use all the help I can get. But weren't you supposed to go on the buggy ride to town?"

The conversation was interrupted again as Aunt Rachel returned to the kitchen, followed by Uncle Elam. Seeing him up close this time, Elizabeth noticed that he wore suspenders.

"Mary!" he cried, striding forward to embrace his sister. "It's wonderful to see you. I've just been getting acquainted with your son," he said, stepping back and looking at her keenly. "He's a fine young man."

"Thank you, *bruder*[19]," Mary said fervently. "It's so good to see you again, too."

Elam turned and spotted Elizabeth. "And this must be your lovely daughter."

"Elizabeth, this is your Uncle Elam," Mary said.

"It's a pleasure to meet you, Uncle Elam," Elizabeth said, stepping toward him and reaching her hand out to shake his.

"I have an idea," Abigail interjected. "Elam, would you be up for taking Elizabeth home for lunch too? That way Elizabeth gets the buggy ride Mamm wants her to have. Then she can help me with supper when she gets back."

"Sure," replied Elam. "I can bring her back when I come back to the shop. Mamm, would you mind picking Eli up from my place on your way back from town? I thought he could stay and play with the boys this afternoon. It would give Ruth a little break."

"Ya, that won't be a problem," Mammi Esh said.

"Oh, and that way I can stop in and meet your boys!" Mary said, overjoyed.

"Excellent," declared Uncle Elam. "Ruth will be glad to see you too."

---

19   Brother

Abigail quickly gathered a few more items in a basket and handed it to Elizabeth. "Take these to add to Mamm's contribution."

Elizabeth followed Uncle Elam out of the house to his buggy, where Eli was already waiting with Mammi Esh's basket of food. Elam helped Elizabeth climb in beside her brother, then settled in the driver's seat, picked up the reins, and made a clucking sound as he gently tapped the reins on the horse's rump. The buggy gently rolled forward, and Eli and Elizabeth grinned at each other.

Uncle Elam's white farmhouse was only ten minutes down the road. As they pulled up, Eli and Elizabeth saw a pregnant woman in a plain dress and bonnet emerge from the front door and walk slowly toward the buggy. Behind her trailed four little boys.

"Elam, is everything okay?" called the woman. "I didn't expect you home."

"Everything's fine. These are my sister Mary's two children, Eli and Elizabeth. They've come to visit Mamm for a couple days. Have you had lunch yet?"

"No," she replied, smiling. "Hello, I'm Ruth. It's a pleasure to meet you. I'm glad you could join us for lunch. Eli and Elizabeth, these are our sons—Abram, Benjamin, and our twins, Daniel and David."

"I'm six!" Abram announced.

"And I'm five!" Benjamin said, not to be outdone.

The twins hid behind their mother's skirt, shyly peeking out at the two strangers. "Come now," Ruth admonished, pushing them forward.

"How old are you two?" Eli asked, squatting down to eye level with the boys.

"We're four," Daniel said.

"Four is fantastic," said Eli. "And so are all the goodies our Mammi sent us for lunch. Can you guess what's in these baskets?" He pointed to the baskets Elam was holding.

"Pie!" Abram shouted.

"Let's get them in the house and we'll see," Uncle Elam said, handing one of the baskets to Eli.

Elam and Eli set the baskets on the kitchen table and Ruth and Elizabeth quickly unpacked and set out the food. Then Elizabeth helped her aunt carry dishes and utensils and arrange eight places around the cozy table.

"Let's enjoy this wonderful food that the Lord has provided," Elam declared. After a silent prayer, he cleared his throat and began serving up plates for the boys. A few moments after they had begun to eat, David, who was next to Eli, reached out and patted Eli's hand, smiling.

"He's asking you to cut his bread for him," Uncle Elam explained.

"Oh." Eli used his knife to cut up David's slice of bread. No sooner had he finished, Daniel patted Eli's other arm. Eli turned to cut up Daniel's food next. It wasn't long before Abram and Benjamin joined in on the game. Between every bite of his own food, Eli was called upon to help his cousins with theirs, each time eliciting fresh laughs from the boys.

At a lull in the laughter, Uncle Elam turned to Eli. "How long have you had that belt?"

Eli glanced down. The belt was faded and cracked in places. "I'm not sure," he said. "I've had it for a while."

Uncle Elam nodded quietly and sat back in his seat as he took another bite of bread.

At the end of the meal, Uncle Elam asked, "How would you all like it if Cousin Eli stayed and played with you this afternoon? I have to go back to work and take Elizabeth to help Aunt Abigail cook supper, but Eli said he'd be happy to stay until Mammi picks him up on her way back from town." All four boys nodded enthusiastically, and their mother smiled.

"We'd love for you to stay, if you want, Eli," Aunt Ruth said.

"Thanks. That sounds fun," Eli grinned.

"We can show you our blocks!" Abram said. "We can build *anything* with them."

"Show me now," Eli said.

All four boys scrambled eagerly from the table. Benjamin grasped Eli's hand to lead him out to the living room.

"Say goodbye to Daed, boys," Ruth called. "He's going back to work."

"Bye!" called a chorus of voices.

"Thank you for allowing me to visit, Aunt Ruth," Elizabeth said, standing to her feet. "I enjoyed it."

"You're welcome, Elizabeth. Abigail is a wonderful cook and a gut teacher, so I'm sure you'll enjoy this afternoon. From what I can tell, you'll be a hard worker and a gut student."

Elizabeth blushed. "Thank you. I'll try."

"See you tonight, my dear," Uncle Elam said as he clapped on his hat.

Elizabeth followed Uncle Elam back out to the buggy. "Sit up here by me," he told her. "I want to hear what you've been up to at the farm."

As they drove back to the farm, Elizabeth told him all the things she had enjoyed so far.

"It's been wonderful," she gushed. "I've read several books about the Amish, but there's nothing like experiencing things firsthand." She was quiet for a moment. "Uncle Elam," she asked. "How did you decide you wanted to go into leatherworking?"

Uncle Elam smiled. "When I left school after eighth-grade, not much older than you are now, I worked in the leather shop with my uncle Benjamin as an apprentice."

Elizabeth's jaw dropped. "You were a school drop-out?"

"Not really," Uncle Elam said, chuckling. "The People only go to school till the eighth grade."

Elizabeth remembered this fact from her reading. "That's right," she said. "But why?"

"It's always good to be smart, but education can sometimes swell your head," said Uncle Elam. "And lead to pride. By the time you get through eighth grade, you know the three R's well enough to get along just fine. We don't need to know anything more than that."

Elizabeth chewed on this. She loved learning and couldn't imagine not graduating from high school. She had even started dreaming about what colleges she wanted to attend in the future. Even though she wasn't quite sure what she wanted to do, she knew she didn't want to give up her education.

Uncle Elam dropped Elizabeth off in front of the farmhouse. After thanking him, she dashed up the porch steps and through the front door, calling, "I'm back, Aunt Abigail!"

"Gut!" said Aunt Abigail. "And not a moment too soon. I was just getting ready to make pie dough. Would you like to learn?"

"Ya," replied Elizabeth, eyes wide with delight.

For the rest of the afternoon, Elizabeth and her aunt worked on the evening meal. They baked homemade fruit and shoofly pies, fresh baked bread, layered salad, fruit salad, baked chicken pot pie, and slippery chicken pot pie. Aunt Abigail even left Elizabeth to tend the oven while she checked guests in to the bed and breakfast.

At 4:30, Aunt Abigail peeked out the window and said, "Ah, gut, Mamm's home."

Elizabeth joined her and saw Mary, Rachel, and Eli all climbing out of the buggy. Moments later, the group swept into the kitchen and were immediately given tasks to help finish preparing the supper food and setting the dining table. As they worked, Eli told Elizabeth of his adventures playing with their young cousins, and Mary echoed her delight at finally meeting them.

At five o'clock, six new guests from the guest house joined them in the dining room. Mammi Esh welcomed them and invited them to sit at the table, along with Mary, Eli and Elizabeth. She then described each dish on the table and concluded, "Dessert will be served on the back porch this evening."

Once everyone had finished the hearty meal, Mammi Esh led her guests to her back porch sitting area. It was a beautiful, warm, deep-blue summer evening. The guests sat and relaxed as Mammi Esh, Rachel, and Abigail set up the dessert table and made coffee. Then Abigail announced to everyone that there was homemade ice cream, shoofly pie, peach pie, apple pie, and a variety of homemade candies to enjoy. Eli and Elizabeth tried a little of everything.

When the sun had set, Mammi Esh stood again to address the group. "The Amish don't have televisions, but we love to play games. Please join us back in the dining room for some table games if you'd like, or feel free to relax back at the guest house."

One guest couple decided to stay and play Dutch Blitz with the Hopewells and Mammi Esh, who, they discovered, was quite funny when she played and more than a little competitive. Laughs abounded, and before they knew it, the clock had struck ten o'clock.

"And that's the signal for bed, I think," announced Mammi Esh.

As Mary walked over to the guest house with her children, she asked them, "Well, what do you think of your visit so far?"

"It's awesome!" Elizabeth said. "I loved working with Aunt Abigail. I can't wait to go home and make a shoofly pie for Dad."

"What about you, Eli? Have you enjoyed yourself?"

"Yes," said Eli. "Uncle Elam's leather shop was really interesting, and it was fun to play with the boys. But..." He hesitated, then admitted, "I wish Dad was here. I miss him."

"I miss him too," said Mary. "I hope he can come next time. But we'll get to see him tomorrow afternoon."

"Really?" asked Eli.

"Yes," replied his mother as they entered the guest house. "I told Mammi Esh we would eat breakfast and then head home."

"Cool," said Eli, taking the stairs two at a time.

Just as Mary opened her bedroom door, Elizabeth stopped behind her. "Mom, wait," she said anxiously.

"Yes, honey?" Mary said, concerned.

"I have to do my chores tomorrow or Mammi Esh won't let me have my doll. We had a deal, remember?"

"You may do your chores while Eli and I load the car," Mary said. "I wouldn't keep you from earning your doll. I know it is important and special to you."

"Oh, thank you, Mom," said Elizabeth, hugging her mother.

Mary looked down into her daughter's eyes. "Are you going to be sad when we leave tomorrow?" she asked.

Elizabeth thought for a moment. "No, I won't be sad. But I definitely want to come back."

Mary smiled and sighed. "Me too. And we will." She kissed the top of Elizabeth's head. "Get some rest, my girl. You've had a busy day."

"Good night, Mom." Elizabeth tripped lightly to her bedroom.

Eli and Elizabeth got in their pajamas and climbed into the big red bed. Eli turned off the gas light on the nightstand beside him, mumbled, "Night," and turned over to sleep.

"Night, Eli." Elizabeth gazed at the ceiling. She didn't feel sleepy at all. "Eli?" she whispered.

"What?"

"Do you think you'd ever want to become Amish?"

Eli rolled over to face her. "What? No. I mean…I don't think so." He paused. "Do you?"

Elizabeth shook her head. "I want to learn as much as I can about them. I want to keep getting to know Mom's family. But… I already know I want to go to college someday."

"I don't know about college," Eli murmured. "But I definitely don't want to live without electricity, or my camera. I like taking pictures too much."

"Yeah, and your pictures are good too," Elizabeth said. "You can't give that up." She breathed deeply. "I'm glad we feel the same."

"Me too," Eli whispered.

"Night, Eli."

"Night."

Their alarm clock woke them up at seven o'clock the next morning. Yawning and groggy, Eli and Elizabeth washed, dressed, and trekked over to the farmhouse with their mother for another lavish breakfast. Elizabeth ate a bit more quickly and was ready when Aunt Abigail rose to go take care of the calves and chickens. While Elizabeth was gone, Mary and Eli helped clear the breakfast table and loaded their bags into the car, along with a generous assortment of canned goodies from Mammi Esh. At last,

Elizabeth came back from the chicken coop, washed her hands in the kitchen, and came out to the front porch, where everyone was waiting.

Mammi Esh held out the promised doll to her. "A deal is a deal, and Abigail tells me you were a natural with the calves and chickens," she said affectionately.

"Thank you, Mammi," Elizabeth cried, pressing the doll to her chest. "It's beautiful."

"Thank you so much for having us, Mamm," Mary said as she embraced her mother.

"It was our pleasure," replied Mammi Esh.

"I'm so glad you came," Aunt Rachel said to Mary as she embraced her. "I've missed you."

After passing around hugs and good wishes, it was time for the Hopewells to leave. As they turned to walk to their car, they saw Elam striding toward the farmhouse with a bag in his hand.

"Oh gut, I got here before you left," he called. When he reached them, he handed Eli the bag.

"For me?" Eli asked.

"Ya." Uncle Elam nodded. "Open it."

Eli reached in the bag and drew out a shiny leather belt. "Wow," he breathed. "Thank you, Uncle Elam."

"You're welcome. Ruth was so grateful for your help yesterday afternoon, and I wanted to make something for you. You see, Amish men don't wear belts, but I noticed yours was looking a little worn, so I came over early this morning and made this for you."

Eli hugged his uncle around the waist. "Thank you, Uncle Elam. I had a lot of fun with your boys. I hope we can do it again soon."

"And if Ruth needs help after the new bobbli comes, let me know," Mary said.

"I'll keep that in mind," said Elam, grinning. "Well, safe travels. I must get back to work."

After another round of hugs, Mary, Eli, and Elizabeth climbed into the SUV. They saw Abigail running after them, waving a sheet of paper. She passed it through the window to Elizabeth and said, "This is our address. Please keep in contact. We would enjoy sharing letters with you."

"Thank you, Aunt Abigail," Elizabeth said. "I will write to you soon."

Eli and Elizabeth waved goodbye to Mammi Esh, Abigail, and Rachel until their mother turned out of the lane.

"It'll be nice to be with Dad again at home," Mary declared.

"Yeah," agreed Eli. "Home." He turned his new belt over and over in his hand, sniffing the new leather. "New for us and old for you, huh, Mom?"

Mary considered this. "I guess you're right. Like I said the other day, you, Dad and Elizabeth are my family and my home. But now I'll get to bring some of my old home into my new home."

"Do you feel better about that now, Mom?" Elizabeth asked, holding up her new doll to examine Mammi Esh's fine stitching.

"I do," Mary replied fervently. "God has answered so many of my prayers in the last week. I…I still can't take it all in. But I am very hopeful. I think many good things lie in store for us."

PART 2

A NEW SEASON

CHAPTER 6
THE GENERAL STORE

"Here we are," announced Mary, turning the SUV into the driveway. "Home sweet home."

"Just like we left it," Elizabeth said, smiling as she took in the sight of the tiny, white house. Four gleaming rocking chairs stood like a welcoming committee on the front porch.

Eli unbuckled his seatbelt. "Is Dad here, Mom?"

"I don't think so," Mary replied. "He's supposed to be working with Mr. Hersh today."

"I can't wait to show him my belt," Eli said, jumping out of the car.

"And my doll!" Elizabeth added.

The siblings joined their mother at the back of the car to unload their bags and gifts. Arms and hands full, they trooped around to the kitchen door and entered the little house.

"Go ahead and put those on the counter," Mary instructed. "And head upstairs to unpack."

"Okay," said Eli and Elizabeth. They set the jars of canned peaches down and marched off toward the stairs.

"We get to sleep in our own beds tonight," Elizabeth said, as she reached the landing and turned toward her bedroom. "Mammi Esh's bed was nice, but it's still not the same as mine."

"Yeah, I like my bed better," Eli agreed, flinging his bag on his bed. "Hey Mom! May we visit Grandpa and Grandma this afternoon?"

"Hmm…" Mary considered as she came upstairs. "I'd like us to stay here today, son. I want to do laundry and clean up the house before your father gets home. And we still haven't unpacked all the boxes in the schoolroom, you know."

"Aw…" Eli began.

"But tomorrow you can spend all day over there if they'll have you," declared Mary as she went into the master bedroom.

"Okay," Eli said. "I've just been thinking about the Sanctuary. I want to take more pictures there again… I got a few good ones last time, but I want to get enough to make an album for Grandpa."

"I think he would love that," said Mary.

"Ooh, I want to make something for Grandma," Elizabeth chimed in from her room. "But I don't know what…"

"I'm sure we can think of something," Mary said. She came out of the bedroom with a laundry basket and set it on the landing. "Okay you two, clean clothes in your dressers and dirty clothes in here. Then meet me down in the schoolroom, please."

Once in the schoolroom, Mary gave each of them a box of books to stack neatly in a tall bookcase.

Eli pulled out a familiar coffee table book. "Hey, I've been wondering where this went!"

Elizabeth peered over his shoulder at the black-and white photographs. "What is it?"

"My Ansel Adams book," Eli murmured, engrossed in the mountains captured in the shots.

Elizabeth went back to unpacking boxes. "Oh!" she exclaimed as she pulled out a Mother Goose picture book their mother used to read to them. "Eli! Remember this?" She leaned over to show him. A book in his box, *Little House on the Prairie*, caught her eye, and she grabbed it out of the box. "It's been ages since I read this!" She read the first page to herself, savoring the words.

"This will take all day if you plan to read the books as you stack them." Mary chuckled as she laid pens and pencils neatly in her desk. "How about this? Pick out one or two books and after chores you may read while I make dinner. And don't forget you have those library books, too."

"Cool," said Eli, setting aside the coffee-table book.

Elizabeth held up *Anne of Green Gables* and *The Little House on the Prairie* in each hand, debating. A second later, she put *Anne* to one side and slid *Little House* onto the bookshelf. Next, she picked up a black, leather-bound Bible from the box. "Hey Mom," she asked. "Are we going to study the Bible for school?"

Mary looked up. "Well…yes, I thought we would. We've read most of the stories, but we've never really studied it together. Now that we're back here, we'll probably be going to church more regularly, so I think it will be helpful."

"Cool!" Elizabeth said. "I've been wanting to learn more about the Bible."

"Two 'Cools' in a row," Mary said in mock surprise. "What have I done to deserve it?"

Eli and Elizabeth grinned at their mother, then returned to their tasks. After the books were put away, they folded laundry, swept the kitchen and front porch, dusted the living room, took the garbage out, and finally collapsed in the living room with their chosen piles of books. It seemed only moments had passed before the kitchen door opened and their father's voice boomed through the house.

"Well, well," he laughed, sweeping Mary into his arms. "My favorite people are back! This is quite a cozy scene."

Eli and Elizabeth laid down their books and bounded over to hug their father.

"We got to stay at Mammi Esh's bed and breakfast, Dad!" Elizabeth gushed. "Aunt Abigail showed me how to feed the calves and the chickens and she also taught me how to make shoo-fly pie! And Mammi Esh paid me with one of her dolls. Here, I'll show you!"

"Oh boy," Jacob grinned as he watched her tear away upstairs.

"And I got a new belt, Dad," Eli said, hooking his thumbs beneath the leather wrapped around his waist. "Uncle Elam made it for me."

"Very nice," Jacob said, nodding. "Uncle Elam is quite the craftsman." Elizabeth skipped back into the kitchen, brandishing her new, faceless doll. Jacob gently took it from her and examined it.

"And Mammi Esh is quite the seamstress." He smiled and handed it back to her. "Do I smell peaches?" He looked hopefully at his wife.

"Yes, Mamm sent some back with us." Mary beamed. "I made a cobbler. We're ready to sit down for supper when you are."

"Excellent," Jacob said, clapping his hands together.

When they were seated around the table, Jacob looked around at his family. "I'm sure glad you're back," he said, his eyes twinkling. After a pause, he said, "How about I say a prayer?"

Mary's gave her husband a curious smile as she, Eli, and Elizabeth bowed their heads.

Jacob cleared his throat. "Dear God, I thank You for bringing us all safely home together this evening to share this delicious meal. You have blessed us in many ways since we came to Pennsylvania. I'm especially thankful for the time we have been able to spend with our family members after so many years apart. Grant us grace as we continue to settle into this new place and new season. Amen."

"Amen," the others murmured.

"So," Jacob began, pulling a dish of fried chicken toward him, "It sounds like you got along well with your Amish relatives."

Eli and Elizabeth both looked at their mother, who smiled and nodded to Jacob. "Eli and Elizabeth were both very helpful and respectful. I was so proud of them. Abigail put Elizabeth to work in the kitchen, and Eli entertained Elam's boys all afternoon. I think they will be inviting them to come back very soon."

"Is that right?" Jacob laughed as he scooped mashed potatoes on his plate. "Well, I'm not surprised. But what did you two think of the farm and how Mom's family lives?"

Elizabeth swallowed a bite of chicken. "I thought it was really interesting. Everyone there can make so many things. They work hard...but they also have a lot of fun together. You should have seen Mammi Esh playing games last night. She was hilarious. The way she slapped those Dutch Blitz cards on the table!"

"Yeah..." Eli agreed, snorting a little at the memory. "It was fun riding in Uncle Elam's buggy too..." Then his face turned serious. "But Dad, we really don't think we could live without electricity."

Jacob nodded. "I know what you mean, son. Thank goodness God loves all of us the same, including those of us who appreciate some modern technology."

Eli smiled broadly at his father. "Speaking of which...Mom said I could go over to the Sanctuary tomorrow to take more pictures."

"Unless you had something else you wanted them to do, dear," Mary interjected.

"Oh no, I'll be at the counseling center tomorrow. I'm sure Grandma and Grandpa would love to see you and hear about your adventure. But I bet *they'll* have things for you to do." He winked at Eli and Elizabeth.

"That's okay," said Elizabeth. "Grandma's food more than makes up for any chores."

"I see how it is" Mary shook her head and eyed her husband wryly.

Jacob shrugged. "Might as well get used to it. My mother likes to feed people." He reached for the peach cobbler. "And so does yours," he added.

"And so do I," Mary, with a slight head-tilt toward the laden table. "In fact, before you two head over there tomorrow, you can pack up some of this and take it over for lunch."

"Or…" Jacob's face lit up and he raised a finger momentously. "You could go to the General Store and get some hoagies to take."

"Oh, can we?" Elizabeth exclaimed. "I saw that place when we went to the library and I've been curious to see what's in there. Wait! What are hoagies?"

"They're subs," Jacob said. "They call them 'grinders' back in Boston. I had one from the General Store yesterday while you were gone. And they were just as good as I remembered."

"Mom?" Eli looked up at Mary hopefully.

"All right," Mary agreed. "We'll head over there just before lunchtime."

"I'll stop by Mom and Dad's on my way to work and let them know you're coming," said Jacob.

* * * * * * * * * * * * * * * *

At eleven o'clock the next morning, Mary, Eli, and Elizabeth piled into the SUV, stowing Eli's camera case and a paper bag containing Elizabeth's doll under their seats. Ten minutes later, they were pulling into the small dirt parking lot beside the General Store. Eli and Elizabeth hurried ahead of Mary toward the front door. As they stepped up onto the covered porch, they saw two, large, cast-iron machines to the right of the entrance. On the left, two gentlemen sat in rocking chairs, chatting and pulling peanuts out from a paper bag between them. Peanut shells littered the floorboards. The men smiled and nodded briefly at Eli and Elizabeth as they crossed the porch and opened the door.

"I wonder what those machines are for," Eli whispered to Elizabeth.

"Maybe they make peanuts," Elizabeth suggested.

"Gosh, it smells good in here," said Eli.

The General Store smelled of freshly baked bread. The children looked up and around, trying to take in the dizzying array of items crammed into the small store. To their right, wooden shelves stood laden with bolts of fabric, spools of thread, buttons, and zippers. Other shelves held stacks of shirts, pants, gloves, and other farm clothing. An assortment of tools hung in a corner over stacks of bins filled with nails, bolts, nuts, and other hardware.

Two chairs and a table bearing a checkerboard, a box of checkers, and a deck of cards stood beside a potbelly stove in the middle of the store. In front of the table were two kegs—one filled with peanuts and the other with empty peanut shells. Large barrels lined the left wall of the store. Eli and Elizabeth stepped over to peer inside them. The first barrel was filled with dill pickles and the second with boxes of crackers.[20] Three other barrels carried roasted peanuts, labeled "light," "medium," and "dark."

20   This is where the term "Cracker Barrel" came from. General stores used to have barrels of loose crackers in them.

"Come on, kids," Mary urged quietly, pointing toward a wooden counter at the back. Eli and Elizabeth followed her, goggling at the sight of a shelf behind the counter lined with candy jars, chockfull with colorful sweets. Other shelves held jars of coffee, tea, sugar, flour, spices, and other small items. An antique scale hung from the ceiling. To the left of the counter stood a cold case with lunchmeat, cheeses, and homemade salads, and a freezer case with buckets of ice cream. The right-hand wall featured a large display of pies, cookies, donuts, and golden-brown rolls and bread loaves.

A short man stood behind the counter, smiling at them. "Hello there! I'm Ed. Welcome to my store. And who might you be?"

Mary nudged Eli and Elizabeth forward.

"I'm Eli Hopewell, sir," Eli declared. "And this is my sister, Elizabeth, and my mom, Mary. My dad is Jacob Hopewell. He told us about your hoagies."

"Oh yes!" Ed's face lit up. "Jacob was here yesterday. He told me all about you moving back here from Boston. I'm sure Samuel and Rebecca must be happy to have you nearby."

"We're going to see them now," Elizabeth piped up. "We wanted to bring them some of your sandwiches for lunch!"

"Well, well," Ed said. "That sounds like quite an occasion. So what kind of hoagies are we having?"

Eli and Elizabeth stepped up to the cold case and began picking out their favorite cold cuts and cheeses. Ed pulled out five freshly baked hoagie rolls, laid them on the counter, sliced them in half, and deftly stacked them with slices.

"Mr. Ed, sir, what are those machines on your front porch?" Eli asked.

"They're roasters," Ed replied. "I roast peanuts in one of them and coffee in the other."

"I thought one of them must be a peanut roaster," Elizabeth said with glee. "I've never seen so many peanuts in my life!"

"Why don't you two go fill up a bag?" Ed suggested. "Your Grandpa likes the medium ones." He winked at them.

"Okay!" said Eli. Elizabeth followed him to the barrel and helped scoop peanuts into a paper lunch sack. They returned to the counter in time to see Ed sliding five paper-wrapped sandwiches into a bag. He reached across the counter, took the peanuts from Eli, and slipped them into the bag. Mary stepped forward, wallet in hand.

"Now wait a minute," Ed said, rubbing his hands together. He turned to survey the many treats around him. "Hmm...I don't want to spoil your appetites, but I think you all need something sweet to tide you over on your way to your grandparents'. Why don't you tell me your favorite kinds of ice cream?"

"Vanilla," Eli stated.

"Chocolate!" squealed Elizabeth.

"And you?" Ed looked expectantly at Mary.

"Oh..." she stammered. "Vanilla for me too, please."

"Excellent. And what about your favorite cookies?" asked Ed.

"Hmm..." Eli craned to look at the cookie jars. "Oatmeal," he decided.

"Peanut butter," said Elizabeth.

"Chocolate chip, please." Mary raised her eyebrows at Eli and Elizabeth and nodded at them.

"Please!" they echoed.

Grinning, Ed retrieved two oatmeal, two peanut butter, and two chocolate chip cookies and laid them on the counter. He laid a scoop of vanilla ice cream between Eli's and Mary's cookies and a scoop of chocolate ice cream between Elizabeth's. Next, he wrapped the three cookie sandwiches in wax paper, placed each in a separate bag, and handed them across the counter.

"Wow! Thank you, Mr. Ed," said Eli, taking his bag.

"Thank you, Mr. Ed!" Elizabeth bounced up and down.

"You're too kind," Mary said. "You really didn't have to do that."

"Consider it my welcoming gift to you," Ed said. "I hope to see you all back in here very soon."

"Oh, I'm sure we'll be back sooner than later," said Mary with a smile, handing him several bills.

"That's what I like to hear," Ed said as he placed the money in the till and counted out some change, which he handed to Mary. He turned to the kids. "Well, goodbye, folks. I've enjoyed meeting and talking with you."

"Same here, Mr. Ed," said Eli.

"See you soon!" Elizabeth said.

CHAPTER 7
PRAYING WITH GRANDMA

"May we eat our ice cream sandwiches in the car?" Elizabeth begged.

"As long as we don't make any messes." Mary smiled.

By the time they reached Samuel and Rebecca's, Eli and Elizabeth had finished the ice cream sandwiches and pronounced them the best they'd ever had.

Mary retrieved her hoagie and handed the bag to Eli. "All right, dears. Have a wonderful afternoon, and please be home in time for supper. Give Grandma and Grandpa my love."

"Yes, Ma'am," they replied as they exited the SUV. They waved at their mother as she pulled away, then scurried up to the door of their grandparents' house.

Grandma Hopewell answered their knocks, smiling wide and throwing out her arms to embrace her grandchildren. "Samuel, look who's here!"

"Aha!" barked Samuel. "Just the two we were waiting for. Your father said you'd be coming."

"We brought hoagies!" Elizabeth announced. "From Mr. Ed!"

"And peanuts," Eli added. "Mr. Ed said you liked the 'medium' ones, Grandpa."

Samuel nodded, then whispered loudly, "So do the squirrels."

"How wonderful!" Grandma said. "Why don't you set your things down and help me set the table?"

In no time, the four of them were seated at the table. Grandpa said a brief prayer, then handed out sandwiches.

"We want to hear all about your trip," said Grandma, unwrapping her hoagie. "Did you like Mammi Esh's farm, Elizabeth?"

Elizabeth and Eli excitedly shared the details of their visit. They displayed Eli's belt and Elizabeth's doll, which Grandma and Grandpa praised. They also explained that while they hoped to visit Mammi Esh again, they didn't think they were cut out to live like the Amish.

"And we missed you, Grandma and Grandpa," Elizabeth confessed.

Eli nodded in agreement. "And the Sanctuary. That's why I brought my camera. I was hoping I could take a few pictures this afternoon."

"Well, we missed you, too." Grandpa smiled as he cracked open a peanut. "Why don't you and I take a walk out by the pond, Eli?"

"That would be great!" Eli lit up.

"And I thought maybe I could help you in some way, Grandma?" added Elizabeth.

"Oh my dear, you are sweet." She thought for a moment, then said, "Would you like to learn to crochet? I can show you how to make a blanket for your doll."

"Ooh, I would love that!" Elizabeth's face glowed with delight.

After helping to wash the dishes and put away the leftovers, Eli hung his camera around his neck and turned to follow Grandpa out the door.

"Let's take these," Grandpa said, snatching the peanut bag. "Bribes for your photo subjects." Laughing, they strode out into the sunshine, as Elizabeth grabbed her doll and joined Grandma on the sofa in the living room.

"Do you mind if I take another look at this very special doll?" Grandma asked.

Elizabeth removed the doll from its bag and held it out with both hands. Grandma took it gently and held it under the lamp, examining it with care. "My, what fine stitching; her stitches are so even. I'm sure her quilt work is outstanding too."

"Yes, we saw some of her quilts in the bed and breakfast," said Elizabeth. "Each one has a different pattern and colors. It must take a long time to make each one."

"But if you do a little each day, you get there eventually," Grandma commented. "That's the key to getting many things done in life, you know." She handed the doll back to Elizabeth.

"Crocheting can go a bit faster than those tiny stiches, though. We'll have a blanket for her in no time once you get the hang of it."

Grandma reached down beside the sofa and pulled out a large basket filled with balls of brightly colored yarns. "Pick a color, dear," she said as she held out the basket.

Elizabeth couldn't resist reaching out to touch the soft yarn. "This blue is pretty," she said, picking up a periwinkle-colored ball. "May I use that?"

"Of course!" Grandma took the yarn from her and selected a crochet hook from the basket. "Let's start by having you watch how I make the stiches."

Elizabeth gazed raptly at her grandmother's aged yet practiced fingers as she wound the blue yarn around a finger, then the crochet hook, and began to weave a chain. After she had several inches, Grandma undid the chain and handed the yarn and hook to Elizabeth. "Now you get to try."

Slowly, with Grandma's patient encouragement, Elizabeth followed the steps, and after a few minutes had completed a fairly even chain of blue stitches.

"That's it!" Grandma praised. "Now let's do the second row. It's a little more complicated." She took the chain from Elizabeth and carefully showed her how to make the pattern of loops. Instead of undoing this row, however, she let Elizabeth take over with the third row. As Elizabeth made her careful loops, Grandma picked up another crocheted piece from her basket and added a row to it.

After completing several more rows, Elizabeth held up her work. "I think I'm getting the hang of it, Grandma!"

"You're doing very well, Elizabeth," Grandma said, looking over the piece. "Oopsy-daisy, it looks like you missed a few stitches—just here." She pointed to the spot.

"Oh no!" Elizabeth cried. Her face fell.

"It's all right, dear," Grandma said brightly. "I'll fix it in a jiffy." She began to unravel the blue yarn.

"I'm sorry I messed up," Elizabeth said.

"Oh, Elizabeth," Grandma laughed. "It's all right. Don't apologize. We all make mistakes when we're learning something new. I still make them from time to time, you know."

"I hate making mistakes." Elizabeth crossed her arms and scowled at the floor.

"I know, they can be frustrating," Grandma sighed. "But I've learned that it's better if we're not too hard on ourselves. We all need grace, don't we?"

Elizabeth thought about finding the Bible the other day and stiffened slightly. "Grandma…" she said.

"Yes, dear?"

"How much should someone read the Bible?"

"How much?" Grandma mused, her fingers flying as she restored the unraveled rows. "Well, I like to read a part of it every day, usually in the morning. Sometimes I'll read a chapter, sometimes a paragraph, and sometimes just a few verses. But my favorite thing is to memorize verses from the Bible. That's how I meditate on God's word and get it deeper in my heart and mind."

"Wow. I don't think I've memorized anything from the Bible," Elizabeth said. "I mean, Mom and Dad have read lots of stories to us…and we're going to start studying it in school!"

"I'm glad to hear that, Elizabeth." Grandma smiled. "I fell in love with God's word when I was about your age. That's when I first came to know Jesus for myself."

Elizabeth looked up. "What do you mean, you came to know Jesus?"

"Well, I learned about Jesus growing up," Grandma explained. "But I was taught how to invite Him into my life, to begin a relationship with Him. I dedicated myself to knowing Him and following Him." She held up the finished rows and handed them back to Elizabeth. "There you are."

Elizabeth took the piece and held it, thoughtfully. "Mom and Dad don't really talk about having a relationship with Jesus," she said. "They pray with us sometimes. Dad just prayed last night before dinner. But he didn't really do that when we lived in Boston. I…I've been wanting to know more about Jesus and the Bible, but I always feel like…like they're uncomfortable talking about it."

"I see," said Grandma. "Well, there's nothing I'd like more than to talk to you about that, Elizabeth."

Elizabeth looked up to see her grandmother smiling warmly at her. "Really?"

"Truly." Grandma nodded. "You can ask me anything you want to know. Why don't you start by telling me what you have learned about Jesus so far."

"Okay…" Elizabeth flushed, then stammered, "Well…I know Jesus is God's Son, and He came to die for our sins so we can go to Heaven. I'm…I'm just not totally sure what all that means," she shrugged and gave an embarrassed smile.

Grandma smiled graciously. "Yes, it's easy to hear such things all the time and wonder why no one takes the time to explain them." She clasped her hands thoughtfully. "Do you know what 'sin' means?"

"Well, yeah…sin is…doing bad things. Things God tells us not to do."

"And why does He tell us not to do them?" Grandma inquired.

"Uh…" Elizabeth's brow furrowed. "Because they hurt people?"

"It may not always seem like it at the time, but yes, sin hurts people," Grandma said. "Not just others, but ourselves. The Bible tells us that sin separates us from God. And God is the source of everything good in our lives. He is life itself. So being separated from Him is…well, it's death."

Elizabeth's eyes widened as she thought about this. "So…so if we don't sin, we won't be separated from God?"

"Well, yes…but there's the problem," Grandma said simply. "The Bible tells us that we have all sinned. Have you read the story about Adam and Eve?"

Elizabeth nodded.

"Well, when Adam and Eve disobeyed God and became separated from Him..." Grandma paused to choose her words. "Somehow they passed that separation, that death, on to every person on earth. And there's nothing we can do restore ourselves to Him. Only He can take away our sins and save us from death."

Elizabeth's mind whirred as she chewed on these words. "So... so is that why Jesus died on the cross?"

Grandma nodded. "Jesus did everything that we could not do for ourselves. We couldn't live up to God's standard, and we couldn't save ourselves from the death we deserved for falling short of it. So Jesus did both. He lived up to God's perfect standard, and then He offered Himself up to die in our place. And somehow, that very sacrifice, that act of love, defeated death once and for all."

Elizabeth's mouth fell open. A thrill of anticipation ran through her. "So...so what does that mean?"

Grandma reached out to clasp one of Elizabeth's hands and patted it affectionately. "It means, you and I are no longer separated from God. By putting our trust in Jesus and what He did, we can draw near to God, come to know Him and walk with Him. We can pray to Him as though He's right here with us and loves us more than we can imagine—because He does!"

"Really?" Elizabeth whispered.

"Oh my dear," Grandma murmured. "You can never get to the bottom of His love. It will take all of eternity to express it fully. I think that's what we'll be doing in Heaven, you know—endlessly discovering God's love."

"I...I want that," Elizabeth faltered. "But how do I...what do I do?"

"Would you like to pray with me?"

Elizabeth nodded.

Grandma beamed at Elizabeth. "We'll do it just like the crocheting. I'll start and you can repeat after me."

"All right," said Elizabeth, bowing her head.

With her hands gently held in Grandma's, Elizabeth softly echoed the words of the prayer, inviting Jesus into her life. After the "Amen," she looked up, smiling, into Grandma's beaming face. Elizabeth felt a refreshed cleanness in her soul, like housekeeping had come in and left everything sparkling.

"Thank you, Grandma. I...I feel different."

"I know what you mean," Grandma laughed. "Everything changes when Jesus isn't something so far away anymore, and you begin to know Him. I will pray for His love to become more and more real to you every day. Now, would you like to learn your first memory verse?"

"Okay!" replied Elizabeth.

Grandma walked into the kitchen and returned a few minutes later carrying a Bible, a 3x5 card, and a pen. "I'll write it down for you. This is a very famous verse, but it's famous for a reason. It's about God's love." After a few moments of writing, she handed the card to Elizabeth.

"For God so loved the world that he gave his one and only Son, that whoever believes in him shall not perish but have eternal life. John 3:16[21]," read Elizabeth.

21   NIV

"There it is in a nutshell," Grandma declared. "Do you think you can get it memorized in, say, a week?"

"Oh yes!" Elizabeth nodded, holding the card up to her face. "I bet I can get it memorized today!"

CHAPTER 8
ANSWERS FOR ELI

They stood on a small rise on the opposite side of the pond, facing back toward the house. Their journey to this spot had been slow and meandering, with many stops for Eli to take pictures, or for Grandpa to tell a story about a certain tree or point out the site of one of Jacob's childhood adventures. Eli was swept up in the shades of green and blue that surrounded them. They had shared the bag of peanuts with various squirrels and birds, creating many opportune moments for Eli to take pictures. It seemed there wasn't a bush, flower, bird, insect, or animal in sight that Grandpa could not name or describe in detail. Eli was feeling a little in awe of his wealth of knowledge. Eli wished the walk would never end. As he took a picture of Grandpa feeding the squirrels, he wished he could live in the camera frame forever, as if he could stay in that captured moment for the rest of time.

"Did your father ever tell you that I grew up on this land too?" Grandpa asked.

"I don't think so," Eli answered, turning to look at Grandpa. "You mean, your parents owned your house?"

"My father built it. His name was Eli."

"Really?" Eli stared at his grandfather, dumbstruck.

"Surely your father has mentioned where he got your name? And Elizabeth's—Elizabeth was my mother's name. You were named after your great-grandparents."

"I...I can't remember him ever telling us that," Eli shook his head.

Samuel sighed. "Well, I hope I haven't overstepped by telling you."

"I'm sure it's okay," Eli assured him. "I'll ask him about it tonight."

Samuel patted his grandson on the shoulder. "All right. Let's head back. There's someone I'd like you to meet back at the barn."

"Who is it?' Eli asked.

"You'll see," Grandpa promised. "He's a very old friend of mine."

Intrigued, Eli followed Grandpa back around the pond and up to the barn. Grandpa led Eli past stacks of hay bales and turned into a small alcove. A striped tabby cat lay sleeping in a towel-lined box tucked in the corner.

"This is my buddy, Tig," Grandpa said. "I've had him ever since your father left home. He's kept me company out here in the barn for many years." He knelt down on the hay, reached out a hand and affectionately scratched Tig's head. The cat slowly opened its eyes and gave a feeble, low meow.

"Wow, ever since Dad left?" Eli's eyes widened. "That's a long time!"

"Yes, he's had a good, long life," Grandpa said.

"He's beautiful." Eli crouched down beside Grandpa to get a closer look.

"Yes, he is a handsome boy," said Grandpa. "But he is in his last days. The vet was here yesterday. He said that he could put him down for me, but I said that I would like to try to keep him comfortable here. I'd like him to spend his last moments in the place he knew as home instead of a sterile vet's office."

A deep pang resounded in Eli's chest as Tig took short, labored breaths. "Oh, Grandpa, I'm sorry."

"It's okay," replied Grandpa. "Tig has had a good life. I'm at peace about it."

Eli leaned forward and gently stroked Tig's back. After a few moments he murmured, "Grandpa...are you afraid to die?"

Grandpa paused and stood up. "Sit with me on this bale, son." They sat down beside Tig's alcove. Grandpa crossed his legs and leaned back against the barn wall. "I'm not afraid to die, Eli," he said slowly. "When I was a young man I worried about it. My little brother, Jacob..." Eli's head spun around. Grandpa nodded in answer to his unspoken question. "Yes, I named your father in his memory. He died in an accident when he was eighteen. I was twenty." Grandpa sighed again, the grief creaking in his voice. "When you see how suddenly someone can go from your life, it makes you think. What if the same thing happens to you, and you leave your family behind? Or what if they leave before you? It can be a frightening thought. But it can also make you thankful for every moment you have together and careful that you don't take it for granted." He patted Eli's shoulder.

Eli looked up at him hesitantly. "I'm really sorry about your brother, Grandpa."

"I still miss him, of course," Grandpa said. "But I know I'll see him again."

Eli kicked at the loose hay on the barn floor. "I don't want to take things for granted. Sometimes…sometimes I wish I could freeze time. When we're all together doing something fun, or when I see something beautiful. I think…that's why I like taking pictures." He stopped as an idea occurred to him. "Grandpa, would it be okay if I took a picture of Tig?"

"Of course," Grandpa nodded.

Eli stepped over and knelt down close to Tig's box. "Hey there, Tig," he whispered as he scratched Tig's head. Tig opened his eyes. Eli raised his camera, framed Tig's face, and pressed the shutter button a few times. Then he stepped back to the bale and held out the camera so Grandpa could see the photo on the screen.

"Very nice," Grandpa said. "You have a good eye, Eli. God has given you a gift."

"Thank you, Grandpa." Eli gazed down at the picture. In a timid voice, he asked, "How long do you think Tig has?"

Grandpa sighed once more. "It could be anytime now. He's still eating a bit, but he's sleeping most of the time. I know he's tired."

"Oh…" Eli frowned as he looked back down at Tig in his box. Then he asked, "Well, do you think I could come visit him again tomorrow?"

"Yes, if you want to," Grandpa said. "Tig always likes company." Abruptly, he slapped his knees and stood to his feet. "Oh boy. Hear that?"

Eli looked up. Loud mooing sounds came in from outside. "Yeah," he said with a grin.

"The heifers always let me know when they're hungry," Grandpa said, wagging a knowing finger. "I could use your help feeding them."

"Okay, sure." Eli jumped to his feet.

"Why don't you put that fancy camera up on that shelf?" Grandpa indicated a row of shelves by the barn door filled with an assortment of tools, buckets, and other odds and ends.

Eli pulled the camera strap over his neck and placed the camera carefully between an old trowel and a seed catalog. Then he followed Grandpa out to the feeding pen, where he saw the heifers crowding around the feeding trough.

"I know, I'm in trouble," Grandpa called out to them. "Eli and I were enjoying some time out at the pond this afternoon. We'll have you fed in a minute."

"What do you want me to do, Grandpa?" Eli asked.

"Why don't you feed them hay while I give them grain and water?" Grandpa pointed to a pitchfork beside a covered stack of hay bales. "Just keep throwing forkfuls over till I say 'stop.'"

"Okay." Eli strode over to the pitchfork and thrust it into a hay bale. With effort, he finally pried a large wedge of hay apart from the bale, stuck it on the fork, and carried it over to the pen.

He thrust the weighty hay through the fence slats. Several heifers immediately lumbered over and swiped up bunches of hay with their long, thick tongues. Eli watched in fascination for a moment, then returned to the bale.

After Eli had served up nearly an entire bale to the hungry cows, Grandpa called, "That'll do it. Let's head back up to the house. I'm sure Grandma will be wondering what's keeping us."

"I'll just grab my camera," Eli said, as he walked over to the shelf. He hung his camera back around his neck and then walked towards the door, where Grandpa was waiting.

"Think you got all the pictures you wanted today?" Grandpa asked.

"I think so," Eli said. "I want to take lots more, but maybe I can take some tomorrow when I visit Tig."

"All right." Grandpa fell into a leisurely stroll toward the house.

"It's really amazing how much there is to see out here," Eli remarked. "Thank you for showing me around the pond, Grandpa. You must know everything there is to know about the animals and plants."

"Not everything." Grandpa laughed. "But God's creation is endlessly fascinating to me. Everything, even the smallest, ugliest, and seemingly insignificant things have a story to them. And there is beauty everywhere if you take the time to look for it."

Grandma met them as they ambled up to the door. "Right on time!" she called. "Elizabeth said they need to be home for supper. Do you want to drive them over, Samuel?"

"Of course," her husband replied, peering curiously at the suppressed delight that sparkled in her eyes. "You two had a good time together, I take it?"

"We certainly did," Grandma said with a wink. "I'll tell you about it later. What about you two? Did you take lots of pictures, Eli?"

"Yes, Grandma. And Grandpa let me meet Tig. He said I could come and visit him again tomorrow."

"Ah, sweet Tig. I'm sure he'll like your company."

Elizabeth joined them, carrying the bag with her doll, the beginnings of its crocheted blanket, and her memory verse card. "May I come back too, Grandma?"

"Oh yes," Grandma said. "Why don't you ask your mother if you can bake with me tomorrow? I'm planning to make a big batch of zucchini bread."

"Oh, I would love to help," Elizabeth breathed.

"And I can help you again, Grandpa," Eli offered. "With the heifers and stuff."

Grandpa stroked his chin. "I've actually been meaning to get that front fence painted…would you be up for helping me with that?"

"Sure!" Eli said.

"Wonderful." He clapped his hands together. "You two go ahead and get in the truck. I'll fetch the keys."

Elizabeth threw her arms around Grandma's waist. "Thank you for teaching me to crochet," she murmured. "And for praying with me."

"It was my pleasure." Grandma squeezed her, then broke away and said, "Ooh, let me send some treats with you. You go along to the truck and I'll bring them out." She disappeared into the house.

Eli and Elizabeth exchanged knowing smiles as they walked to Grandpa's truck. They had just buckled their seatbelts when they saw Grandma and Grandpa heading toward them. Grandma passed a paper bag through the passenger window while Grandpa climbed in the driver's seat.

"More whoopie pies," she mouthed.

"Thank you, Grandma!" they cried, waving goodbye as Grandpa backed out of the drive.

"I'll peek in and say hello to your mother," Grandpa told Eli and Elizabeth as they turned down the lane. "Make sure she's okay with us having you back over tomorrow. In fact, the painting project will probably take a few days, Eli, if you can be spared."

"Definitely," nodded Eli.

No sooner had they climbed out of the truck than Jacob drove up beside it in the car.

"Dad!" called Eli and Elizabeth, hurrying around to meet him.

"Jacob!" called Grandpa as he stepped down from the truck. "Just returning a few valuables of yours."

Jacob laughed as he gave Eli and Elizabeth a quick hug. "Thank you very much! I trust they were on their best behavior?"

"As always," Grandpa nodded. "In fact, we're finding them so helpful that I've come to ask if we could borrow them again. I'm going to be painting the front fence over the next few days and Eli would sure be a great help. And Grandma wants to introduce Elizabeth to the art of zucchini bread."

"It's fine with me," Jacob grinned. "Unless your mother has something she needs you to do."

"What about their mother?" Everyone turned to see Mary walking toward them, wearing an apron.

Elizabeth ran over to her mother, gave her a hug, and handed her the bag of whoopie pies. "Grandma wants me to make zucchini bread with her tomorrow, Mom," she said.

"And Grandpa wants me to paint the fence with him," Eli added.

"I see," said Mary, smiling fondly at their avid faces. "Well, we'll have to find some old paint clothes for you, won't we." She ruffled Eli's hair. "That's fine with me."

"Great! Grandma and I will plan on seeing these two around eight."

"We'll see you then, Grandpa!" said Eli as Elizabeth waved.

Grandpa waved goodbye, climbed into the truck, and drove away.

"Dinner's on the table," Mary announced as they walked back to their kitchen. "Let's wash up and sit down before it gets too cold."

A few minutes later, they were all diving into Mary's macaroni and cheese with relish and taking turns telling each other how the day had gone. Jacob had enjoyed his day at the counseling center, and Mary had spent the afternoon planning lessons for Eli and Elizabeth's math courses. Eli told them about his walk around the pond with Grandpa, meeting Tig, and feeding the heifers. Lastly, Elizabeth described Grandma's crochet lesson. Abruptly, she broke off.

"What's up, Elizabeth?" asked Jacob.

Elizabeth took a deep breath. "I prayed with Grandma today." She hesitated.

Mary's eyebrows popped up in surprise. "Oh? What about, honey?" she asked gently.

Elizabeth tried not to let her words out in a rush. "She talked to me about having a relationship with Jesus. I said I wanted that, so she helped me pray and ask Him to forgive my sins and come into my life. And she gave me a memory verse."

Mary and Jacob gazed at each other, their faces flushed with joy, while Eli stared at his sister, wide-eyed.

"That's wonderful, sweetheart," said Jacob.

Mary reached over to squeeze Elizabeth's hand. Eli gave his sister a brief smile and busied himself with his macaroni.

Then Eli said, "Hey Dad, Grandpa told me that you named me and Elizabeth after his parents and he that you were named after his brother, the one who died."

It was Elizabeth's turn to be surprised. "What?"

Jacob tilted his head. "Haven't I told you that before?" Eli shook his head no.

"I don't remember either," seconded Elizabeth.

"Hmm..." Jacob pondered this. "Well, yes, you were named for my grandparents. Sadly, they died before you were born, just like my uncle died before I was born. But I guess my dad and I have a thing for keeping names in the family."

"So what did Grandpa Eli do?" asked Eli.

"He was a pastor. And he was very good at building things—he built the house that Grandma and Grandpa live in now, in fact. I can still remember sitting in church as a boy, listening to him preach. He could be quite intimidating, but also very gracious." He paused and smiled fondly. "I still remember one of my last conversations with him. I was eighteen, and I had just decided to marry your mom and become a social worker. Grandpa Eli heard about my plans from my parents, and one Sunday after church he asked me to come over for a talk. We walked around the pond and he asked me how I had come to my decision to leave the community. I explained that I felt called to help people outside it, and that Mary felt the same." He shook his head and laughed. "Boy, I was so nervous to tell him that."

"Why, Dad?" asked Elizabeth.

"Oh, I think Grandpa had a not-so-secret hope that I would become a pastor too. He hoped I would follow after the same dream my uncle had. So I thought he might feel disappointed."

"So what did he say?" Eli asked.

"Well...he told me that he loved me, that he trusted that God would show me my path, and that he would pray for me. He blessed me to follow my heart and God's leading," Jacob said simply.

His eyes twinkled. "You know..." He eyed Mary keenly. "I wonder what he would say about us coming back here. I think he'd be pleased that we're back home."

Mary replied, "I'm sure he'd be pleased."

"Dad..." Eli interjected suddenly, his face reddening.

"What is it, Eli?"

Jacob, Mary, and Elizabeth watched and waited as Eli struggled to compose his thoughts.

"I...I don't know," he said finally. "I know when we left Boston you told us there was a lot you hadn't really explained about... our family and stuff. But now that we're learning some of it...I guess I just don't understand why you haven't talked to us about it before."

Jacob sighed, his head bowed in apology. "I know, Eli...and I'm sorry." He looked up at the ceiling, considering. "I think... we were just in a different season of our lives—practically in a different world. And it was a good season. But in that season, there were some things that were too painful to talk about, like your mother's family. Now we're in a new season, in this world, and we've found healing for those old wounds. So it's easier for us to talk about those things now. Plus, here, you don't just have to hear Mom and me tell you about our family and how we grew up; you get to experience things for yourselves. All of that gets to come alive for you now. Does that make sense?"

"I think so..." Eli said.

"I know it's a lot, Eli—a lot of change," Jacob continued. "But when I look at what's happened since we've come back here, I have to conclude that God led us here in His time and for His purposes. It was His timing for Mom's reconciliation with her family..." Mary nodded in agreement. "And I think you two are just now at the perfect age to really understand about the Amish, about faith..." Elizabeth, who smiled glowingly back at him. "And about our families," he finished, returning his gaze to Eli, who still looked perplexed. "And..." Jacob added dramatically, "You may have noticed that this new season has brought a lot of delicious treats into your life." He gestured at the plate of whoopie pies.

At this, Eli's face broke into a grin. "That's for sure." With a sigh, he reached for a pie and said, "Okay, a new season. I guess we just have to go with it."

"Bingo," said Jacob.

CHAPTER 9
GOD MAKES BEAUTIFUL

The next morning, Eli and Elizabeth wolfed down their breakfasts, promised their mother they'd be home right after lunch, and tramped through the backfields to Grandpa and Grandma Hopewell's. They met Grandpa outside, and he and Eli strode off to feed the heifers before tackling the fence painting. Elizabeth entered the house to find Grandma laying out bowls and ingredients for the zucchini bread. Ten loaf pans were on the table, all arranged in a straight line.

"That's a lot of bread pans!" Elizabeth said, slightly shocked. "Who is all this zucchini bread for?"

"Oh, lots of people." Grandma laughed. "I'll freeze a few loaves for the winter and donate some to a local bake sale. And I'll share the rest with family and friends. I like to let them choose between my spicy raisin zucchini bread and the plain kind, so I make lots of each. It's more fun when you give people what they really like," she explained, her eyes twinkling. "Why don't you put this on?" she asked, holding out a calico-print apron.

"Okay!" Elizabeth said. She tied the apron around her waist and then walked over to wash her hands in the sink.

"Good girl," Grandma said. "Now how's that memory verse coming?"

"I worked on it last night," Elizabeth said. "Let's see…" She carefully recited the verse, pausing only a few times to remember the words.

"My goodness," Grandma said. "Very impressive. I think I'll need to give you a new one after we finish our baking."

Meanwhile, Grandpa was showing Eli the proper way to paint fence boards. "Don't overcoat your brush. And work with the grain of the wood," he instructed, demonstrating with his own brush.

Carefully, Eli dipped his brush in the paint bucket, wiped the drips on the edge, and swiped the brush slowly across the boards.

"That's it, son," said Grandpa. "Why don't you work on this section while I get started over here?"

"Okay, Grandpa," said Eli.

The pair worked quietly for a few minutes. As Eli fell into a rhythm of his strokes, he started thinking about Jesus. *Why did Mom and Dad get so excited when Elizabeth told them she invited Jesus into her life? And why do Grandma and Grandpa love Jesus so much?* Then, without warning, Grandpa started to sing.

"Amazing grace, how sweet the sound, that saved a wretch like me…"

Eli stopped and stared at Grandpa.

"I like to praise God as I work," explained Grandpa.

"Why?"

"Well, Eli, I'm very thankful for what He's done for me. See, God sent Jesus, His Son, down to earth so we can be free from the bondage of sin. It's in Jesus that we're able to find the beauty in life, and through Him, we don't have to be weighed down by the worries of the world. I'm so glad He loves me enough to save me from evil." He peered down at Eli. "Do you know that hymn?"

"I've heard it before...but I don't really know the words," Eli confessed.

"Would you like me to teach it to you?" Grandpa offered.

"Okay," said Eli.

"Let's take it a line at a time. I'll sing a line and you sing it back to me, okay?" Eli nodded. In a slow, deliberate tempo, Grandpa sang, "Amazing grace...how sweet the sound..." Quietly, Eli echoed the line. "That saved...a wretch...like me..." When Eli had finished the first verse, Grandpa grinned and said, "You have a very nice voice, Eli. All you need is a little confidence. Want to try again?"

When they finished the third section of the fence, Eli could sing three verses of "Amazing Grace" from memory with Grandpa. After deciding to give their singing voices a rest, Eli filled Grandpa in on the conversation at the dinner table the previous night.

"Dad said he thought Great-Grandpa Eli wanted him to be a pastor," said Eli.

Grandpa pursed his lips. "My father did tell me he thought Jacob would make a good pastor," he admitted. "I think he saw that Jacob was outgoing, compassionate, and loved to serve people. Jacob just decided to use those qualities for social work, which, after all, is similar to pastoring in many ways." He paused. "I think your father needed the challenge of serving people who were very different than he. He wanted to see the world a bit and broaden his perspective. And you know, sometimes that's a good way to help you appreciate where you came from." He raised his eyebrows at Eli.

"Yeah, Dad said that he feels like Boston was one season, but now we're in a new season where we get to learn about where he and Mom grew up and experience it for ourselves," Eli said.

"A new season…" Grandpa repeated. "That puts me in mind of some verses I memorized when I was about your age." He took a deep breath and began to recite, in a slow, sonorous tone:

"For everything there is a season,

a time for every activity under heaven.

A time to be born and a time to die.

A time to plant and a time to harvest.

A time to kill and a time to heal.

A time to tear down and a time to build up.

A time to cry and a time to laugh.

A time to grieve and a time to dance.

A time to scatter stones and a time to gather stones.

A time to embrace and a time to turn away.

A time to search and a time to quit searching.

A time to keep and a time to throw away.

A time to tear and a time to mend.

A time to be quiet and a time to speak.

A time to love and a time to hate.

A time for war and a time for peace.

What do people really get for all their hard work? I have seen the burden God has placed on us all. Yet God has made everything beautiful for its own time. He has planted eternity in the human heart, but even so, people cannot see the whole scope of God's work from beginning to end. So I concluded there is nothing better than to be happy and enjoy ourselves as long as we can. And people should eat and drink and enjoy the fruits of their labor, for these are gifts from God.[22]

A hush fell in the wake of Grandpa's words. Something stirred inside Eli like a flutter of light, but he could not fathom it. He wasn't sure how, but the passage had touched something in him. Finally, he said, "That was beautiful, Grandpa."

"Thank you, son."

"Where is it from?"

"Ecclesiastes," said Grandpa. "And I think it's true, you know. I think God is going to make things beautiful in this season for you."

---

22   Ecclesiastes 3:1-13

An hour later, Grandpa told Eli it was time to call it a day on the fence painting. They trekked to the barn, wrapped their brushes and stowed them with the paint buckets, washed their paint-spattered hands, and stopped briefly to check on Tig before heading into the house for lunch. There they found Grandma and Elizabeth setting the half of the table that wasn't covered by bread pans. A light, warm cinnamon scent filled the room.

"Wow, it smells amazing in here!" Eli said.

"And we get to take some home," Elizabeth whispered to him as they sat down with Grandma and Grandpa.

"Elizabeth, dear, would you like to pray?" asked Grandpa.

Elizabeth's face lit up. "All right, Grandpa."

Wordlessly, they bowed their heads.

"Dear God," Elizabeth began. "Thank You for this day and for this food. Thank You for the time that Eli and I had with Grandma and Grandpa Hopewell today. Also, thank You for bringing us to Pennsylvania so we could learn more about Your love for us. I pray these things in Jesus' name, Amen."

As Grandma's chicken salad began to make the rounds, Grandma said, "Grandpa and I were wondering if you all wanted to come over after church again on Sunday for another cookout in the Sanctuary."

"Definitely," Eli said, as Elizabeth nodded fervently.

"Wonderful. Are you two planning to come back over tomorrow?" Grandma asked.

"I am," Eli said, catching Grandpa's eye. "We have a lot more fence to paint."

"What about me, Grandma?" Elizabeth asked.

"I think we could probably finish your blanket tomorrow," Grandma suggested. "And maybe start another project."

"Great!"

"Ask your parents tonight about Sunday," Grandma urged them, "and let us know their answer when you come in the morning. Tell your mother she can bring anything she likes, but we'll cover all the main dishes."

By one o'clock, Eli and Elizabeth had hugged their grandparents goodbye and set off for home, Elizabeth carrying a still-warm loaf of zucchini bread.

"Grandma is giving me verses to memorize," said Elizabeth, showing Eli the card Grandma had given her.

"Grandpa quoted a long verse to me today while we were painting," replied Eli, handing her back the card. "It was all about times and seasons. He said it was from Ecclesiastes. I liked it." He considered telling her how it made him feel, but he shrugged it off.

"Cool," Elizabeth said. "I think Grandma and Grandpa must have a lot of verses memorized. Grandma says she's been memorizing since she was my age."

"Yeah, Grandpa said he had too." He looked back over the fields. "So tell me more about praying with Grandma yesterday."

She smiled nervously. "Well...she just told me that she has a 'relationship' with Jesus. And I just felt like I didn't really have that. I know Mom and Dad have talked about God and read the Bible to us, but...I haven't felt like I really know Him."

"I think I know what you mean," said Eli. "So...did it feel different when you prayed?"

"Yeah, it did!" Elizabeth said. "I felt...really peaceful. And excited. I felt like Jesus was right there with us as we prayed to Him, and I felt His love. It was...beautiful."

"Beautiful," Eli whispered. Before he could say more, he saw his mother waving at them from the kitchen door.

*   *   *   *   *   *   *   *   *   *   *   *   *   *   *   *   *

Eli and Elizabeth wasted no time in passing on the invitation to Grandma and Grandpa's on Sunday. Their mother told them to let Grandma know they would be delighted to come, and would bring along dessert and a salad. Then she announced that they were free to amuse themselves that afternoon—after they wrote thank you notes to Mammi Esh and Uncle Elam for their gifts. Eli finished this task first and headed upstairs to sort through photos on his camera. Elizabeth, who wanted to thank Mammi Esh and Abigail in detail, took a bit more time with her letter, then set off for her room to read *Anne of Green Gables*. At four, Mary called them down to help her with dinner, which they decided to eat on the porch in their rocking chairs—with zucchini bread and a few rounds of UNO for dessert.

The next day passed in similar fashion. Eli and Grandpa painted another third of the fence and spent some time visiting Tig. Grandma helped Elizabeth finish her doll's blanket and start a new, more complicated project: a crocheted hat. In the afternoon, Elizabeth helped her mother mix up a bowl of pasta salad for Sunday's picnic while Jacob and Eli drove in to town to buy s'more ingredients.

After church that Sunday, the Hopewells stopped at home to change and load the food in the SUV before driving to Grandma and Grandpa's. Elizabeth and Mary commissioned Eli and Jacob to take the food they had brought out to the Sanctuary while they went to help Grandma in the kitchen.

Grandpa stoked the fire as Jacob and Eli walked up to the table. They set the bowl of pasta salad and bag of s'mores stuff beside a large platter of hotdogs and hamburgers. "Hey, there!" called Grandpa.

"Hey Grandpa," Eli said. "How's Tig today?"

"He was fine when I checked on him before church, but I haven't been out to see him since I got home," Grandpa replied. "Would you go ahead and do that for me?"

"Okay, Grandpa." Eli jogged over to the barn. Reaching Tig's alcove, he knelt down and reached out to gently scratch Tig's head. The moment his fingers touched the cat, he knew something was wrong. He pulled his hand back and watched for signs of breathing. Tig was entirely still. Eli sat frozen in shock for a few moments, then walked numbly back to Grandpa. With every step he dreaded more the news he was about to give. He was about halfway back to the Sanctuary when Grandpa saw him and walked swiftly to meet him.

"He's…" Eli felt a lump rise in his throat, choking his words.

"It's all right, son," said Grandpa. He put a hand on Eli's shoulder and led him back to the barn. When they reached the alcove,

Grandpa knelt down and stroked Tig's fur slowly. "Ah, Tig. You were a good friend." He sighed. "Now you can rest. I'll miss you, buddy."

At the sight of this tender farewell, Eli's eyes welled with tears, then spilled over. Grandpa stood up. "Come here, son," he said, pulling Eli into a warm embrace.

Eli began to sob on Grandpa's shoulder. He couldn't understand what was happening, but it felt like something had broken open in him. All the emotions of leaving Boston, meeting Mom's family for the first time, and getting to know Grandpa finally showed themselves. Something else that had affected him was watching how Grandpa and Grandma lived their lives made him want to know Jesus more personally. He no longer wanted information. He wanted a relationship.

After a minute or two, Eli pulled away and swiped at his running eyes and nose. "Grandpa?"

"What is it, son?"

"Elizabeth told us that Grandma prayed with her. To have a relationship with Jesus."

"That's right," Grandpa said, nodding.

"Will you pray with me?"

Grandpa put a hand on Eli's arm and led him over to the hay bale by Tig's alcove. "I'd love to pray with you."

"We're going to do something very simple. We'll do it like you learned 'Amazing Grace'."

After Eli had finished the prayer, Grandpa gave him another hug. "What a day." He shook his head. "I get to say 'See you later' to an old friend and help my grandson take his first step in his walk with Jesus. I feel very blessed."

Eli blew out a sigh. "Thank you, Grandpa."

"Thank *you*, Eli."

"Everything okay in here?" Jacob had appeared in the barn door.

"Just fine, Jacob," said Grandpa. "Old Tig's time finally came."

Jacob reached them and peered down into Tig's box, then reached out to hug his father. "I'm sorry, Dad. I know how special he was to you."

"Thank you, son," Grandpa said. "Well, he's in a better place. But since you're all here, it would be pretty nice to have a ceremony for him. Would you help me bury him, Eli?" Eli nodded. "I'll carry his box out if you can grab that shovel." He pointed to the far wall where a row of tools hung.

Grandpa carefully covered Tig in his blanket, picked up his box, and led Eli and Jacob out of the barn and back toward the Sanctuary. The ladies hurried over to meet them.

"Oh, Tig," Grandma said as she saw the box.

"We're going to go ahead and bury him now, Rebecca," Grandpa said.

Grandma, Mary, and Elizabeth joined the procession behind Grandpa as he walked slowly toward the corner of the Sanctuary closest to the pond. Finally, he stopped, put Tig's box down, and pointed to a spot under a large oak tree. "Go ahead and start digging there, Eli."

Eli stuck the spade in the soft earth and dug a hole deep and wide enough for Tig's box. Grandpa gently lowered the box into the hole and stood back. He looked at his wife, and she recited Psalm 23.

When she had finished, Grandpa said, "Dear Lord, we give You back our dear friend, Tig. Thank You for his long life and his company. May he rest in peace. Amen."

"Amen," the group intoned.

Then, suddenly, a voice began to sing. "Amazing grace, how sweet the sound…" Everyone looked around, their faces astonished as they realized Eli was singing. "That saved a wretch like me…" Joining him, the five other Hopewells took up the refrain. "I once was lost, but now am found; was blind, but now I see."

"Thank you for that, Eli," said Grandpa warmly. "I'll take that spade now." He scooped the dirt Eli had dug and tossed it in the hole to cover Tig. When he had finished, he said, "Let's all head back over to the fire pit. I'm just going to put this back in the barn, stop at the house to wash up, and then I'll be right out to join you."

Later, Grandpa returned to the Sanctuary carrying a large sack. He set the sack on the table as Grandma looked at him, surprise twinkling in her eyes. She joined him at the table.

"What's that, Grandpa?" Elizabeth asked.

"It's something that Grandma and I would like to give to you."

Eli and Elizabeth immediately hurried over, Mary and Jacob following. Grandpa reached in the bag and pulled out a stack of Bibles. Two of them appeared to be very old, while the other two looked brand new.

Grandpa held up the older books in each hand. "These Bibles belonged to my parents, Elizabeth Ann Hopewell, and Eli Jacob Hopewell." Eli and Elizabeth looked at each other, eyes wide. "It seemed obvious to us that you, their namesakes, should have them. And seeing as you both have just prayed some very significant prayers, the time for you to have them has come."

Elizabeth looked at Eli quizzically. He raised his eyebrows and nodded slightly to confirm his own conversion.

"However," Grandpa continued, laying down the old Bibles and picking up the new ones. "Seeing as these Bibles are in the King James Version, and are a little more challenging for you to read, we thought you also ought to have your own Bibles in a more contemporary version."

"Wow! Thank you, Grandpa!" cried Elizabeth.

"Yeah, thank you," said Eli. "And you, Grandma."

"You are so welcome dear," said Grandma. She picked up Eli's Bibles and handed them to him, while Grandpa handed Elizabeth hers.

Jacob shook his head. "You always outdo yourselves, Mom and Dad," he said. "Thank you for loving our kids."

"They are easy to love, you know." Grandma winked at him.

Mary examined the leather cover of Elizabeth's new Bible. "These are so beautiful, Samuel and Rebecca," she said. "What special gifts."

"They are beautiful," Eli said. He paused and looked over at Grandpa, whose face was shining with joy. "You were right—it's a beautiful season."

"It certainly is," Grandpa agreed. "And don't forget the next part. It's time to 'eat and drink and enjoy the fruits of our labor.'"

Laughing, they all sat around the table and began to celebrate.

PART 3

THE LETTERS

Love is patient and kind. Love is not jealous or boastful or proud or rude. It does not demand its own way. It is not irritable, and keeps no record of being wronged. It does not rejoice about injustice but rejoices whenever the truth wins out. Love never gives up, never loses faith, is always hopeful and endures through every circumstance. (1 Corinthians 13:1-7)

"For I know the plans I have for you," declares the LORD, "plans to prosper you and not to harm you, plans to give you hope and a future." (Jeremiah 29:11 NIV)

CHAPTER 10

TRANSITION

The rest of the summer went smoothly. Eli and Elizabeth continued to help Grandpa and Grandma Hopewell on their farm. Eli helped Grandpa finish painting the fence and also had the opportunity to help him with the fieldwork. He and Grandpa baled hay and straw. While Eli was helping Grandpa, Elizabeth was helping Grandma in the garden and with housework. She and Grandma canned chow-chow and froze freezer slaw. They also took a Sunday trip to Mammi Esh's, so that Jacob could go along. While they were there, they were able to see their new baby cousin, Esther. Yes! A girl! Finally!

The day after Labor Day, the Hopewell children started their homeschooling studies. They were studying many subjects: home economics, earth science, American history, Christian history, Bible, basic math, English, literature, and writing. At first Eli and Elizabeth thought their mother had gone overboard. However, once they realized how their mother had planned her lessons to make everything flow together, they really began enjoying their new school setting. Once a week they had what was known as Adventure Days. On Adventure Days their mother would take them to the library and on some other practical, educational adventure. Eli and Elizabeth never realized how much they could learn through this type of learning.

Eli and Elizabeth continued going to Grandma and Grandpa Hopewell's when school started. Now they were not only going over to assist their grandparents, but they had to keep a journal about what they did while they were there and what they thought of the experience. This was one way that Eli and Elizabeth practiced their writing.

Mary also found ways for her children to incorporate their hobbies into their schoolwork. For example, Eli was required to do something with photography for several of his assignments and Elizabeth was making blankets for the local nursing home and hospital.

Mary and the children were not the only ones having educational experiences. Since Jacob was told that he had to begin taking continuing education courses for his counseling job, he decided to start his master's degree. He wasn't sure how he was going to pay for such an endeavor, but the Lord provided. He qualified for financial aid. So, he was working for Mr. Hersh five days a week, going to class two evenings a week, and working at the counseling center three evenings a week. Even so, he made time for his family and God. He did his major studying on Saturdays. Sundays were devoted to church and family time.

Things were going very well and the family was enjoying the fall as the leaves were changing, the fields were being cleared, gardens were ending, and homes were being decorated with pumpkins and other fall décor. Everyone was getting into a comfortable routine.

CHAPTER 11
ELIZABETH'S LETTER

It was a school day in late October when the first letter came. Mary and the children were just getting home from one of their weekly field trips when Elizabeth noticed it lying on the kitchen table. She recognized Ann's address and tore open the envelope. Her excitement quickly turned to sorrow as her tears gathered in her throat.

Dear Elizabeth,

How's Pennsylvania? I bet you guys have been really busy with homeschooling. Do you like it? What's it like? I sometimes wish I were homeschooled, though Samantha hasn't been giving me as much trouble lately—I almost think she misses messing with you. But I can't complain about her being off my back.

Here's my news: I ended up in the Emergency Room last week. I was invited to a back-to-school get-together. I'm usually careful about going to stuff like that, but I figured I'd be okay since the family hosting the event knew about my condition.

They did everything they could to make sure I could enjoy myself. They had veggies, fruit, and gluten free rolls—everything I could ask for. They also had burgers, hot dogs, and chicken, and that's what made me sick. They had added a seasoning to the meat that had gluten in it. I thought it was just salt and pepper, so I ate some. But I'm okay now. I hope things are going well with you.

Miss you,

Ann

Mary came into the kitchen and noticed a tear sliding down Elizabeth's cheek. She walked over and put her arm around her. "Honey, what's wrong?"

Elizabeth thrust the letter into her mother's hands. "Mom, everyone knows that Ann has issues. Why can't they be more careful?" Her face crumpled as she imagined Ann in the hospital, the pain boiling in her stomach.

Mary skimmed the letter. "Elizabeth, I'm sure the hosts tried their best and feel terrible about what happened. They didn't mean to make her sick."

"I hate that she has to be so careful," Elizabeth burst out. "It just seems that she misses out on so much fun." Pain filled her heart. "Mom, may I go over to Grandma's for a little while? I need to work out my frustration."

"Sure, go ahead. Just be sure to come home for dinner. Would you like to call Ann and see how she's doing when you get back?"

"No, that's okay. I'll just write her a note back."

After giving her daughter a quick hug, Mary sent her on her way.

As Elizabeth approached her grandparents' place, she saw them out in the garden picking pumpkins. She took off in a dead run towards her grandmother, tears streaming down her face. By the time she got to her grandmother she was sobbing. Grandma Hopewell stopped what she was doing and gathered Elizabeth in her arms.

"Child, what's wrong?" asked Grandma. Elizabeth told her grandparents about the letter she had received. "Why don't you come inside with us?" Grandma asked. I was just about to start supper."

"Oh, I can't stay."

"That's fine. I'm just going to start fixing ours. Let's get your mind off your troubles for a while. Dear, would you mind bringing that pumpkin inside for me, please?"

"Coming right up," Grandpa said. He wasn't sure what Rebecca was up to, but he knew she was on a mission. He picked up the pumpkin, carried it into the kitchen, and set it on the counter.

Suddenly a green and white, pumpkin-shaped thing caught Elizabeth's eye. "Grandma, what's that?" she asked.

"That's a pumpkin," replied Grandma.

"Huh," replied Elizabeth. "I thought pumpkins were orange."

"It's just a different type of pumpkin," said Grandma. "I'm going to fry the neck of that green and white pumpkin. Then I'll make pumpkin custard out of what I call the bowl of it. However, you and I are going to make some special things out of the orange pumpkin that Grandpa brought in. There are some newspapers on that chair over there. Would you spread some of them on one end of the kitchen table, please?"

Grandma washed the orange pumpkin in the sink and dried it off with paper towels. She carefully set it on the newspaper-strewn table and got out several knives, a large spoon, a bowl, and a baking sheet. After everything was ready, she looked at Elizabeth and asked, "What do you see?"

"I see a pumpkin and a bunch of cooking stuff," replied Elizabeth.

"What do you see, Grandma?"

"Well, I see two things. First, I see a way to praise God. I also know that there's a wonderful snack inside."

"Huh?" replied Elizabeth.

"Watch." Grandma took one of the knives, cut a circle in the top of the pumpkin, and she popped the lid off. "Look inside. What do you see?" She pointed down into the pumpkin's bowl.

Elizabeth peeked inside and backed away. "*Eww*, I see seeds and strings." She stuck out her tongue.

Grandma smiled for a moment. "Elizabeth, have you ever seen pumpkin seeds at the grocery store?"

Elizabeth thought about it. "Well, yes, but they were in packages."

"Well, now you know where they come from. First, we're going to roast some pumpkin seeds. Then we're going to create a fall decoration that will praise the Lord."

Cautiously, Elizabeth replied, "Okay." *Where is Grandma going with this?* she wondered.

"Before we continue, though, I'm going to call your mom and tell her what we're doing. Grandpa will take you home."

After she had talked with Mary, Grandma showed Elizabeth how to scoop the seeds out of the pumpkin and how to separate the strings from the seeds. Then they arranged the seeds on the baking sheet, seasoned them, and put them in the oven to roast.

"Now, we'll have to keep an eye on those. We'll need to stir and turn them." Rebecca turned to her granddaughter. "Do you remember the day that you accepted Jesus into your heart?"

"Yes, ma'am."

"What did I tell you that day?" asked Grandma.

"You told me that I was a new person."

"That's right. And you know what else? You don't need to be ashamed or embarrassed about people knowing that you follow Jesus. He is the light of the world, and you have His light in you to share with others. Now, we're going to make our fall creation a little different than other folks do. Do you remember what Galatians 5:22-23 says?"

Elizabeth recited, "But the fruit of the Spirit is love, joy, peace, patience, kindness, goodness, faithfulness, gentleness and self-control."

"Excellent!" said Grandma.

Suddenly, it dawned on Elizabeth. "Oh, I get it!"

"Now, which word would you like to use?" asked Grandma.

"I'd like to use the word 'Love' since God is love."

"I think that's a great choice."

For the next hour, Grandma and Elizabeth stirred pumpkin seeds and carved the pumpkin. When they were finished, Grandma packed some of the seeds and gave Elizabeth the pumpkin to take home.

"But Grandma, that's your pumpkin."

"We can carve one for me tomorrow. I want you to take this one home since you showed such love and concern for your friend."

Elizabeth hugged her grandmother tightly, "I love you," she whispered. Then, with a slight spring in her step, she walked to her grandfather's truck. Grandma smiled inside and out as she watched her go. *Thank You God, for helping her grow*, she prayed silently.

Mary went out to meet Samuel and Elizabeth when they pulled into the driveway. She smiled when she saw Elizabeth carrying her gifts.

"Look what Grandma and I did!" Elizabeth held up her pumpkin, her face gleaming with pride.

"You did a great job! Let's put the pumpkin here, so Dad can see it when he comes home from class, and you take the seeds inside with you. I'll be in after I talk to Grandpa."

"Okay," replied Elizabeth, bouncing into the house.

Mary walked over to Samuel. "Thank you for bringing her home."

"Oh, Mary, it was nothing. What granddad wouldn't help his granddaughter when she's hurting?"

Mary smiled and said, "I'm glad she has you two. Would you please tell Rebecca that I'll be bringing the children over tomorrow? I would like to thank her for her help."

"I'll let her know. See you in the morning."

As she walked in the house Mary heard Eli say, "Boy, I sure hope I get to carve a pumpkin too."

"I'm sure you'll get to do one," Elizabeth replied.

Eli peered up at Mary. "Mom, may I go out and see Elizabeth's pumpkin?"

"Sure, go ahead, then we'll eat dinner."

While Eli stepped outside, Elizabeth gave her mother a hug and said, "Thank you for letting me go."

"You're welcome. I'm glad you're feeling better."

Eli bounded back into the house "That's neat! I wonder if she'd let me carve one that says 'Believe'."

"I'm sure she would," said Elizabeth.

Once hands were washed, Eli, Elizabeth and Mary sat down to a dinner of fried ham, sweet potatoes, green beans, and pumpkin pie. Mary asked, "Elizabeth, would you like to say the blessing?"

With her head bowed and eyes closed, Elizabeth said, "God, thank You for being with my friend Ann, and thank You for helping her feel better. Thank You for my wonderful family and for this food. Let it make us strong so we can do the work You want us to do. I pray these things in Jesus's name. Amen."

Once the leftovers were put away and the dishes were washed, Elizabeth headed to her room to write to Ann.

Dear Ann,

I'm sorry you went to the ER, but I'm glad you're okay. If something like that happens again, please call. I would really like to know so I can pray for you.

Things are going well here. My dad is working and going to grad school. I'm really enjoying being home-schooled. We have Adventure Days every week to go with our lessons. I also get to see my grandparents almost every day, which is a lot of fun.

I got to meet my mom's family for the first time this summer. I never knew my mom grew up Amish until after we moved here.

Anyway, I'm glad you're feeling better, and I'm glad Samantha's leaving you alone. I hope to hear from you soon. Take care!

Blessings,

Elizabeth

Once she had finished her note, she got ready for bed. It had been a long day, and her eyelids grew heavier with each moment. Five minutes after she snuggled beneath the covers, she was asleep.

CHAPTER 12
VISITING WITH GRANDMA

As soon as Mary parked the car at Grandma and Grandpa Hopewell's the next morning, Eli went toward the barn to find Grandpa. Elizabeth and Mary headed to the house and found Grandma cleaning up from breakfast.

"Good morning, you two!" she said. "Mary, would you like a cup of coffee? It's fresh."

"No, no thank you," replied Mary. "I had some at the house. I just came to thank you for helping Elizabeth yesterday."

"Oh, you're welcome. I'm always glad I can help."

"Elizabeth, would you like a tall glass of cold milk?"

"No thank you Grandma, I'm fine."

Just then, Grandpa and Eli walked in through the back door, each with a pumpkin in their arms.

"Well, what's this?" Mary asked.

"You and I each get to carve a pumpkin, Mom!" said Eli.

"Oh well, I really don't have time. I have to prepare lessons for next week and go to the bank. And Jacob needs me to..." Her mind whirred with her mental to-do list.

"Please, Mom," Eli begged. "Please stay and carve a pumpkin."

Mary shrugged. "All right. I suppose I can carve one." In no time, the pumpkin seeds were roasting. Eli carved "Believe" into his pumpkin and Mary chose "Joy." While they worked on their pumpkins, Grandma whipped up some pumpkin custard, several types of pumpkin cookies, and pumpkin whoopie pies.

After a little more coaxing, the three of them stayed and had lunch with Grandma and Grandpa. While they were eating Grandma asked, "Mary, are you and the children doing anything special on Saturday?"

"Nothing out of the ordinary," replied Mary. "Why do you ask?"

"Well, I got to thinking after Elizabeth left. My friend's daughter, Noelle Newcomer, and her husband, Nick, homeschool their children, Naomi and Noah, because of some health issues. Naomi has type 1 diabetes and Noah has congenital adrenal hyperplasia. They're about Eli and Elizabeth's age. Anyway, they have a stand at the farmer's market in town. I thought maybe we could visit them on Saturday morning."

Mary was quiet for a moment before answering. "Are you sure it would be okay with their mother? I don't want to be pushy or anything."

Grandma blushed slightly. "I called Noelle this morning before you came. There aren't many people in our area who homeschool, and she would love to be friends with another homeschool mom. And her children would enjoy some new friends as well. Some people don't know how to relate to the family because the children are adopted. Plus, with their health issues, they can't do some of the things that other kids do. Your kids have such a heart for people, and I think they would be great playmates for the New-comers." She took a bite of her soup. "I hope I didn't overstep my bounds. I just saw an opportunity for a wonderful friendship. Also, for what it's worth, Jacob knows Nick. They used to go to high school basketball games together. Maybe you all could have a family outing sometime."

Mary's eyes darkened for a moment. Rebecca thought Mary might be angry with her.

A slight smile crept across Mary's face. "Oh, why not?" she said. "I would have liked if you would have talked with me first. But, yes, we'll be available on Saturday. It will give the children a chance to meet some new people and allow Jacob more quiet time to study. We'll pick you up at nine on Saturday morning."

As they headed home with many goodies, Mary realized that Rebecca's actions had frustrated her. She thought to herself, *I could have shown my disapproval. I could have told her about our plans with Jacob. I could have said, 'How could you?' But what good would that have done? What example would that have set for my children? Besides, even though what she did has rubbed me the wrong way, she did it out of Christian love and I'm blessed to have in-laws who want to help us make friends.*

Mary talked in private with Jacob about what happened. He chuckled. "That's Mom for you," he said. "Always trying to con-nect people. You'll like Noelle, she was a year or two behind Nick and me in school. They're both a lot of fun. At least, they were in school. Go and have a great time on Saturday. As for me carving a pumpkin, tell the children that I'll carve mine on Sunday afternoon. I have a lot of homework to catch up on."

Mary told him she would share his decision with Eli and Elizabeth. Though she felt that Jacob had not taken the situation as seriously as she thought he should, she thanked God for allowing her to have this experience. It gave her the opportunity to show gentleness towards her mother-in-law and help her grow as a believer and made her realize that one has to choose one's battles. Some things are not worth arguing about.

CHAPTER 13
SATURDAY MORNING

Mary had to smile at how quickly her children got up and got ready to go. After wishing Jacob a successful morning of studying, they were out the door and on their way. They arrived at Grandma and Grandpa's a little before nine.

"Now you all go and have a good time," said Grandpa as they were getting ready to leave.

"Samuel, are you sure you don't want to come along?"

"Rebecca, look, I'm a big boy. I can take care of myself. Go! Have a good time."

"We'll bring something back for you and Jacob. Mary, are you sure you don't want me to drive?"

"Rebecca, will you stop?" said Grandpa. "Mary is very capable of driving. You put the plans together and you're buying lunch. You've done your part."

"I agree," said Mary. "You've done enough." Her voice came out a little rougher than she intended. She cleared her throat and tried again, a smile on her face. "Relax and enjoy yourself." *She arranged this out of Christian love,* she reminded herself. After one final goodbye, they were on their way.

Grandma directed Mary to the brick building that housed the market. As they entered, the smells of bacon frying and coffee brewing surrounded them. The sights overtook Eli and Elizabeth. There were rows and rows of vendors. Some offered prepared foods, breakfast sandwiches, platters, coffee, and smoothies. Others sold meat, fresh and jarred vegetables, a variety of fruits, and handmade items.

They wandered to Noelle and her children's stand, The Servant's Servants. There they found Noelle speaking with customers. When she finished taking care of them, Noelle turned to Grandma, beaming. "Rebecca, it's so good to see you. These must be the folks you were telling me about."

"Yes, yes," replied Grandma. After the introductions, Grandma said, "I was hoping we could all go to lunch after your stand closes. I would love for you to get to know each other a little better."

Noelle smiled. "I thought you might like to do that. So, the children and I have prepared some things and we'd like to invite you back to our home for lunch. We thought it might be a little more relaxing."

"Oh, Noelle, I didn't want to put you to any work. I simply wanted to create an opportunity for everyone to make some new friends."

"It wasn't any problem, Rebecca. I simply wrote it into my lesson plans. The children had fun planning the meal."

Grandma blushed. "It's fine with me if it's okay with Mary." Mary nodded her assent.

"Great," said Noelle. "Why don't you meet us here about 11:45 and we'll get ready to go."

For the next hour and a half, Grandma, Mary, Eli and Elizabeth walked the market. They bought some meat, vegetables, and a mince pie. When it was time to leave, they put their purchases in a cooler Mary had brought along with them.

They followed Noelle to her beautiful home in the country. The gravel lane led to a two-story log and stone house with a large, roofed porch at the front. Two maple trees stood in the front yard, draped in brilliant, fall color. The stone end of a barn peeked out from behind the house. To the right of the house was a green chicken hutch and yard, with a cleared-off garden just behind them.

A miniature collie came bounding up to them as they approached the house, followed by a cat with no tail. "These are Faith and Patience," Naomi said.

Elizabeth bent down to pet the cat. "Where's the cat's tail?" she asked as the cat rubbed itself against her legs.

"Patience is a Manx cat," Noah said. "Manx cats don't have tails."

About that time Noelle's husband Nick came out of the house. "I have lunch ready and waiting. Do you need me to carry anything in for you?" he asked.

"No," replied Noelle. "I think we're fine, but thank you."

Nick held the door open for everyone as they came into the house. The smells of coffee and chocolate greeted their senses. Nick had set the long farm-table with places for everyone. Two large platters stocked with sliced fruits and vegetables lay in the middle of the table.

"You went to too much work," said Grandma. "I didn't expect you to do all of this."

"Oh, it was nothing," replied Nick. "I cook at the station all the time."

"Station?" Eli asked. He remembered his friend Josh telling him once about how his dad worked to put out fires downtown.

"Yep," said Nick. "I work as a paid firefighter. Now, who's ready for some vegetable soup and grilled sandwiches?"

"We are!" cried Naomi and Noah.

"Well okay then! Why don't you show Eli and Elizabeth where to wash-up?"

"Okay, this way," said Naomi, leading them down the hall to the bathroom.

"Don't forget to check your sugar, Naomi," Noelle called.

"Yes ma'am!"

"Check your sugar?" asked Elizabeth.

"Yes, I'm a diabetic. So I have to check my blood sugar before meals."

"Does it hurt?" asked Eli.

"A little," said Naomi. "Would you like to see what I have to do?" She reached up, swung the medicine cabinet open, and extracted a lancet, a small meter, and a box of test strips. After she washed her hands, she pricked her finger with the lancet. Eli and Elizabeth winced. "Don't worry, guys," said Naomi. "It really doesn't hurt that much." She squeezed her finger, letting out a drop of blood. She touched a test strip to the bright red bubble and inserted the strip into the meter. The blood soaked into the test strip, and a number popped up on the screen.

"Okay," said Naomi. "I'm good to go!" After they all washed their hands, she led the kids back to the kitchen.

They found Grandma, Mary, and Noelle eating soup. "Are you guys ready for some sandwiches?" asked Nick.

"Yes, sir," they replied.

Eli and Elizabeth couldn't believe the choices they had: wheat bread, potato bread, gluten free bread, sharp cheese, Swiss cheese, ham, turkey or beef. As everyone placed their order, Nick grilled the sandwiches on a large griddle on the stove. Eli thought it was cool that all the sandwiches could be made at the same time. Nick had the children sit as he served each one a bowl of soup with their sandwich order before moving on to making the ladies' sandwiches.

"Now ladies, are you ready for yours?"

"Oh I don't know if I have enough room," said Mary.

"Oh come on," said Nick.

"I'll eat one if you eat one," said Grandma to Mary.

Four more sandwiches, made to order, were on the griddle in no time. When he noticed that the children were finished eating, Nick said, "Noah, why don't you take Eli downstairs and show him your train set?"

"May I show Elizabeth my crafts?" asked Naomi.

"That's a great idea," said Nick.

"Let's go, Elizabeth," said Naomi.

As the children scampered off to play, Noelle kissed her husband on the cheek. "Thank you, dear," she said. "Lunch was delicious."

"No problem, I'm glad to help. I wanted you gals to have a chance to relax and talk."

"So Mary, Rebecca tells me you just started homeschooling Eli and Elizabeth this year?"

"Oh, yes," said Mary. "It's something I've always wanted to do, and I'm so glad I finally have a chance to do it. The kids are having so much fun while they're learning, and I am, too!" She smiled. "How did your family decide to homeschool?"

Noelle dabbed at her lips with a napkin. "I think Rebecca told you about my kids' conditions," she said. "They want to have as normal a life as possible, and after talking it over with them, it seemed to be the best option." She took a sip of coffee. "Noah's able to rest whenever he needs to, and Naomi has more control over her schedule so she can quickly grab a snack when her blood sugar gets too low."

"They seem like sweet kids," Mary commented.

Noelle smiled. "Oh, they are. I love them so much." She took another bite of her sandwich.

"When did you decide to adopt?" asked Mary.

When Noelle had finished chewing, she said, "Nick and I realized there are a lot of kids in the world who still need someone to love them. So we decided to bring Naomi and Noah into our lives."

"Wow," Mary murmured. "What was that like?"

Nick joined in on the conversation from the sink, where he was washing the dishes. "It wasn't easy at first, but our church really helped us out a lot as we were getting started. They were there for us with tips for bonding with the kids when they first came to live with us, and they helped us get counseling when we needed it." He came to Noelle's side and put an arm around her. "It was definitely stressful, but I wouldn't have traded it for the world."

Noelle nodded. "Luckily, with my nursing education, I can support the kids in helping them live like other kids. It's really been a wonderful adventure, a blessing." Her eyes sparkled as she looked back at Mary. "Anyway," she said. "I would love to do some homeschooling activities together if you're willing."

"I would enjoy that very much. Elizabeth loves to help however she can, and Eli really needs a friend here."

"Well, maybe we can have Naomi and Noah teach Elizabeth and Eli about their medical conditions. We could work it into their science and language arts curriculum."

"That would be great," said Mary.

"I could teach all four of them about gluten. Rebecca told me about Elizabeth's friend. How is she doing?"

"Ann's doing better now," said Mary. "But Elizabeth was very upset about it when she heard."

Noelle nodded knowingly as Naomi burst into the kitchen. "Mom! Mom!"

"Goodness, what is it Naomi?"

"Elizabeth and I were wondering, could she make some things for our market stand? She would like to send the money to an organization that teaches about gluten intolerance."

"I think that would be a wonderful idea."

"It looks like they've already started working together." Mary said.

"Yes, I think they have."

Meanwhile, as Eli descended the stairs, he noticed the train track that made its home on a well-constructed platform, with an inside and outside track and detailed scenery attached to it. On the outside track was a freight train with a green engine with a long coal car behind it. Next several cars that matched the engine, alternated with red cars. All of them were painted with shiny gold numbers. A passenger train, with a little red caboose, lived on the inside track.

"Wow, Noah, this is neat!" Eli said.

"Thanks," said Noah as he started telling Eli about the different types of cars. "This one's called a boxcar. It's often used to haul stuff around." He handed it to Eli to examine. "My dad and one of his friends from the station, who is a train collector, built this train table for me. I got the train set for Christmas and Mr.

John, who knows how much I love trains, came over and helped us build the platform. Would you like me to show you how it works?"

"Sure," replied Eli. Noah turned on the power box to the system and slowly turned a knob. Just then, the train started to move. "Wow, this is super! You have one cool dad!"

"Yeah, I do," Noah murmured.

"You know, I have a friend back in Boston named Josh. His dad's a firefighter, too."

"Really?" said Noah.

Eli watched as Noah moved the train to show him how to attach another car to it. "Josh told me about how scary it can be sometimes to watch his dad go off to work." He peered at Noah. "Is it scary for you, too?"

Noah shrugged. "Sometimes," he said. "But Mom always reminds us that God is watching over him and over us, and even if something really bad happens to Dad, we'll be okay." He sighed. "Some days are a little scarier than others, though." He offered Eli a turn at running the train. "Wanna try?"

"Sure, thanks." Eli cautiously took his turn. He didn't want to cause a train wreck. After a few minutes of fun, he turned to Noah. "So Grandma said you had con...congen..."

"Congenital adrenal hyperplasia." The syllables rolled expertly off Noah's tongue.

"Yeah, that," said Eli. "What's that like, if you don't mind me asking?"

Noah sighed again. "My adrenal glands don't work right, so I get tired easier than most kids," he said. "It's hard for me to keep up with other kids when they play games and stuff. I guess that's why I like playing with these trains so much. When I'm playing with my trains, I don't feel like I have to save my energy. I can just have fun."

Eli nodded. "I get that. What else do you like to do?"

"I like to read, which Mom makes me do a lot of, anyway." He beamed. "But I don't mind. I get to read a lot about trains and fire trucks. I like reading about fire trucks more than fire engines because my dad rides on the ladder truck."

Eli smiled back. "So you like being homeschooled?"

"Oh, yeah," Noah said. "It's a lot easier for me, too," he said. His eyes got cloudy. "I had gone to school before, but the kids treated me different there, and their parents did, too."

"Their parents did?" Eli raised his eyebrows. "Why would they do that?"

"They're afraid their kids are going to get what I have," said Noah. "And they can't. I was born with this, it's not something you can catch. Though I *will* catch whatever cold their kids have."

"Wow," said Eli, taking it all in. "That must have been hard for you."

"Yeah." Noah shrugged. "Luckily, Mom's a nurse, so she knows how to help me, and it makes my life a lot easier." He looked up at Eli. "How do you like homeschooling?"

"Oh, it's great," said Eli. "At first, I thought Mom had gone overboard—she's teaching us home ec, Christian history, earth science, algebra, Bible, English, and American history. But I like how I can get my work done as quickly as I want, or if I need more time to understand something, I can go as slowly as I need to. Mom's also scheduled time for us to have fun, like our Adventure Days. We go someplace new and then check out books from the library on what we learned."

"That's neat!" Noah said. "What's the best place you guys have been so far?"

Eli told him about a recent visit to their Amish relatives when he and Elizabeth went with their mom to meet and help care for their new baby cousin. "I got to feed her," Eli said. "She was so small, but she guzzled it down like a hungry calf!"

Noah laughed and crinkled his nose. "I don't know if I could hold a baby," he said. "I'm too scared of breaking it! Speaking of food, I'm ready for dessert. How about you?"

"Sure!" They bounded up the stairs to the kitchen.

"Hey Dad, we're ready for dessert," said Noah.

Nick smiled at Noelle. "Sit still," she said. "It's my turn."

Within a few minutes, everyone had brownies and ice cream. "How are you able to eat brownies and ice cream?" Elizabeth asked Naomi.

"I don't overdo it," replied Naomi. "Planning, moderation, and exercise—that's the name of the game."

Before Eli and Elizabeth knew it, it was time to leave. After expressing their thanks for a wonderful lunch and afternoon, the Hopewells exchanged phone numbers with the Newcomers and shared their goodbyes. Grandma, Mary, and the children then headed for home, hearts warm with affection for their new friends.

When they got home, Eli and Elizabeth raced into the living room to tell their dad all about their day, their mother following them. But when they found him, he was fast asleep, a textbook open in his lap. The children fell quiet instantly.

"Poor Daddy," Mary whispered. "The farm work and the studying must have really tired him out." She peered over at her children and felt a pang when she saw their deflated moods. She wrapped her arms around them and squeezed them. "We can tell Daddy about our new friends after dinner, okay?"

CHAPTER 14

SHARING WITH JACOB

After church the next day, Elizabeth and Eli quickly said goodbye to Grandma and Grandpa and hurried to the car. "Are you doing something special this afternoon, Jacob?" Grandpa Hopewell asked as the adults strolled out to their cars. "The children seem anxious to get home."

"I'm supposed to carve my pumpkin this afternoon and roast pumpkin seeds with the kids." Grandma Hopewell looked towards Mary and smiled. "Why are you smiling that way, Mom? What are you two up to?"

"Let me put it this way, dear," she said. "You won't be the only one carving a pumpkin this afternoon. Your dad will be carving his too."

"Well how about that? The women went behind our backs," said Grandpa.

"Should we even bother telling them that we're making sure that they get fed?" Mary replied with a grin on her face.

"I don't know. That just might be too much for them," said Grandma.

"Food? There's food involved with this?" Grandpa said.

"Of course we're going to eat, silly! You didn't think your daughter-in-law and I would let you starve, do you? After all, you will need strength and energy to carry and carve your pumpkin," said Grandma.

"Well then, dear, we should get going. I'm anxious to get this event started."

Jacob quietly chuckled and said, "Okay, Dad, we'll see you in a bit."

As Jacob and Mary got into the car, Jacob glanced at Eli and Elizabeth in the backseat. He saw tear tracks glistening on Elizabeth's red cheeks. "Elizabeth, what's wrong?" Jacob asked.

"Nothing. I'm okay." Elizabeth turned to look out the window.

Mary turned and peered at her. "Do you want to talk about it at home? What's the problem?"

Elizabeth burst out crying. "I've been waiting for this afternoon all week. Dad doesn't seem to care about our special afternoon. We've been spending all this time with you, Mom, but we don't even get to see you anymore, Dad. You're always working and studying. I know those things are important, but Sunday afternoons are important too because that is the time we set aside just for us." She sobbed, her unexpected anger bubbling out of her.

Jacob was speechless as he looked at Elizabeth. He felt his heart crack a little, and it cracked even more to see a tear streaking Eli's face, too. *How long had they felt this way?* he wondered.

Shocked by Elizabeth's outburst, Mary looked at her husband with troubled eyes. "I've been doing my best to take care of them," she murmured. "I thought I was doing okay."

"I'm sure you're doing a great job, Mary." Jacob glanced up at his forlorn children again, wondering what to do.

Elizabeth chimed in, "Mom, you are doing a wonderful job taking care of us and we love you, but we miss Dad."

With that, Jacob looked at Mary and said, "You drive. I'm going to sit in the back with the kids."

When he got into the backseat, Jacob wrapped an arm around each of his children and held them close. Jacob prayed silently as they drove. *I thought I was doing the right thing for my family. I brought them to Pennsylvania so they would have love and support while we got back on our feet. I've had Mary stay home while I provide for the family so they would always have a parent around. I've been thrilled that they have wanted to spend time with my folks and have made new friends. I'm not working this hard so we can keep up with the Joneses, Lord. I thought I was trusting You. I thought I was doing what You wanted for my family. Please, Father, show me what to do.*

As Mary pulled into the driveway, Elizabeth squeezed Jacob's arm. "I love you, Daddy," she whispered. "I didn't mean to be nasty, and I'm sorry if I made you feel bad. I've just missed you so much. I know you work so hard for us, but I look forward to Sundays with you."

Jacob looked down at Elizabeth. "I understand, sweetie. I've missed you, too. I'm so sorry I haven't been able to spend as much time with you as I want to. What can I do to make this better? How can I fix it?"

"Daddy, you can't make it better and you don't need to fix it." She hiccupped. "I know you have to work and study. Those things are important. But Sundays are our special time and I just don't want to miss a single moment."

"I've missed you, too, Dad," Eli croaked on the other side of him.

Jacob squeezed Eli closer to him. "I've missed you, too, son." He rubbed his shoulder. "Hey, kids, come here." Jacob gazed at Eli and Elizabeth. "I love you kids so much. Thank you for sharing your feelings with me. Sometimes we have to go through some difficult times to get to better times. Please know I'm touched to know you love me so much. That's refreshing. Often I hear children telling their parents that they hate them."

"Really, Dad?"

"Really, Eli. It's sad to see and hear. Now, I think it's time for us to have some fun, just us as a family. So, why don't we get ready for some pumpkin carving?"

Eli cheered and scampered toward the house. Then Jacob got out, with Elizabeth following close behind. In his heart, Jacob knew his kids needed him, and now, he knew how he could be there for them.

CHAPTER 15

A SPECIAL AFTERNOON

When they entered the house, Mary said, "We need to get changed before helping Dad with his pumpkin project." Elizabeth and Eli raced up to their rooms, eager to spend time all together again.

Jacob looked at Mary and put his arms around her. "I had no idea…"

"Neither did I," she replied. She squeezed him tight. "I've missed you, too, you know."

Jacob grinned and said "So many of my favorite people have missed me. I feel loved." He gave her a quick hug before jogging upstairs to change.

As Elizabeth was going to change, she heard a vehicle pull into their driveway. "Hey, everybody!" she squealed. "Grandma and Grandpa are here and they have more pumpkins with them."

The rest of the family quickly finished changing and went down to greet them.

"Grandma, Grandpa, what are you doing here?" asked Elizabeth.

"Well, we thought it might be nice if Grandpa had a chance to carve a pumpkin too. Would that be okay?"

Eli and Elizabeth looked at each other. Eli replied, rather nonchalantly, "Sure. Why not?"

Perplexed by the lackluster greeting, Grandma looked at Mary as the children dashed to the kitchen. "Is everything all right?" she asked.

At that moment, Jacob stepped in. "We'll talk about it later, Mom. Right now, let's enjoy ourselves, okay?" He ushered them into the house.

As the adults entered the kitchen, Eli and Elizabeth laid the last plates on the table. Elizabeth straightened the knives and forks for a finishing touch. "Well, I guess they're ready to get this party started," Mary said, smiling at her mother-in-law.

While Eli and Elizabeth filled glasses with ice, Mary and Grandma Hopewell unpacked and arranged a smorgasbord lunch on the counter. As usual, Grandma had outdone herself. "I wasn't sure what everyone would want." Grandma laid out chicken salad, ham salad, sliced turkey, sliced roast beef, Swiss cheese, American cheese, homemade bread, chow-chow, canned pickles, canned peaches, and, of course, whoopie pies. Mary laid out her offerings, as well: macaroni salad, potato salad, Waldorf salad, lettuce leaves, sliced tomatoes, and sliced onions.

As the women and children prepared lunch inside, Jacob and Grandpa Hopewell unloaded the pumpkins, laid out newspaper, and got a pan to put the seeds in to roast.

While they were working, Grandpa said to Jacob, "The children didn't seem very excited about us carving our pumpkins together."

Jacob looked at his father. "Dad, my children love you and enjoy spending time with you. However, my family hasn't really seen a lot of me lately since I started grad school. The kids were so anxious to get home and spend time with me that they got upset when Mary and I stopped to talk with you and Mom. They really miss me, Dad, and they relish spending Sundays with me. I'm glad we're able to get together as we do, however, I think if we plan on doing anything on Sundays as a family, we need to plan it well in advance. I don't think surprises are going over very well right now. We're all going through some growing pains at the moment and we need our space sometimes."

"Would you like for your mother and me to go home? We can do that if it will help," said Samuel, hurt pinching his voice.

"Absolutely not!" replied Jacob. "You saw how the kids took charge of lunch. They're fine. However, I do think we need to plan things openly instead of doing surprises right now. That will help Eli and Elizabeth. It will also keep you and Mom from getting your feelings hurt."

Samuel looked and his son and nodded. "That's fair. Son, when did you become so wise?"

Jacob grinned. "You taught me well, Dad. You taught me well."

Eli and Elizabeth came bouncing out the door. "Lunch is ready," announced Eli. "Come on, Grandpa." They grabbed at his hands to pull him into the house. "We need to eat so you and Dad can carve your pumpkins and roast pumpkin seeds."

"Hold on, kids, I need to say something first." He knelt down so he could look them in the eye. "I want to apologize. I'm sorry if Grandma and I spoiled your afternoon with your dad."

Elizabeth shrugged. "You didn't spoil our afternoon. We just weren't expecting it. That's all."

"Yep," said Eli. "Now the afternoon is extra special. We get to help both of you. Now come on, the food is ready!"

Samuel looked at his son. "What can I say, Dad? Those are my kids. I told you they love you."

With that the Hopewell family spent the rest of the afternoon happily feasting and carving pumpkins.

CHAPTER 16

LEARNING FROM NAOMI

Two weeks after meeting at the market, Mary, Eli, and Elizabeth were once again invited to Noelle and Nick Newcomer's home for some oral presentations. Naomi and Noah were anxious to teach Eli and Elizabeth about their challenges, so Noelle gave the children a public speaking assignment and invited the Hopewells to be their audience.

When Mary, Eli, and Elizabeth arrived, Noelle welcomed them back. "We're so glad you could come," she said.

As they walked into the house, they found Naomi and Noah getting ready for their presentations. When Noelle announced their guests' arrival, Naomi and Noah went to greet Mary, Elizabeth, and Eli.

"Thank you for coming today," said Naomi. "It means a lot to us."

"We wouldn't have missed these for the world," replied Mary.

Once everyone was seated, Naomi started her presentation. "Today I will be speaking on diabetes. During my presentation,

I will be explaining how type 1 diabetes is different from type 2 diabetes. I will also explain what it's like to live with type 1 diabetes.

People with type 1 diabetes like me are born with a pancreas that doesn't make insulin, which makes us dependent on insulin. In other words, we need insulin injections to manage our blood sugar. However, those who live with type 2 diabetes develop the condition over time. They can sometimes control their blood sugar by changing their lifestyle, exercise and by taking oral medicines."

After comparing the two types of diabetes, Naomi explained why it is a challenge for her to live with her condition. She shared that she gets tired of all the needles and planning ahead. "It's exhausting sometimes to plan so much." Her hands shook as she shared her heart with her newfound friends. "When I went to school, the staff tried to support me, but I never really felt understood. I always felt like I just didn't fit in. I hope you can understand now who I am a little more."

With tears slowly trickling down her cheeks, Naomi took a deep breath before giving out her hand-outs and thanking her audience for their time. Then she let all her tears out, reliving her pain and discomfort. Noelle quietly got up and wrapped her arms around Naomi. As Naomi cried, Noelle looked at Noah and asked, "Would you mind if we listened to your presentation after lunch?"

"That's fine, Mom," replied Noah. "I'll start setting the table."

"We'll help too, said Mary. "Just tell us what to do."

Elizabeth didn't follow Noah, Eli, and her mother. Instead, she walked over and sat down with Naomi and Noelle. She put her arms around Naomi and, with tears now coming down her face said, "I can't understand everything you're feeling, but I do understand what it's like not to fit in."

"You do?" Naomi asked.

"Yes," said Elizabeth. "I wasn't accepted by many people at my old school. Sure, I had some very close friends, but some kids would make fun of me because I always had my nose in a book and because I was friends with Ann, and they didn't understand her gluten issues. The only thing that kept me going was that I had a family at home who loved me."

Mary came back to check on the girls. "You know," said Noelle. "I think we have two very special girls who need some lunch."

"I agree," replied Mary, smiling. With that, they went into the kitchen and joined the boys for a feast made up of chicken salad wraps, homemade tomato soup, and fruit salad.

CHAPTER 17

NOAH'S PRESENTATION

After a very satisfying and relaxing lunch, everyone gathered in the living room for Noah's presentation.

"Today I will be speaking on congenital adrenal hyperplasia (CAH). First, I will briefly mention the different forms of the disease. Then I will explain how the disease is treated. Finally, I will share what it is like to live with this disease."

Noah began by pulling down a chart of the human body and pointing out the adrenal glands located on top of the kidneys. He explained that, for people with his condition, these glands don't function properly. Because of this, those with CAH don't have a natural fight-or-flight response, making it harder for them to handle stressful situations.

"Like diabetes, CAH has two types: classical and non-classical," he explained. "Also like diabetes, classical CAH is a condition you're born with, while non-classical CAH can be developed later on." He also shared that, like him, some individuals with classic CAH have a type called salt-wasting CAH. These people are unable to retain the sodium their bodies need due to their condition.

He shared that he takes Prednisone and Fludrocortisone daily to help with his condition. "If I'm sick or really upset, I have to increase my Prednisone so my body doesn't shut down."

Noah held back tears as he continued. "I asked to be home-schooled because I was sick and tired of being sick and tired. I worried if someone in my class had a cold because I knew I would be sure to catch it. I had difficulty keeping up with the other kids in gym class and at recess. I was also tired of other parents pitying me or being afraid that their children could 'catch' the condition I live with, which, of course, isn't true."

Noah swallowed, and a warm wave of pride rose in Eli's heart. This must have been difficult to share, but he was glad Noah could trust him and his family with his story. Noah, he thought, was a real trooper.

CHAPTER 18
ELI'S LETTER

Jacob entered the kitchen. "Man, something smells good in here! What have you all been working on this morning?"

Mary looked up from the pot of soup she was stirring. "The children have been studying and I've been making some treats since it's cold out today."

Jacob wrapped his arms around his wife's waist. "Mmmm, I am very blessed to have a wife who is such a good cook."

Eli and Elizabeth entered the room and started setting the table. "Hi, Dad," said Elizabeth.

"Did you have a good morning?" asked Eli.

"Mr. Hersh and I have been busy," replied Jacob. "But it was pretty good. How about you two?"

"We worked on some social studies. Now we're writing down some ideas for a short story that Mom told us we have to write," said Elizabeth.

"That sounds interesting," said Jacob. Are you writing this story together?"

"No," replied Eli. "We both have to write one." His voice fell flat.

"Oh stop," said Mary. "It won't be that bad." Eli rolled his eyes, but didn't say anything.

Once they washed their hands, they sat down to pray over their meal of vegetable soup, toasted cheese sandwiches, and fruit salad. When everyone was finished Mary asked, "Do you have time for some gingerbread, Jacob?"

"Is there lemon sauce to go with it?"

"Of course there is, silly."

He smiled. "Then I have time. Oh gosh, I almost forgot. Eli, I got the mail before I came in and I saw that there was a letter for you."

"Really?" said Eli, intrigued.

"Yes." He handed Eli the letter. "I think it's from Josh."

Eli carefully slit the envelope and started reading. All of a sudden, he tossed the letter on the table and ran to his room.

"What in the world?" said Mary as she headed up the stairs after him.

Jacob picked up the letter and read...

Dear Eli,

I hope everything is going well for you in Pennsylvania. School is going okay, but it's not as fun without you being here. I'm sorry that I haven't written you sooner but things have been a little crazy here.

Please keep my family in your thoughts. My dad was badly hurt in a fire the other week. I don't know when he's going to get out of the hospital. I don't know who else to talk to, and I'm kinda scared.

Anyway, I can't wait to hear from you. Tell the rest of your family I said hi.

Take care,

Josh

"Elizabeth," said Jacob. "Would you go tell Mr. Hersh that I'm going to be a few minutes late? Just tell him something came up here that I needed to take care of."

Elizabeth grabbed her jacket and ran out the door.

When Jacob reached Eli's room, he found Eli crumpled on his bed. Mary sat by his side, stroking his hair as he cried.

"It's not fair," Eli sobbed. "I can't help that we moved. What can I do? He's all alone...I'm here and he's there."

Jacob knelt on the floor next to Eli's bed and listened as Eli's sobs gave way to hiccups. "Son," he said. "I want you to know that I'm very proud of you."

Eli looked up in disbelief, his face red and tear-streaked. "Proud?"

"Yes, proud."

"Why? I didn't do anything. I can't do anything."

Jacob looked his son in the eye. "Eli, a person doesn't get a letter like that unless he has been a very good friend. Josh obviously thinks a great deal of you and trusts you."

Eli looked at his dad and said, "Yeah, we are pretty good friends. The other guys didn't understand why he worried about his dad so much. But I understand."

"I'm curious Eli. How could you understand Josh?"

"Well, I know firefighters have a dangerous job. But, I overheard you tell Mom one night how you were lucky that you weren't killed during a home visit. I also remember you saying that you had to go to court because of parents that were mistreating their kids. It was then that I knew you had a dangerous job too."

"Yes, I had some very interesting days." Jacob hugged his son and said, "You know what? I bet Josh would really like to talk to you about what's going on. Would you like to call Josh and tell him that you're thinking of him?"

"Yes, may I call him now?"

"The kids won't be home from school yet, but you can leave a message," said Mary. Mary got her cell phone and handed it to Eli so he could dial. The phone on the other end rang and rang till the answering machine picked up. "Hey, Josh," he said. "This is Eli. I got your letter today. If you want to talk about it, you can call me back later." Then he left his mom's cell phone number and hung up.

Eli looked up at his mother, his eyes drooping. Mary gently stroked his cheek. "Honey, that's all you can do right now. We'll just have to wait and see if he calls back."

Eli looked at his mom again and asked, "Mom, may I go to Grandpa's for a little while? I just want to take some pictures and be alone."

"Sure," replied Mary.

Eli grabbed his camera and headed out the door.

CHAPTER 19
FIREFIGHTING

Grandpa Hopewell was walking out of the house just as Eli came up the driveway. "Well, hello Eli," Grandpa said cheerfully. "To what do I owe this special visit?"

Eli explained what had happened. A concerned look crossed Grandpa's face, "How bad was he hurt?"

"I really don't know. All he said in his letter was that he was hurt. I called and left a message for him, so I guess I'll find out when he calls back."

Grandpa sat down on the porch steps. "Yeah, firefighting is a tough business. I've been hurt myself once or twice."

Eli's eyes widened. "You're a firefighter, Grandpa?"

"I sure am. I'm a member of the volunteer station down the road here. I don't run calls anymore but I still help with the dinners and the Mud Sale."

"Mud Sale?" Eli scrunched up his eyebrows.

"Yep! We have a Mud Sale every spring to help keep the station operating."

"Why do you call it a Mud Sale?"

"Think for a minute Eli. What happens to the ground when it starts to thaw in the spring? Now I know there's a lot of concrete in Boston, but there's got to be some grass somewhere."

"Sure, there are grassy places in Boston. One of those places is Boston Public Gardens, next to the Commons."

"Okay," said Grandpa. "What happens to the grass when it starts to get warm out?"

Eli thought for a moment, then his face lit up. "Oh, it gets muddy! Now I get it!"

Grandpa just smiled and shook his head.

"Grandpa, could I help with the Mud Sale next spring?"

"Of course you can."

Eli's face fell again, "But what can I do until that time comes? I want to do something to help now."

Grandpa smiled again. "How about this? You and I will take a ride down to the station tomorrow and talk to the guys about it. I'm sure they can help you come up with something."

"You mean it?"

"Sure. We'll go down in the morning. Now, why don't you go and take those pictures. Don't stay too long. It's beginning to get cold out here."

"Okay, Grandpa, thanks for your help."

"You're welcome Eli. You're welcome."

When Eli returned home, he shared with his mother the plans that he and Grandpa had made. "That's fine, Eli," she said. "I don't want you getting in the way, though." Secretly, she thanked God he was too young to run calls, but also for her son's kind heart.

Not long after Eli told his mother about his plans her cell phone rang. The young voice on the other end said, "Mrs. Hopewell?"

"Yes?"

"This is Josh, Eli's friend. May I speak with him?"

"Sure, he's right here. By the way, Josh, we want you to know that we are keeping you and your family in our thoughts and prayers."

"Thank you, Mrs. Hopewell," said Josh. "I appreciate that."

Mary handed Eli the phone. "Hello?"

"Hello, Eli," said Josh. "I was glad to get your message."

"I'm sorry about what happened," said Eli. "How is he?"

"Well, he got some really bad burns, especially on his hand. They had to amputate it, so he won't be fighting fires anymore. Another guy got hurt, too, but not as bad as my dad, and even worse than that, one guy got killed."

"Wow," said Eli, the weight of Josh's words falling on him. "That must be so hard for everyone. I wish I could make this better for you, but I can't. You can always write me though, or call."

"Thanks, man," said Josh. "Talk to you soon."

As Eli finished his phone call with Josh, Mary wiped tears from her eyes. Her son was growing up into an empathetic young man.

The next morning, Eli was up bright and early, brimming over with anticipation for his field trip. After breakfast, Eli and Elizabeth walked to their grandparents' house. As they walked in the door they heard Grandma call, "Good morning! We're in here."

Grandma and Grandpa Hopewell were just finishing up breakfast. "Are you ready to go to the station?" said Grandpa.

"Yes sir," replied Eli.

"Okay then, let's get this adventure started," said Grandpa with a smile. "We'll see you ladies later."

It was a short drive to the station. As he and Eli walked into the station, one of the firemen said, "Well, look who's here! Good morning Samuel, would you like a cup of coffee?"

"Yes, Frank, I would. Thank you."

"And who is this young fellow?" asked Frank as he patted Eli's shoulder.

"Well, this is my grandson. Eli, this is Mr. Frank, Mr. Lew, and Mr. Norm. They help run the station during the day."

After exchanging pleasantries, Mr. Frank offered Eli a cup of hot chocolate, which he readily accepted.

"Guys, Eli received a letter in the mail yesterday that upset him. He would like to know how he could help others in the community now, since he's too young to run calls and the Mud Sale's a few months away."

Mr. Lew was the first to speak. "Well, Eli, there are many things you can do. You could always go and read to the folks at the nursing home. I know they like when young folks come to see them."

"Eli, do you go to church?" asked Mr. Norm.

"Yes sir," replied Eli.

"Well, maybe you could get a couple of names off the shut-in list and send those folks a card once a month."

"You might want to volunteer some of your time down at the food bank," said Mr. Frank.

"I don't know," said Eli. "That seems so unimportant compared to what you guys do."

"Eli, anything you do to help make the world a better place *is* important." Mr. Lew held up his coffee cup. "For instance, do you realize that we're helping people by drinking this coffee?"

"Huh?" said Eli.

"He's right," said Mr. Frank. "We buy Land of a Thousand Hills Coffee to help people in another country earn a living. We figured we're going to drink coffee anyway, so why not do it in a way that helps somebody else. So, we all chipped in and bought a subscription. The coffee gets shipped here and it's all good."

"Eli," said Grandpa, "You don't have to do big things to serve. You can serve every single day, in little ways. The Bible tells us this in Matthew 25:34-36. It says, 'Then the King will say to those on his right, 'Come, you who are blessed by my Father, inherit the Kingdom prepared for you from the creation of the world. For

I was hungry, and you fed me. I was thirsty, and you gave me a drink. I was a stranger, and you invited me into your home. I was naked, and you gave me clothing. I was sick, and you cared for me. I was in prison, and you visited me." Serving in small ways is just as important as serving in big ways."

Grandpa and Eli thanked the firefighters for allowing them to visit.

"Come back soon!" said Mr. Frank.

"You're now part of the crew," said Mr. Lew.

CHAPTER 20
ELIZABETH'S IDEA

After sliding the last pan of molasses cookies out of the oven, Grandma asked Elizabeth, "Since Grandpa and Eli aren't back yet, would you like to go and help me feed the squirrels?"

"Feed the squirrels?" asked Elizabeth.

"Yes, feed the squirrels," replied Grandma. "Your Grandpa enjoys feeding the birds. I enjoy feeding the squirrels."

"Sure, I'll help," said Elizabeth.

Grandma and Elizabeth went out back to the waterproof containers at the edge of the patio. One of the containers held ears of corn and another held peanuts. "Here," said Grandma. "You fill this bucket with peanuts and I'll fill this one with ears of corn."

Once they were ready, Grandma and Elizabeth walked out to the feeders by the patio. Grandma showed Elizabeth how to put peanuts in two of the feeders. Then she said, "I'm going to go down to that wheel and attach these ears of corn."

"Okay, Grandma." Elizabeth watched her grandmother walk a little farther to a thing that looked like a Ferris wheel. She watched Grandma twist the ears of corn onto the spikes that were attached to the wheel.

Out the corner of her eye, Elizabeth noticed that she wasn't the only one watching Grandma. Sitting by an oak tree was a squirrel with a fluffy tail holding an acorn. As Grandma walked back towards the patio, Elizabeth saw the squirrel drop the acorn and run toward the corn wheel. The squirrel ran to the post holding the wheel, climbed it, and vigorously gnawed at an ear of corn.

When Grandma reached Elizabeth, she said, "Aren't you done yet?"

Elizabeth blushed. "I'm sorry. I was enjoying watching you and that silly squirrel."

"Oh, that's the one I call Susie. She often sits by that tree and watches me fill the wheel."

"How do you know it's a girl, Grandma?"

"I watched her with her young'uns earlier this year. I enjoyed that. There's another squirrel that I call "Farmer Squirrel." He is forever planting corn kernels instead of eating them. I can't tell you how many corn shoots I pulled out of this yard this past spring," Grandma said with a smile. "He's a very good farmer. I just wish he would plant his crop in another spot."

Elizabeth's imagination churned with thoughts of the two squirrels. As Grandma and Elizabeth topped off the peanut feeders, they heard Grandpa and Eli pulling into the driveway. "It sounds like the men are back." Elizabeth took off running toward the truck. *I wonder what got into her all of a sudden,* Grandma said to herself.

Elizabeth ran around the side of the house as Grandpa and Eli hopped out of the truck. "Grandpa, Grandpa!"

"Elizabeth, is everything alright? Is your Grandma okay?" Grandpa asked.

"Everything's fine, Grandpa. I didn't mean to scare you. I just wanted to know if you would be willing to go on another adventure."

"Well, I guess, where do you need to go?"

"I need to go into town for an assignment Mom's given us. Please Grandpa, I'll work an extra day."

"No, no, that won't be necessary." Grandpa said.

Just then Grandma walked around the corner of the house. "Goodness, child! I've never seen you move that fast!"

Grandpa smiled. "Elizabeth would like me to take her to town. There's something she needs for a project Mary has assigned. Would my taking her interfere with your plans for today?"

"No, that would be okay. Eli could help me finish making frozen banana s'mores dessert for lunch while you're gone, if he wouldn't mind."

"Oh Eli, you want to help with that project," said Grandpa. "That is some good eating."

"Okay, then," said Grandma. "You take Elizabeth, and Eli and I will work on the dessert. When you get back we'll have lunch."

Elizabeth didn't have to be told twice to get into the truck. As they started out the drive Elizabeth said, "We have to stop at my house first, Grandpa. I have to get my money."

A few minutes later Grandpa pulled up in front of Elizabeth's house. Mary walked out onto the porch. "Elizabeth, is everything alright?"

"Everything's fine Mom. Grandpa is taking me to town so I can get something for my short story."

"Something for your short story? Elizabeth, all I asked you to do is write a story. What would you possibly need?"

"Mom, I'm not only going to write it. I'm going to perform it for you. Please let me. I'm paying for it with my own money."

Mary sighed and smiled. "Okay, sweetie but you know how I feel about you spending your money. Have you thought about what you're about to do?"

"Yes ma'am, I have. I know that I have to put 10% of my allowance in the offering plate at church every week, another 10% in the savings account you opened for me, and the other 80% in my bank for when I want or need something."

"Okay, you obviously have thought this through. Go and get your money."

Elizabeth scampered into the house to make a withdrawal from her piggy bank. After she collected a sufficient amount, she dashed back downstairs, where her mother and grandfather were talking.

"I don't know what she needs for this assignment, Samuel," said Mary.

"I don't know, either" replied Grandpa. "But it must be pretty important. Say, why don't you come over to the house for lunch? I heard a rumor that frozen banana s'mores dessert is on the menu."

Mary smiled. "Thanks, but I'd like to eat with Jacob today. I'll be over to get the kids and have some dessert later, though."

"Very good," said Grandpa. "Now Elizabeth, let's get this adventure started. I'm anxious to see what you're so excited about."

As they came into town Grandpa said, "You're going to have to tell me where we're going, honey."

"I will, Grandpa. Just stay on the main street." A green awning stretched out over a sidewalk, bearing the name "Tom and Tina's Books and Gifts" in gold script. "There it is, Grandpa," Elizabeth cried, pointing it out.

"I should have known," said Grandpa. "A bookshop."

Grandpa hardly had the truck parked before she approached the door and was halfway through the store by the time Grandpa entered the shop.

"Well, good morning, Samuel! Here to buy the Mrs. a little something?" asked Mr. Tom.

"No, no," replied Grandpa. "I'm just the chauffeur. My granddaughter, Elizabeth, needed something you have here for a school assignment."

You don't say," replied Mr. Tom, looking at his wife, Mrs. Tina.

Elizabeth slowly came around the corner carrying a squirrel puppet. "Isn't she beautiful?" asked Elizabeth. "I think she looks just like the one Grandma calls Susie." Now things started to make sense for Grandpa.

Mr. Tom looked at Elizabeth and said, "I hear you need this puppet for a school project. What's the project?" asked Mr. Tom.

"My brother and I are supposed to write a short story," Elizabeth said. "However, I want to do more than just write a short story. I want one of the characters to tell it."

"What is your story about?" asked Mrs. Tina.

"It's going to be about a little girl who talks to a squirrel. The squirrel is going to tell her about her friends that live with her in the forest."

"That sounds interesting," said Mrs. Tina.

"Very creative," said Mr. Tom. He looked at his wife and she nodded. Then he turned to Elizabeth and said, "You know, Mrs. Tina and I give a discount on things that are being used for school. So young lady, you just got a 25% discount."

"Really?" asked Elizabeth. "That's so kind of you. Thank you!"

Grandpa broke in, "Tom, you really don't have to do that."

"Yes, Samuel, I do. However, I do have one request."

"Okay," said Elizabeth nervously.

"You have to come and perform that short story for us."

"It's a deal!"

Elizabeth paid her bill, thanked Mr. Tom and his wife, and headed for the truck.

"That's one special little girl you have there, Samuel," said Tom.

"Yes, she is," replied Samuel. "She and her brother, Eli, are both very special. I have been richly blessed by God."

After eating dessert with Grandma and Grandpa, Eli, Elizabeth, and Mary headed for home. "Mom, may I work on my short story this afternoon?"

"Of course," replied Mary.

"I'd like to work on it in my room, if I may."

Mary looked at her daughter and replied, "I guess that would be okay. What about you Eli, what are you planning on working on this afternoon?"

"My short story, I guess. I'm not quite as far as Elizabeth."

"I'm sure you'll come up with something. Would you like to work in your room as well or are you going to work in the schoolroom?"

"I think I'll work in my room, too," replied Eli.

"That's fine," said Mary. "Just make sure you get something accomplished."

When they walked in the house, Eli and Elizabeth immediately headed upstairs. "Now remember, schoolwork. No napping or goofing off."

"Yes, ma'am," they replied.

When Eli got to his room, he lay back on his bed and let his mind whir for a few minutes. His mind swirled with what his friend Josh was dealing with and how life had slowed down since coming to Pennsylvania. Inspiration dawned on him. He scrambled to his desk and started scribbling his story. After a few minutes, he tiptoed to Elizabeth's room and pointed to their meeting place.

Once they were settled in Elizabeth asked, "How was your trip with Grandpa this morning?"

"It was good. The guys are really nice. They're going to let me help with the Mud Sale next March."

"That's great," said Elizabeth. "Have you decided on what you're going to write your short story about?"

"That's what I wanted to talk with you about. Elizabeth, I've been thinking about my friend Josh and his dad a lot. Handing her the pad he had been writing on, he said, "I'm going to write a fire department story. Here are some of my ideas. What do you think?"

"I think these are great! All you have to do is organize your thoughts," replied Elizabeth.

"How about you? What are you going to write about? And why did you have to have the squirrel puppet all of a sudden?"

"Well, my squirrel puppet, Susie, goes along with my short story. I got the idea this morning when Grandma and I were filling the squirrel feeders. I started thinking about what I could write and then suddenly remembered about the squirrel puppet that was at the shop in town. So then I thought I could not only write the story, but read it to others using my puppet."

"That's really neat," said Eli.

"Thanks," replied Elizabeth. "I'm not sure exactly how I'm going to write it yet, but I have some ideas. Anyway, we need to get to work. If Mom comes upstairs and finds that we're talking and not working, we'll be in big trouble."

"Yeah, you're right. Let's go."

Quietly, Elizabeth opened her closet door. She and Eli quickly got out of the closet, and made their way to their desks. What they didn't know was that their mother had already snuck upstairs to check on them. However, when she heard the whispers coming from the closet, she knew they were having one of their "secret meetings." Instead of getting upset with them, Mary thanked God that her kids were close and willing to share their thoughts and feelings with each other.

CHAPTER 21
MORE TIME

Mary had given Eli and Elizabeth a week to work on their short stories but the night before they were due the brother and sister went to their mother and asked for more time.

"Mom, we simply cannot get this assignment finished in a week. We need more time." Elizabeth said.

Mary knew that both of her children had been working very hard on their stories because while they were at their grandparents' home she had snuck upstairs to see what they had accomplished. She was not surprised to find that Elizabeth was well on her way to writing a book instead of a short story. What did surprise her was that Eli was well on his way to doing the same thing. So, when her children asked for more time, Mary decided to grant their wish but not without having a little fun.

In a semi-stern voice Mary said, "So, you need more time. I would think a week would be long enough to write a short story. Bring me what you have so far. I want to see what you have accomplished."

Eli and Elizabeth quickly went to their rooms to retrieve their work and brought it to their mother.

"Your writing is very good. However, I asked for a short story, not a book.

"We know that you only wanted a short story but when we started writing our stories they sort of, well, grew," replied Elizabeth.

"I see," said Mary. "Eli I also have to say that I am very surprised but pleased at the amount you have written. I thought you didn't like writing,"

"I don't enjoy it as much as Elizabeth, but I have a lot to say, what happened to Josh and his family has been bothering me. It has made me think about things. I guess writing this for you is my way of dealing with that."

Mary softened her voice and said, "I know that has been bothering you and you wish you could be there in person for him. Eli, Josh knows that you care. We'll call again soon and ask how things are going."

"Thank you, Mom! That would be great. Do you think we could send a little care package too?"

"We'll talk to Grandma Hopewell about that. I know she used to send things to your dad when he was at Messiah. Let's see what she suggests."

"Okay," replied Eli.

"Now, as for this assignment, I am going to grade one of your chapters as your short story and your entire writing as another assignment. Deal?"

"Deal!" shouted Eli and Elizabeth together.

"You have until November 1st to finish."

With that, Eli and Elizabeth hugged their mother, said good-night and were off to bed.

For two weeks Eli and Elizabeth worked feverishly on their short stories. Over those two weeks, they found their stories growing into books. When they weren't writing, they worked on putting a care package together for Josh and his family. Grandma Hopewell told them that she used to send their dad cookies, whoopie pies, and other goodies to him while he was at Messiah. So, Eli decided to send his friend a Pennsylvania care package. Just like their books, the care package grew into packages, two boxes filled with Pennsylvania goodies: whoopie pies, shoo-fly pie, chow-chow, and apple butter. Grandma Hopewell asked a friend at the post office to help her pack the boxes so nothing would get broken.

Grandpa Hopewell, who didn't want to be left out of the fun, paid for the goodies to be shipped overnight. The night before the packages were shipped, Eli called his friend Josh to alert him of a surprise coming in the mail for him.

"Cool, thanks!" said Josh. "I'll let you know when it comes."

"Sounds good," said Eli. "How's your dad doing?"

Josh shared that his dad was slowly improving. "He misses firefighting. And learning to live without his hand is pretty hard. But he likes spending more time with us."

"That's good to hear," said Eli. "Take care, Josh. Looking forward to hearing from you."

CHAPTER 22
NOVEMBER 1ST

November 1st was a special day at the Hopewell house. Not only was it the day that Josh would get his packages, it was also the due date for Eli and Elizabeth's stories. Mary invited Grandma and Grandpa over for dinner to make the evening memorable for Eli and Elizabeth and to show them what the children had accomplished.

When the time came to eat, Mary had baked ham, baked macaroni and cheese, green beans, baked acorn squash, freshly baked bread, apple butter with cottage cheese, and homemade apple pie. Grandma Hopewell brought pepper slaw and apple-sauce that she had made that afternoon to add to the already scrumptious fare.

Between dinner and dessert, Eli and Elizabeth went and brought their assignments for everyone to see. Both children had placed their writing in a three-ring binder, along with some artwork they had added. While the adults paged through the children's creations, Mary's cell phone rang. Mary smiled when she saw Josh's number.

"Hello?" She wasn't prepared for the crying she heard on the other end. "Hello?"

A shaky voice came through. "Miss Mary, it's Josh. My family and I wanted to call and thank you for the things you sent us. I had been afraid…" Mary heard sniffling on the other line.

Suddenly Mary heard a female voice. "Hello, Mary, this is Elaine, Josh's mom."

"Hi, Elaine. Is Josh alright?" asked Mary.

"He's fine," said Elaine. "He's just very touched by what you sent. He thought once you moved that Eli would make new friends and forget about him."

"Oh no, Elaine, Eli wouldn't do that."

"I'm glad to hear that," replied Elaine. "He misses Eli so much."

Eli motioned for his mom to give him the phone. "Miss Elaine, it's Eli."

"Hello, Eli. We just wanted to call and thank you for what you sent."

"You're welcome, Miss Elaine, but the goodies weren't just from me. They were from all of us. Listen, would you give Josh a message for me?"

"Sure," replied Miss Elaine. "I'd put him on but he's a little emotional right now. He's really glad to have a friend like you. Now, what would you like me to tell him?"

"Tell him another package will be coming in the mail. I'm not sure when because my mom has to grade it first. I hope it doesn't upset you, but I wrote it because of what happened to Mr. Walt and because of some other things I have learned since moving here."

Josh's mom, who had her phone's speaker setting on, replied because her son couldn't speak, "Thank you. We look forward to reading it."

"And please tell Mr. Walt that I asked about him."

"Thank you, Eli!" Mr. Walt's voice came over the line. "I'm hanging in there."

"I'm glad," said Eli. "We'll talk soon." After hanging up, Eli sat down in the middle of the floor and cried.

His dad got up and put his arm around him. "I'm very proud of you," said Jacob. "You showed the love of Christ during that phone call."

"Dad, I wish I could do more. I feel such a connection to guys who are firefighters. They're, they're like family to me."

"I know, son. I've felt like that before, too." He rubbed his son's shoulder. "But you've done all you can for right now. You just need to take one day at a time and remember that we're all here for you."

"Thanks, Dad."

"Now, how about we get some dessert? I bet that'll cheer you up a little."

"I'd like that," said Eli.

The evening ended with the family enjoying apple pie, vanilla ice cream and a few hands of Dutch Blitz.

After their children were tucked in for the night, Mary sat frowning at her children's books.

Jacob plopped down on the couch next to her. "What's wrong?"

"Jacob, I don't know how I'm going to be able to grade these."

"Why, what's the problem?" He put his arm around her. "You've never had a problem grading their work before."

"Their work has never had this much emotion in it," she said. "It feels like I'm seeing a whole new side of them, and...I don't know how I'm feeling about it."

"Give me one of the books. Let me take a look," said Jacob.

Mary handed him Eli's book. After skimming through the first few pages, he said, "I see what you mean. Would you be willing to team grade these assignments? You grade for grammar and I'll grade for content."

"Do you have time for that?" Mary asked.

"I'll make time," replied Jacob.

"I would love the help," said Mary.

"Okay, which one do you want first?"

"I'd like to read Elizabeth's first," said Mary. "I think I can emotionally handle hers."

"Here you go," said Jacob, handing her Elizabeth's binder. "I'll start on Eli's."

For the next two hours the two snuggled up, each with a cup of tea, to read what their children had written.

PART 4

COUNTRY
CHRONICLES

By Elizabeth Hopewell and Susie Squirrel

DEDICATION

THE RADIANT BRIDE

Who could ever find a wife like this one—

she is a woman of strength and mighty valor!

She's full of wealth and wisdom.

The price paid for her was greater than many jewels.

Her husband has entrusted his heart to her,

for she brings him the rich spoils of victory.

All throughout her life she brings him what is good
and not evil.

She searches out continually to possess

that which is pure and righteous.

She delights in the work of her hands.

She gives out revelation-truth to feed others.

She is like a trading ship bringing divine supplies from the merchant.

Even in the night season she arises and sets food on the table

for hungry ones in her house and for others.

She sets her heart upon a nation and takes it as her own, carrying it with her.

She labors there to plant the living vines.

She wraps herself in strength, might, and power in all her works.

She tastes and experiences a better substance, and her shining light will not be extinguished, no matter how dark the night.

She stretches her hands to help the needy and she lays hold of the wheels of government.

She is known by her extravagant generosity to the poor,

*for she always reaches out her hands to those in **need**.*

She is not afraid of tribulation,

for all of her household is covered in the dual garments

of righteousness and grace.

Her clothing is beautifully knit together

a purple gown of exquisite linen.

Her husband is famous and admired by all,

sitting as the venerable judge of his people.

Even her works of righteousness

she does for the benefit of her enemies.

Bold power and glorious majesty are wrapped around her

as she laughs with joy over the latter days.

Her teachings are filled with wisdom and kindness

as loving instruction pours from her lips.

She watches over the ways of her household and meets every need they have.

Her sons and daughters arise in one accord to extol
her virtues,

and her husband arises to speak of her in glowing terms.

"There are many valiant and noble ones,

but you have ascended above them all!"

Charm can be misleading,

and beauty is vain and so quickly fades,

but the virtuous woman lives in the wonder, awe,

and fear of the Lord.

She will be praised throughout eternity.

So go ahead and give her the credit that is due,

for she has become a radiant woman,

and all her loving works of righteousness deserve to
be admired

at the gateway of every city! (Proverbs 31:10-31 TPT)

Susie Squirrel and I would like to dedicate this book to Grandma Hopewell, a great friend and a wonderful grandmother.

Elizabeth Hopewell

HOW I MET SUSIE

One warm afternoon, I was sitting out in the Sanctuary, where I sometimes go to read. I was embarked on a Civil War adventure when I was interrupted by a squeaky voice.

"Hi, Elizabeth, are you enjoying your book?" I looked over the top of my book and saw a gray squirrel sitting on the arm of the chair next to me. She wore a white blouse with a frilly collar and a flowered skirt. I didn't know whether to scream and run or stay and chat. So I quietly sat there, staring, as the squirrel talked.

"My name is Susie. I've seen you come out here with your grandma."

Eventually, I found my voice. "You're Susie, the squirrel that my grandma talks about."

"That is correct. The squirrel your grandma calls Farmer Squirrel is my brother, Sammy."

"You never had a dress on when Grandma and I were out here," I said.

"I wasn't sure if you were ready to see me like that. However, I'm on my way home and I saw you reading. So I thought I would stop and say hi."

"You're on your way home? Where are you coming from?" I couldn't believe that I was truly having a conversation with a squirrel.

"Oh, I'm coming from church. Pastor Peacock and I had a meeting to discuss me doing what he wants to call 'A Moment of Encouragement' over the next several weeks," replied Susie. I couldn't believe this squirrel went to church, much less that she was telling me about it. "I go to Lovington Community Church in Hopeville Forest. Over the years I've written little stories and given them to people to encourage them. Well, I kept a copy of all the stories that I've written and I've turned them into a book. Now the pastor wants me to share what I've written with the congregation. Each one has a scripture to go with it and some questions for folks to think about at the end. So, using one of my puppets, I will read a story to the congregation each week and then ask them the questions about what they heard. I'm also going to encourage them to memorize the Bible verse that accompanies the story."

"You own puppets?" I asked in disbelief.

"Oh, yes," said Susie. "I have quite a collection. I'll bring you a copy of my book if you would like one."

"I would like that very much." I needed some proof that this conversation actually did happen. "Do you and my grandma ever talk like this? Has she ever seen you in your dress? Does she know that Farmer Squirrel is your brother?"

"Oh, your grandma and I have talked many times. She knows all about me and my brother." She scampered up the chair to peek over my shoulder. "So, what are you reading?" she asked.

"I'm reading a book about the Battle of Gettysburg," I said. "My brother, Eli, and I have been studying the American Civil War this year for our history class and, in a few months, we're going to take a Civil War field trip."

"Sounds exciting," said Susie. "Will you tell me about your trip when you return?"

"I'll make you a deal," I said. "I'll tell you about my field trip and the assignments that go along with it since you're going to share your stories with me."

"It's a deal," she said. She held out her paw to shake on it. Then she jumped off the chair and scurried into the woods.

SPECIAL DELIVERY

The next morning Eli and I went to help our grandparents on their farm. After having a treat of milk and homemade apple dumplings with our grandparents, Eli and Grandpa went out to do some outside work while Grandma and I made some treats.

Once we were alone, Grandma turned to me and said, "There's an envelope for you in my crocheting basket." I gave her a strange look before going to the living room to look in the basket. Sure enough, there was an envelope tucked carefully in the basket. I cautiously removed it and saw this on the front, written in beautiful handwriting.

To: Elizabeth

From: Susie Squirrel

Happy Reading

I gingerly opened the envelope to find a handmade book along with a note. I put the book beside me on the couch and opened the note to read it.

Dear Elizabeth,

I enjoyed our chat at the Sanctuary yesterday. As I promised, here is a copy of my book. I hope you enjoy what I have written. I'll see you soon.

Blessings,

Susie Squirrel

"When did this come?" I asked Grandma.

"Susie delivered it this morning. She was sitting in the yard when I came downstairs to make coffee." She pointed to the backdoor. "So, I went outside and talked with her. She told me that you two had visited with each other yesterday afternoon and asked me to give this to you."

After lunch, Eli and I headed home with our arms filled with baked goods and, of course, my package.

As we entered the house, our mother asked, "How did this morning go?"

"It was great," replied Eli. "Grandpa and I worked on some special projects in the barn."

Mom smiled, then asked me, "What's in the envelope?"

"It's some stories that one of Grandma's friends wrote. She's going to be using them at church and thought that I might like to read them." I didn't dare tell her that they were from a squirrel. "I would like to quickly glance at them just to see what she did before I start my afternoon schoolwork."

Again, Mom smiled and said, "Sure, go ahead."

I ran up the stairs and got comfortable on my bed. Then I carefully opened the envelope, took the book out, and started reading. Susie's stories were enjoyable and interesting. They made me think.

When I saw Susie again, I asked her if she would mind if I had her stories published as an actual book so other children could read them. We decided to tell the story of how we met and have the remainder of it be her stories.

Anyway, I've done my part. I hope you enjoy her stories as much as I have.

Your friend,

Elizabeth Hopewell

ANNABELLE:
THE AMIABLE ALPACA

I delight to fulfill your will, my God, for your living words are written upon the pages of my heart.
(Psalm 40:8 TPT)

Amiable – having or showing pleasant, good-natured personal qualities; affable, friendly, sociable, agreeable; willing to accept the wishes, the decisions, or suggestions of another or others.[23]

One Saturday morning, on a farm near Samuel and Rebecca Hopewell's, Annabelle, the amiable alpaca, looked forward to the day. Annabelle enjoyed greeting the children who came to visit with her at the Angelic Alpaca Farm. She also enjoyed watching them take home items made from her fleece.

Annabelle was basking in the sun when she noticed her owner, Alice, and a family with a little red-haired girl happily walking towards her corral.

---

23   All definitions in Country Chronicles are from dictionary.com

Alice walked up to her and stretched out her arm to stroke Annabelle's face. "Annabelle, today is a very special day. It's this little one's fourth birthday. Not only that, guess what her name is? Her name is Annabelle."

Annabelle moved her head up and down in approval.

Alice turned to little Annabelle. "Would you like to pet her?"

The little girl wasn't sure. Alpaca Annabelle was awfully big.

"It's okay," said Alice. "She won't hurt you."

"Would you like me to do it with you?" asked Annabelle's dad. The little girl nodded. He picked Annabelle up with one arm and stretched his other arm to rub Alpaca Annabelle's nose.

The little girl laughed. "I want to try!" Carefully, the little girl stretched out her hand and petted Annabelle. Alpaca Annabelle stood still for a few seconds because she didn't want to scare little Annabelle. She slowly started moving her head up and down. She wanted little Annabelle to know she was enjoying her visit.

"What do you think of that?" asked Annabelle's mom.

"I think it's neat," replied Annabelle, her eyes aglow.

"Would you like to see the rest of the farm now?" asked Alice.

"Okay," said Annabelle, still stroking Alpaca Annabelle's nose.

"I'll be back in a little while," said Alice to Alpaca Annabelle. Alpaca Annabelle bobbed her head up and down. As the group walked away the little girl called out, "Goodbye Annabelle! It was nice to meet you and thanks for making my birthday special!" Alpaca Annabelle, once again, moved her head up and down.

About an hour or so later, Alpaca Annabelle heard someone calling her name. It was little Annabelle. "Look," she called, holding up an alpaca puppet her parents had bought for her. "I'm taking you home with me." Alpaca Annabelle smiled.

After she closed the gift shop, Alice walked up to see Annabelle. Annabelle saw her and went over to the fence to greet her. As Alice stroked Annabelle's nose, she said, "Thank you for being so friendly and gentle, Annabelle. You really helped make that little girl's day." Alpaca Annabelle smiled inside. She liked to make people feel special and happy.

Questions:

1. Do you like to help make people feel happy?

2. What kinds of things make you feel happy?

BECKY:
THE BENEVOLENT BULLDOG

*So be strong and courageous, all you who put your
hope in the LORD!* (Psalm 31:24)

Benevolent – characterized by expressing goodwill or
kindly feelings; desiring to help others; charitable

Mr. Hersh's grandson Brian, a hard-working college student, knew his English bulldog Becky was special from the day he got her. Becky loved to go for car rides and visit people. Since he was preparing to become a visitation minister, Brian got Becky certified as a visitation dog. The two of them often graced the halls of rehabilitation centers and nursing homes. Many of the patients would brighten as Becky made her rounds.

There was one particular patient, however, that they never seemed to get to smile. He always seemed to have a tear in his eye when they came. So, one day, before leaving, Brain asked the head nurse, Brenda, if his bringing Becky was a problem.

"No, Brian. Ben actually loves when you come. It just brings back memories for him and makes him miss what he used to have."

233

"What do you mean?" asked Brian.

Brenda continued, "You see, Ben grew up in England and Becky reminds him of home. He and his wife, who passed away a few years ago, always had a bulldog as a pet. Simply put, he misses his wife, his bulldog, and how his life once was. I guess he's just a bit lonely."

Brian was silent for a moment, then asked, "Brenda, would it be okay if I brought Ben a present?"

Brenda looked at him and said, "Sure, as long as it doesn't need walked or fed. If you think you have a way to make him smile, go for it."

"Becky and I will be back in a bit."

"Okay," replied Brenda. "See you then."

As Brian and Becky were walking down the hall, one of the aides asked Brenda, "Where's he going in such a hurry?"

"I have no idea," said Brenda. "But he's on a mission."

Before long, Brian and Becky walked into Tom and Tina's Books and Gifts. "Good afternoon, Mr. Tom." said Brian.

"Good afternoon, Brian," he replied. "What can I do for you?"

"Do you still have that English bulldog puppet I saw the other day? Becky and I would like to buy it for a friend of ours."

"I sure do," said Mr. Tom.

Brian smiled, paid Mr. Tom, and said while walking out the door, "Thank you helping us Mr. Tom."

"Anytime, Brian, anytime."

When Becky and Brian returned to the nursing home, they found Ben catnapping in his wheelchair in the sunroom. Brian, followed by Brenda, quietly walked up to Ben and sat down on a chair beside him. Then he gently shook Ben's shoulder. "Mr. Ben, are you awake? It's Brian. Becky and I brought something for you."

After a few minutes, Ben was awake enough to realize something was laying on his lap. His eyes filled with tears as he asked, "For me? Really?" With Becky taking a nap at their feet, Ben shared his story with Brian. He told him about his wife and how she would take walks with their dog every morning, and how his kids got so excited when they discovered their new dog on Christmas morning. Eventually, Ben's head started nodding. Brian suggested that he go rest in his room. Just before leaving, Brian turned to Ben and asked, "What are you going to name your friend?"

Ben smiled. "Bristol, after my home land, of course."

Questions:

1. Have you ever done something special for someone in an attempt to cheer them up?

2. Has anyone ever done something nice for you to help you through a hard day?

CANDY:
THE COMFORTING CAT

"Then these righteous ones will reply, 'Lord, when did we ever see you hungry and feed you? Or thirsty and give you something to drink? Or a stranger and show you hospitality? Or naked and give you clothing? When did we ever see you sick or in prison and visit you?'

"And the King will say, 'I tell you the truth, when you did it to one of the least of these my brothers and sisters, you were doing it to me!' (Matthew 25: 37-40)

Comfort – to soothe, console, or reassure; bring cheer to

For several months, Rebecca Hopewell had noticed that her neighbor, Mr. Hersh, seemed less cheerful than usual. At church, instead of greeting her and Samuel enthusiastically, Mr. Hersh would glance at them for a moment, as if trying to place them, before waving a limp hand. It unnerved her. So, one morning, over a cup of coffee and fresh sticky buns, she shared her concern with his wife. "Rose, is everything okay? Reuben doesn't seem like himself lately."

Tears sprang to Rose's eyes. "No, Rebecca. I took him to the doctor the other week, and we found out he's in the early stages of dementia."

"Oh Rose, I'm so sorry. That must be so hard for you." She took Rebecca's hand. "What are you going to do?"

"The doctor gave us several suggestions to make life a little easier and more enjoyable for him," said Rose. "One of those suggestions was getting an indoor pet. He says having a pet will provide company and comfort for him."

"Have you gotten him one yet?"

"No, no. I'm trying to keep things as normal as possible. I want him to help with the farm as long as possible. But, as a precaution to keep him safe, I've shared the news with Jacob," said Rose. "One thing I have started to do is play quiet music for him when he's in the house, which was also something the doctor suggested. But I haven't gotten him a pet yet."

"One of our cats had kittens about six weeks ago," said Grandma. "If you would like, we could go look at them and see if there's one you'd like to take home for him."

"I would like to do that," said Rose.

After finishing their coffee and sticky buns, Rebecca and Rose walked out to the barn. In a barrel, they found a mother cat and three kittens. One kitten was gray with black stripes. Another was a tan color with black stripes, and the third was yellow with orange stripes. "You're cute," Rebecca said, picking up the yellow one. She stroked its soft fur.

Just then Samuel walked over. "So how many are you taking home with you?" he said.

"Just this one," Rose said. Samuel raised his eyebrows. He had been kidding but realized Rose wasn't. Rebecca and Rose had Samuel sit on a straw bale as they shared the news with him.

When they were finished, Samuel said, "Rose, if there is anything Rebecca and I can do, please let us know."

"I will," she said.

"What are you going to do with the farm?" Samuel asked in a shaky voice. He and the Hershes had been neighbors for almost fifty years. Though he knew things couldn't stay the same forever, it would be a shame to watch the farm get torn down.

"Well, the children and I have been discussing that," said Rose. "But we haven't made a decision yet. I'll let you know when we do."

"Very, well," replied Samuel. He wanted to offer to buy Reuben's farm right then and there but Rebecca wouldn't appreciate it.

Rebecca went to the house for a basket and a towel to transport the kitten before Samuel drove Rose home. Reuben would soon be coming to the house for lunch.

As they pulled in the drive, Jacob and Reuben came out of the barn. "Good morning Reuben," said Samuel.

"Well, good morning, Samuel. What brings you here?"

"Well, said Samuel, "Rebecca and I have something that we want to give to you." As Jacob and Samuel watched, Rose pulled back the towel and showed Reuben the kitten. "I shared our news with Rebecca and Samuel this morning," said Rose.

Reuben's eyes filled with tears. "Samuel, I'm angry and I'm scared but I'm also touched by your thoughtfulness. Thank you for the gift." He touched Jacob's shoulder. "I'm also thankful for your son, Jacob. Samuel, you have a special boy. He's willing to stand by me and help me farm for as long as possible. He's also using his education. He has agreed to help my family decide on the best way to take care of me."

Blushing, Jacob said, "Reuben, you were there for my family when we needed help. Now we're going to be there for yours. Now, what are we going to name this new addition?"

Reuben looked at the kitten for a moment. "She reminds me of butterscotch candy, so let's call her Candy."

"That's a wonderful name. Now, may I make a suggestion?" said Jacob.

"Of course," replied Reuben.

"Would you be willing to allow Candy to live with my family and come to visit you and you come to visit her? I'm concerned you may trip and fall if she lives with you fulltime."

Jacob and Samuel could both see the disappointment in Rose's and Reuben's face. Rose smiled gently at Reuben to assure him that this was a good idea. Reuben replied, "If you think that'd be best, that's what we'll do."

Jacob said, "Why don't you take your little buddy to your home for a visit and I'll have Elizabeth come and get her later."

"We'll take Candy home with us for now and we'll see Elizabeth in a little while," said Rose. And with that, they all headed to their own homes for lunch.

Questions:

1. Have you ever done something special for someone in an attempt to cheer them up?

2. Has anyone ever done something nice for you to help you through a hard day?

3. Do you have a pet that cheers you up when you're feeling sick or upset?

CHARITY:
THE COMPASSIONATE CHICKEN

*All praises belong to the God and Father of our Lord
Jesus Christ. For he is the Father of tender mercy
and the God of endless comfort. He always comes
alongside us to comfort us in every suffering so that
we can come alongside those who are in any painful
trial. We can bring them this same comfort that God
has poured out upon us. And just as we experience
the abundance of Christ's own sufferings, even more
of God's comfort will cascade upon us through our
union with Christ.* (2 Corinthians 1:3-5 TPT)

Compassion – A feeling of deep sympathy and sorrow
for another who is stricken by misfortune, accompanied
by a strong desire to alleviate the suffering.

One fall day, Grandma Hopewell's friend Beverly showed up
at Grandma's front door crying.

"Beverly, what's wrong?" asked Grandma Hopewell.

"Oh, Rebecca, I miss Blake so much since he's gone off to college and today's his birthday." She blew her nose into a handkerchief. Just then, Charity the chicken appeared on the scene. She stood at Beverly's feet clucking. "What do you want?" asked Beverly.

"She wants you to pet her," said Grandma Hopewell.

"Pet her!" exclaimed Beverly. Grandma Hopewell nodded. Cautiously, Beverly leaned down and petted Charity. "Well, I can't say I've ever done that before. I can't believe it. A chicken that likes to be petted."

"Come with me Beverly," said Grandma Hopewell. "Let's give her a treat."

"A treat!?!"

"Sure, just follow me." The three of them walked around to the back of the house, Grandma leading and Charity bringing up the rear.

Once they reached the walkway at the rear of the house, Grandma stopped at a trash can and pulled out a scrap. "Now you know what you have to do to get this," said Grandma. She drew circles in the air with the scrap. "Let's go this way. Now, let's go the other way."

Beverly giggled as Charity unwound herself. "Rebecca, I've never seen anything like this," said Beverly.

"She's special." Grandma smiled. "Listen, it's nice out. You go sit at the table and I'll bring out some treats for us."

"Oh, Rebecca, you don't have to do that."

"I insist. Now scoot!"

Blushing but grateful for her friend, Beverly made her way to the table on the patio. When Beverly sat down, Charity stood beside her.

"Now what do you want?" asked Beverly. Charity stood there, her head cocked. Before long Beverly found herself petting and talking to Charity. When Grandma and Grandpa Hopewell walked up with some cheese, crackers, fruit and iced tea, Charity clucked happily.

"Goodness Samuel, I didn't mean to take you away from your work."

"You didn't take me away from anything," replied Grandpa Hopewell. "I came inside for a drink and Rebecca said you were here. So, I decided to come and visit for a bit."

"Well, I'm glad you did."

Suddenly Beverly asked, "Where did Charity go?"

"Look beside you," said Grandpa. Beverly looked down to see that Charity had made herself comfortable beside Beverly's chair.

"She loves to socialize," said Grandma. "She especially enjoys going to see Mrs. King."

"You mean she goes visiting with you?"

"That's right. I put a chicken diaper on her and away we go."

"Now I've heard everything," said Beverly, her hands in the air. Grandma and Grandpa just smiled at her.

"Now," said Grandpa. "How are you doing?"

"Oh," said Beverly. "It's just that I'd grown so used to Blake coming to see me that life just doesn't seem normal with him being away at school."

Grandpa nodded. "We felt that way when Jacob went off to college and we'll most likely feel the that way again when Eli and Elizabeth move on to new things in their lives."

Just then Beverly looked at Grandma. "Do you think Charity could come and visit me once in a while?"

"Sure!" Grandma said.

"You know you're always welcome to come and visit her, too," said Grandpa.

"I appreciate that. I'll make sure to stop in from time to time."

"Now," said Grandma Hopewell, "I think it's time for us to enjoy our treats."

"I agree," said Grandpa. Charity, still full from the snack she had earlier, plopped down next to Beverly's chair for a nap.

Questions:

1. What is one way you can show others compassion?

2. Has anyone ever shown you compassion?

ELMER:
THE EMPATHETIC TREE

So encourage each other and build each other up, just as you are already doing. (1 Thessalonians 5:11)

Be happy with those who are happy, and weep with those who weep. (Romans 12:15)

Empathetic – of, relating to, or characterized by empathy, the psychological identification with the feelings, thoughts, or attitudes of others.

Elmer is a dear friend of mine. Not only did he give me shelter as I grew up, he also encouraged me to do my best and to follow God's lead. When I got older, I moved to another part of the forest, but I never forgot Elmer and visited him often.

For instance, one sunny autumn afternoon, when I was feeling down, I went to visit Elmer. His smile faded as he saw my sadness. "Susie," he asked me, "What's wrong?" His leaves and branches drooped.

I looked up at him with sad eyes and said, "What purpose do I serve? Odessa the Opossum recently lost her home, and she's so sad. I don't know what to do to comfort her. It makes me sad to see her so sad."

His leaves and branches drooped even more. "I know how that feels," he said. "Sometimes I wonder what my purpose is now that you're gone. I can't move around and do things like you do because I'm stuck in one place. I would have been cut down and removed from the forest a couple of years ago if you wouldn't have talked Mr. Hersh out of it. I enjoy your visits, and I always feel better after I talk to you. Even if you're just stopping by to store some acorns for later, you always bring a ray of sunshine with you. You're a wonderful friend, Susie, great at encouraging people. How are you doing with your stories?"

I shrugged. "They're coming along all right. I'm not sure what I'll do with them when I'm done." Tears came to my eyes as I spoke.

After a few quiet moments, Elmer, looked down at me and said, "Why don't you put them all into a book? I know those stories really brightened my day; they'll likely cheer Odessa up, too."

"You really think so?" I asked.

"I know so," said Elmer. "And you know what? After you write your book, I'll even host story time for you. I can see your stories speaking to all the animals of the forest. We can call this space here The Gathering Place."

Tears started falling from my eyes. In a shaky voice I said, "Thank you for loving me so much."

"Thank you for loving me, Susie. You're a great friend."

After that, Elmer and I snuggled together and took an afternoon nap.

Questions:

1. Has anyone ever encouraged you?

2. Have you ever encouraged anyone?

GINGER:
THE GIVING GUERNSEY

You must each decide in your heart how much to give.
And don't give reluctantly or in response to pressure.
"For God loves a person who gives cheerfully." And God
will generously provide all you need. Then you will
always have everything you need and plenty left over
to share with others. As the Scriptures say, "They share
freely and give generously to the poor. Their good deeds
will be remembered forever. (2 Corinthians 9:7-9)

Giving – To present voluntarily and without expecting
compensation

As Eli and Elizabeth walked up the lane to their grandparents'
house, they saw Grandpa standing at the barn door motioning
for them.

"Good morning!" he called. "Here, follow me a second. I
want you to help me do something. Then, I want you to take
something in to Grandma. We have a special day planned for
you." Eli and Elizabeth smiled at each other. "What are you smiling at?" asked Grandpa.

"Oh, nothing," said Elizabeth. "We were just talking on the way over about how we like to come and see you and Grandma. There's always something interesting going on here."

Grandpa shook his head, smiled back, and thought about how thankful he was to have his grandchildren living next door to him.

"Well, then if you came over to do interesting stuff, we'd better get started. The first thing we have to do is milk Ginger."

"Milk Ginger?" said Eli and Elizabeth simultaneously, sounding very unsure about this adventure.

"That's right, I'm going to teach you how to hand milk. Come on, you two love Ginger."

"Well, that is true," said Elizabeth.

Just then Ginger turned around and gave out a soft moo. "See?" said Grandpa. "She loves you, too, and she wants milked. That bag is getting heavy. So, who's first?"

Eli nudged Elizabeth forward a little as he said, "She is."

"Eli, I'm surprised at you," said Grandpa.

"I don't mind going first," said Elizabeth. "What do I do?" Grandpa showed Elizabeth how to pet Ginger so she would know Elizabeth was there. After cleaning the udder and giving the teats a few squeezes to clean out the dirt, he sat Elizabeth on the stool and put the bucket underneath Ginger's bag. "You have to squeeze your thumb and finger like this and pull like this." He gently pinched the teat between his thumb and forefinger and rolled the rest of his fingers down it. "Now, you try," said Grandpa.

"If you want milk to come out," Elizabeth asked. "Why do you squeeze? Why don't you just pull?"

"You squeeze so the milk doesn't go back up in the bag. If the milk goes back into the bag, it can give the cow a really bad infection, and we don't want that. Go on, give it a try."

Gently, Elizabeth started pulling. "You have to pull harder than that or you won't get anything. This poor girl doesn't want to stand here all day," Grandpa said. Elizabeth swallowed hard. Then, with all the strength she could muster, she squeezed and pulled at the same time. Kerplunk! She did it again. Kerplunk!

Elizabeth's eyes got wide. "I did it! I did it!"

"You sure did," replied Grandpa. "Now it's time for you to use both hands and milk opposite teats." It took a little practice but before long Elizabeth established a rhythm and was finished with her part of the job. "You're next," said Grandpa to Eli.

Eli swallowed hard as he sat on the stool. Grandpa instructed him just as he had Elizabeth.

Before too long, Eli was successfully getting milk. His rhythm was a bit slower than Elizabeth's, but he still got the job done. When Eli finished, Ginger let out a soft moo.

"See, she's thanking you," said Grandpa. "Now, I'm going to put some of the milk in this small milk can for you to take in to Grandma. While you do that, I'm going to put the rest of the milk in the tank and let Ginger out. Tell Grandma that I'll be in in a few minutes."

As they entered the house Grandma called out, "Well, good morning, you two. How did milking go?"

"It was an experience," said Eli.

"It was sort of cool," said Elizabeth. "I didn't know you had to be able to keep a beat while milking."

Grandma smiled. "Well, are you ready for the next part of this adventure?" she asked.

"That depends," said Eli.

"Well, do you think you can handle making butter and churning ice cream?"

Eli and Elizabeth's faces brightened up. "Sure, we can handle that," said Elizabeth.

After everyone had a little snack, Grandma, Grandpa, Eli, and Elizabeth washed their hands for the next milk adventures. When everyone was ready, Grandma put some of the milk into two one-pint canning jars.

"Now," said Grandma, passing the jars to the children. "I want you to sit there and shake these jars. Be careful not to drop them."

As Eli and Elizabeth shook the jars, Grandpa explained that the milk in the jars was called raw milk. "It's called raw because it hasn't been pasteurized," he said. As he was talking, Elizabeth's eyes widened. "What's wrong?" he asked her, a smile on his face.

"It's changing, Grandpa. It's getting, well, solid."

"That's because it's changing into butter," he said.

"Just like that?" asked Elizabeth.

"Yes," he replied, "just like that." Once they were finished making their butter, Grandpa showed them how to stamp an image on the butter with a butter print.

Once that was done, they moved on to making ice cream the old-fashioned way. Grandma put the ice cream mixture into the canister, Grandpa assembled the ice cream churn. Next, Eli and Elizabeth alternated layers of ice and rock salt in the bucket until they surrounded the canister.

"Okay," said Grandpa. "Start cranking." Eli and Elizabeth turned the handle of the churn for what seemed like *forever*. By the time they were finished, their hands and arms were sore and they were exhausted. But as the first bite of their ice cream melted on their tongues, they felt it was all worth it.

Questions:

1. Have you ever given a gift to someone? How did you feel when you did that?

2. Has anyone ever tried to teach you a new skill? How did that make you feel?

HOLLY:
THE HAPPY HOLSTEIN[24]

*Now may God, the inspiration and fountain of
hope, fill you to overflowing with uncontainable joy
and perfect peace as you trust in him. And may the
power of the Holy Spirit continually surround your
life with his super-abundance until you radiate with
hope!* (Romans 15:13 TPT)

Happy – delighted, pleased, or glad, as over a particular thing

One morning I was out and about when I ran into my friend
Holly, a Holstein cow. As I approached Holly, I noticed that my
friend seemed especially happy. Holly swished her tail from side
to side as she walked back and forth along the fence. She even let
out a joyous moo every now and again.

When I was close enough for Holly to hear me, I asked, "How
are you this morning, Holly?"

---

24   This story is dedicated to Reese Burdette, a very special Franklin County
farmgirl. Reese, you are an inspiration and a blessing.

"I'm happy, very happy," replied Holly. "I get to see my favorite little girl today. I was told that I need to go see her to help her feel better so she can come home. She's been in the hospital for months."

As I sat on the fence, I said, "You must miss her very much. I'm delighted you'll finally get a chance to see each other. Life isn't always easy but knowing that someone else cares helps to make things a little better."

"That's true," replied Holly. "I'll let you know how my little friend is when I return."

When Holly returned from her trip, she told me her friend, Hallie, was very glad to see her. She told me how Hallie patted her nose and how she mooed softly to Hallie, telling her to get better. She also said that the hospital had a little picnic for Hallie and her family, including some hay for her. She was very happy to be included. It was hard for Holly to say goodbye when it was time for her to go home, but Hallie promised that she would join her soon.

Questions:

1. Have you ever gone to a hospital to visit someone? How did that make you feel?

2. How do you think the person you visited felt when you came to see them?

3. Have you ever been in the hospital? Who came to see you while you were there?

HOPE:
THE HELPFUL HOUND

Now, this is the goal: to live in harmony with one another and demonstrate affectionate love, sympathy, and kindness toward other believers. Let humility describe who you are as you dearly love one another.
(1 Peter 3:8 TPT)

Hope – n – the feeling that what is wanted can be had or that events will turn out for the best

v – to feel that something desired may happen

Henry started out life as a preemie, born before his due date, which resulted in some health issues.

One evening, after Henry was in bed, his parents started talking about getting him a puppy for his birthday. "I think he could handle walking a dog," his dad, Jerry, said. "You know, he loves *The Fox and the Hound* and a girl I work with has a Basset Hound that had puppies a few weeks ago. Would you like me to see if she has any that aren't spoken for?"

"That would be wonderful," his wife, Cara, replied. Suddenly, Jerry looked down at the floor.

"What's wrong, dear?" asked Cara.

"Oh, nothing. I'm just glad you agree because I already did," he said, blushing like a little boy who got caught stealing a cookie from the cookie jar.

Cara smiled. "When do we go to pick our new family member?" she asked.

"Tomorrow," replied Jerry.

"What were you going to do if I said no?"

"I was going to text her and tell her that I got in trouble with the teacher."

Cara smiled as she shook her head. Then she said, "Come on, you. We need to get some sleep. We're going to have a busy day tomorrow."

The family slept in like they would any other Saturday. While eating breakfast, Jerry said, "Henry, Mom and I have been talking about what to get you for your birthday and were wondering if you would like to get a puppy?"

A smile grew on Henry's face and he bounced a bit in his seat.

"Now, if you don't think that's a good idea," Jerry teased. "We can come up with something else."

Cara chuckled to herself as she watched her two boys talking things over.

"When do we get to go pick our puppy, Dad?"

"Our puppy? I thought it was going to be your puppy," said Jerry.

"I know, but isn't he going to be part of the family? After all you *and* Mom take care of me. Aren't you going to talk and play with him, too?"

"Of course we will, sweetheart," Cara said.

"Why are you worried about it?" his dad said.

"I know what it's like to be ignored," Henry said. "Some kids won't play with me because I can't do certain things. It hurts, and I don't want to hurt my puppy. If you're not going to be friends with him, then I don't want a puppy."

His parents' jaws dropped in amazement. He had never told them how deeply his challenges affected him before. But in his care for their puppy, they saw how these challenges strengthened him.

After he found his voice, Jerry spoke. "We will love the puppy just like we love you. We're so sorry you've struggled with this. That would be hard for anybody, and we hate that it's happening to you."

Henry said, "They just don't understand. But as long as I have you, Mom, and God, I'll be okay. We're a team."

Once again, Henry's parents were amazed at what they were hearing. How in the world did their little boy get such wisdom at such a young age? His dad cleared his throat. "Would you like to go find OUR puppy?"

"I sure would," Henry said, beaming.

"Well, go get your shoes on."

About twenty minutes later, Henry and his family arrived at the home of Jerry's coworker, Alica. After trading introductions, the group went to see the puppies, milling about their mother. Immediately, Henry's eye's focused on the smallest one in the group. "That's the one."

"Dear, don't you want to look at the other..." Cara said.

"No," Henry interrupted. "That's the one."

"She's had some rough times," said Alicia.

"That's okay," replied Henry. "I have too." The four of them watched the pup play, toddling behind her brothers and sisters. Even though she couldn't keep up with the others, she seemed very friendly and happy. She trotted up to Henry's leg and sniffed at his ankles, giving them a tentative lick. Henry giggled.

"Are you sure that's the one you want?" asked Jerry.

"I'm positive," said Henry.

"Okay," said Alicia. "I'll keep her for you. I need to keep her for about another two weeks. That way I'll know that she'll be strong enough to go to her new home. She has a little more growing to do before you take her home."

"Two weeks!" said Henry. "That's when my actual birthday is!"

"Well then, that's perfect," Alicia said. As they got ready to leave, Henry's dad pulled out his wallet to pay for the pup. Alicia stopped him. "No charge."

"No, that's not fair."

"No, seriously, I want to," said Alicia. "I wasn't sure if I would be able to find her a home."

"You have to promise us one thing then," said Jerry. "Promise you'll come to Henry's birthday dinner."

"I'd be honored. How about if I bring, bring..." Alicia turned to look at Henry. "Who am I going to bring with me to your birthday dinner, Henry?"

"You're going to bring Hope," replied Henry.

"Hope...that's a beautiful name."

"Yep! There's hope for both of us," said Henry, his face aglow.

Questions:

1. How have you offered someone hope? How did doing so make you feel?

2. How has someone given you hope when you were facing a tough situation? How did that make you feel?

HELEN:
THE HELPFUL HORSE[25]

*Those who live to bless others will have blessings
heaped upon them, and the one who pours out his
life to pour out blessings will be saturated with favor.*
(Proverbs 11:25 TPT)

Helpful – giving or rendering aid or assistance of service

Hannah and Helen, a Morgan horse, had competed in equestrian events for years. However, Helen got older and competing got harder, and Hannah worried that Helen would fall and take her down with her. So, Hannah left her home to relax in the pasture while she competed with a younger horse.

While Helen enjoyed her home pasture, she felt empty inside when she stopped competing. That is, until she met Heidi Taylor. Heidi had recently moved with her parents to the home beside Helen's pasture.

Heidi fell in love with Helen at first sight. She would stroke

---

25   In memory of Mr. Michael Shipley – artist and horseman

Helen's nose and bring her apples and carrots when she came to visit. They quickly became good friends.

One day Helen whinnied loudly to Hannah as she was getting ready to put her in the barn. Helen was upset because she heard Heidi crying. Since school started Heidi cried frequently. "I know, girl. I know," Hannah coaxed. "I don't like hearing Heidi so upset either. I'm sure she'll be all right soon, though."

That didn't matter to Helen. She whinnied even louder. Hannah started getting concerned. "Helen, what do you want, girl?" she asked as Helen kept trotting towards Heidi's house.

Finally, Hannah didn't know what else to do but go and knock on Heidi's door. Heidi's mother answered.

"Hi, Hannah," said Mrs. Taylor. "I'm sorry if you heard Heidi. I just can't get her to read her homework assignment without getting upset."

"May I make a suggestion?" asked Hannah.

"Sure," Mrs. Taylor said. She chuckled. "At this point, I'm open to anything."

"Let her take her book and read it to Helen. It might calm both of them down, and Heidi will get her homework done."

"Helen's been upset?" asked Heidi's mom.

"Yes," replied Hannah. "She heard Heidi crying and has been pacing back and forth along the fence."

"Well, I guess it wouldn't hurt to try," said Mrs. Taylor. "Heidi, would you like to take your book out and read it to Helen instead?" Heidi poked her head around the corner, cheeks still red, eyes still puffy from crying, and nodded. "Alright, put your jacket on and go read to Helen." Heidi grabbed her jacket, her book, and a carrot from the fridge, and ran out the door to join Helen.

Helen trotted to meet Heidi. Heidi climbed up on the fence and fed Helen the carrot. "I didn't come to just feed you. I came to read you a story about a horse." Carefully, so Helen could see the pictures, Heidi leaned against the fence and read the book to Helen. She took her time, pointing to the pictures and stroking Helen's nose every now and again.

Hannah and Mrs. Taylor quietly walked toward them, watching and listening. "Well, would you look at that!" Mrs. Taylor said. "Heidi isn't only calm, she's actually reading the story correctly. I can't get over how calm Helen has become."

"I wish you would have seen her a little while ago," said Hannah.

Then Mrs. Taylor thought of something. "Hannah, would you mind if Heidi came over in the evenings to read to Helen? I don't see any other way of getting her to do this."

"I wouldn't mind at all. She can even come on the weekends when I'm out competing. I just ask that you come with her so I know she's safe."

"Of course. Thank you for your help."

"It's not a problem. I appreciate the chance to help you. I think Helen will like it too."

When they reached Helen and Heidi, Hannah said, "Heidi, would you help me with something?"

"Sure," said Heidi. "What can I do?"

"Well," said Hannah. "I've noticed that Helen has been a little sad since I haven't been taking her to competitions. I noticed how happy she was to have you read to her this evening. Would you be willing to come and read a story to her every evening?"

"I would love to, Miss Hannah!" replied Heidi, jumping up and down.

"Now, there are some rules to this. Your mom has to come with you so I know you're safe. She's not going to do anything except hang around to make sure you don't get hurt because sometimes I won't be home."

Heidi thought for a minute then said, "You mean I can come even when you're away?"

Hannah smiled. "That's exactly what I mean."

Heidi jumped into Hannah's arms and gave her a big hug. "Oh, thank you, Miss Hannah. I'll do an awesome job for you and Helen."

Hannah smiled as Heidi hugged her. Then she put her down and said, "Okay now, you go home with Mom and finish the rest of your homework without fussing. I need to put Helen to bed."

"Okay," said Heidi. "'Night, Helen." Heidi took her mother's hand and they walked home together.

Hannah turned towards Helen and said, "I'm sorry you've missed competing. I just didn't want either of us to get hurt. You mean a lot to me." Helen rubbed her nose against Hannah's shoulder. "Do you think you can handle this job?" Hannah said.

Helen whinnied softly. She knew she still had a purpose. "That's what I thought," said Hannah. "Now, let's get you to bed."

Questions:

1. Have you ever helped someone feel like they have a purpose?

2. Has anyone ever shown you that you have a purpose?

MOSES:
THE RESCUED MACAW

The Lord is close to the brokenhearted; he rescues those whose spirits are crushed. (Psalm 34:18)

Rescue – to free or deliver from confinement, violence, danger, or evil.

My friend Noah lives with a salt-wasting type of congenital adrenal hyperplasia. He went to his endocrinologist, Dr. McCaw, for his six-month checkup, and to share his school presentation. I rode along on top of his mom's van, without anyone knowing and listened to everything through an open window as I sat on a tree branch. It was an adventurous afternoon.

Dr. McCaw strolled into the examination room, a blue macaw with yellow around its eyes and beak sat on his shoulder. "I hear that you have something to share with me," said Dr. McCaw.

"Yeah," replied Noah. "Mom told me I had to share my presentation with you."

"Well, let's hear it," said Dr. McCaw. The macaw squawked in greeting.

"Who is that?" asked Noah, pointing to the bird.

"Nope, you first. I'll tell you about my new buddy after you give your presentation."

"Okay, fine." Then, after giving Dr. McCaw a copy of his handout, he started to speak on his condition and his struggles living with it. Toward the end of his presentation, he said, "But the biggest thing that frustrates me is knowing I'll never be able to be a firefighter like my dad. I have no idea what I'll be able to do when I get older because...I'm not normal." His voice broke.

Dr. McCaw put the macaw on his portable perch as he put his arm around Noah. After a few minutes Dr. McCaw said, "Noah, that had to be one of the most honest and informative presentations I've ever seen. I can see why you received an A on your project."

"Thank you, Dr. McCaw." He wiped away his tears. "Now, will you tell me about your new friend?"

"I will in a minute, but first I'd like to ask you a few questions."

"Okay," said Noah.

"You said that you're not normal. Noah, what is normal?"

"Normal is being able to do what other folks can do."

"You can work on building your model railroad by yourself. Correct?"

"Sure. Why?"

"Well, I don't have any idea how to do that. Shoot, I can't even change the oil in my lawnmower and my dad used to change his all the time. So does that make me abnormal?"

Noah considered this for a moment. "No, it doesn't make you abnormal. You can just do different things."

"That's right," said Dr. McCaw. "I can't change my oil but I can help sick people. My dad couldn't do that."

"What did your dad do for a living?"

"He was an engineer who helped build things. When the time comes, we'll talk about what you're good at and talk a little further about what you can do for a career. Right now, though, enjoy what you're doing and enjoy being a kid. You might have to do things a little differently but that doesn't make you abnormal. That just makes you unique."

"Now, you've been asking me about my new friend." Dr. McCaw tapped his shoulder with his hand, inviting his friend to join him. The bird hopped onto his shoulder. "Noah, this is Moses."

"Hi, Moses," said Noah.

"Hello," Moses squawked.

"Moses is a macaw," said Dr. McCaw.

"A macaw?"

"That's right; same name, different spelling. He's a hyacinth macaw. Moses hasn't always been treated nicely. His previous owners didn't know how to care for him because he didn't fit in. To them, you might say he was abnormal. They didn't realize how much care and attention he would need.

"Anyway, a neighbor saw that Moses seemed very sad and encouraged his owners to take him to a bird sanctuary instead of getting upset with him all the time. So that's what they did.

After staying at the sanctuary for a time, Moses was put up for adoption. We told the folks at the sanctuary that I was an endocrinologist and a blue macaw would be a perfect companion for us. We also explained that Moses would come with me to my office and enjoy the company of me and my family when I was at home. So, the folks at the sanctuary taught us how to care for Moses and how to transport him. Now, he's part of my family and my practice. So Noah, even though you might sometimes feel like you're abnormal and don't fit in, remember that there's always hope. You may feel that you don't fit in and have no idea what you want to do or could do as a career, but you'll find the answer. Just be patient and let God show you in His time."

Questions:

1. Have you ever felt like you didn't fit in?

2. Have you ever been there for someone who felt like they didn't fit in?

OWLBERT:
THE OBEDIENT OWL

Love means doing what God has commanded us,
and he has commanded us to love one another, just
as you heard from the beginning. (2 John 1:6)

Obedience – the act or practice of obeying; dutiful or submissive compliance

Even though Owlbert had a teaching degree, he decided to teach at a daycare, instead of an elementary school. When he wasn't at the daycare or taking care of his home, he spent his time tutoring or stocking grocery shelves, except on Sundays. Owlbert made sure he followed God's direction about having a day of rest.

Everyone knew Owlbert to be a nice, honest, and law-abiding individual. He taught Sunday School and helped with church events when he could. One Sunday after church, Pastor Peacock asked Owlbert to join him and his family for lunch. Over dessert, Pastor Peacock said, "Owlbert, I would love for you to tell me more about why you do what you do."

Owlbert said, "Pastor Peacock, let me ask you something. How many children are growing up without a father or positive role model in their lives?"

"I can't give you an exact number," said Pastor Peacock. "However, I am sure there are many."

"Well, I feel God has given me several mission fields. The daycare I work at is a mission field, one where God has shown me I get to be a positive role model to children who need it. My tutoring business and even the grocery store are mission fields too. Yes, you can minister to people when showing them where the ketchup is. I even had the privilege of leading one of my co-workers to Christ. I simply go where I feel God leading me."

The pastor sat for a moment, amazed. "Owlbert, would you mind if I share about your obedience to God in a future sermon? I feel led to preach on listening to God and trusting Him enough to go wherever He leads. You are a wonderful example that God has purposes greater than we can see, which is why we must trust and obey Him, even in stocking ketchup."

Owlbert grinned. "I feel honored that I have inspired a sermon. My heart's desire has always been to go wherever God leads."

Owlbert went home, grateful to have been seen and valued.

Questions:

1. Have you ever been misunderstood for a choice you made?

2. Have you ever wondered why someone made a certain choice?

JOSIAH RAT'S
REVERENT REUNION

And out of your reverence for Christ be supportive of each other in love. (Ephesians 5:21 TPT)

Love is large and incredibly patient. Love is gentle and consistently kind to all. It refuses to be jealous when blessing comes to someone else. Love does not brag about one's achievements nor inflate its own importance. Love does not traffic in shame and disrespect, nor selfishly seek its own honor. Love is not easily irritated or quick to take offense. Love joyfully celebrates honesty and finds no delight in what is wrong. Love is a safe place of shelter, for it never stops believing the best for others. Love never takes failure as defeat, for it never gives up. (1 Corinthians 13: 4-7 TPT)

Reverent – feeling, exhibiting, or characterized by reverence; deeply respectful

Josiah Rat had not seen his cousins since a family disagreement that happened ages ago. As a result of the feud, his uncles moved their families out of the area. Though the cousins often spoke secretly on the phone, things weren't the same. However, Josiah was preparing to bury his father, and he felt it was time for them all to get together. So he and his cousins, Jonny and Jackson, planned for them to visit Josiah's place in Pennsylvania. While they knew they would probably not arrive in time for the funeral, Jonny and Jackson were looking forward to reuniting with their cousin.

Late Friday evening, Jackson hopped on a Pennsylvania-bound train in Texas. At about eight o'clock on Saturday morning, Jonny left his Brooklyn apartment, located above an Italian grocery, to do the same thing. Both hoped to be at Josiah's place by early Sunday morning. They had agreed to meet at Elmer, a tree that they played around when they were young, and then go to Josiah's together.

The cousins met at Elmer. They were surprised at how much Josiah had changed over the years. He wasn't nearly as tall as they had remembered, and he had since grown a mustache. Then again, once they stopped and thought about it, they were surprised at how much they all had changed over the years. They were no longer the energetic rats they once were. Instead, they were a little grayer and a little heavier. They were all married and had families of their own.

The three of them went back to Josiah's home. They sat and talked about how things were when they were little, reminiscing on the hours spent together as kids. Then, out of the blue, Jackson said, "You know, this is crazy. We've been talking to each other for years, but our kids don't know their cousins. I think it's time for a family reunion.

Josiah and Jonny looked at each other for a moment. "I agree," said Josiah.

"What will our dads think?" Jonny asked.

"We'll have to come clean," Jackson said. "We can also tell them, if you want, that we don't want to lose our friendship like they did."

"This isn't going to be easy," said Jonny.

"Since when is anything that is worth doing easy?" asked Jackson.

"True," said Jonny.

So, for the rest of their time together, the three cousins talked about the family reunion. They decided to meet at Josiah's home so they could show their kids where they grew up.

Immediately, Josiah, Jackson and Jonny sprang into action to prepare for the big event. It felt like Christmas all over again. Once Jackson and Jonny arrived home, they told their wives and families about the reunion. After sharing the news, both Jackson and Jonny went to speak with their fathers. Jonny's father was very angry with him and said that he couldn't believe what had happened. His mother, however, was a little more understanding. She, too, had secretly been corresponding with Jackson's wife, who was her sister.

When her son went to the door, she whispered, "I'll help you get ready for this and I'll go with you."

"But what about Dad?" asked Jonny. "He'll be very upset with you."

"Don't worry about him. I'll simply tell him that I have missed my sister and I want to see her."

Jackson's father responded differently. He rubbed his chin as he took in the news. "Well, son, I wish you would have told me sooner," he said. "But I understand. It would be good to see the boys again. I'll come with you. What can I do to help?"

The day for everyone to travel to Josiah's home finally came. Josiah and his family put the final touches on sleeping and dining areas for the family while his cousins' families embarked on their journey.

Just before they left, Jonny asked his father, one last time, if he would like to go with them. His father scoffed and turned away from them. So, sadly, without his dad, Jonny started towards Josiah's home with his mom and the rest of his family.

Two days later, the cousins and their families met at Elmer. Elmer was honored to be included in the glorious event and asked me, Susie, to be there with him. After they greeted each other, the families asked me if I would like to join them. Of course, I said yes. I also told Elmer that I would share what I saw and did with him later.

When we arrived at Josiah's, I was put in charge of the little ones. While the adults unpacked, the children and I played games, read stories, and explored the forest.

Once everyone had found where they would be staying, things really started to get interesting. The women gathered and started cooking. Smells of chow-chow, black-eyed peas, and Manhattan clam chowder filled the air. The men gathered under an old oak tree and talked.

Out the corner of my eye I saw Josiah and his cousins visiting quietly with Jackson's father, Jeff. A tear dropped down the old man's whiskers.

Over the next four days the rat families ate together and played together and I reported everything I saw and did to Elmer. I even took some of the little ones to visit him, which he enjoyed. However, I didn't see Jackson, Jeff, or Jonny during that time. Then, on the fifth day, I saw Jackson and his father, Jeff, along with Jonny and his father, Joel, eating breakfast with the rest of the family. Little ones were crawling up on Jeff and Joels' laps to say hi. They gave out many hugs with tears in their eyes. When I got a chance, I asked Jackson about what had happened. He told me that he and Jonny went to New York to speak with Joel. They explained that the family would really like to see him and finally close the family feud. So Joel changed his mind and came.

For the next three days, old hurts were forgiven and were replaced by new memories as the families spent time together. The women cooked and swapped recipes while the men worked on various projects in order to keep the homeplace looking nice. When the children weren't helping with projects, they played games and enjoyed the forest.

When it was time for each rat family to go their separate ways, they exchanged tearful goodbyes. The families decided to make this gathering a yearly tradition, and that they would keep talking to each other. They no longer had any secrets to keep.

Questions:

1. Has your family ever had a disagreement? How did they handle it?

2. How did your experience make you feel?

SAMMY:
THE SHARING SQUIRREL

There is a special time for everything. There is a time for everything that happens under heaven. There is a time to be born, and a time to die; a time to plant, and a time to pick what is planted. (Ecclesiastes 3:1-2 NLV)

When you are generous to the poor, you are enriched with blessings in return. (Proverbs 22:9 TPT)

Sharing – giving something to someone else without expecting anything in return

Sammy was a squirrel who liked to plant and collect things, and he loved to share what he grew and collected. Every spring Sammy, with the help of some younger squirrels, would plant corn and sunflowers. During the growing season he would lovingly care for his crops. When he wasn't tending his fields, he spent his time gathering nuts. At harvest time he picked his corn and his sunflowers. After storing enough for himself, he would share the rest with those who were less fortunate than he.

He loved helping others. When asked why he did what he did, he would say, "Because I feel that's what God wants me to do. He's blessed me and I want to be a blessing to others, whether it's sharing my harvest or teaching the next generation how to plant and harvest."

One year Sammy tore his paw, preventing him from planting his crops. He had so much to do. *How am I going to get it all done?* he wondered.

When the younger squirrels heard Sammy was injured, they immediately went to visit him. "We'll take care of everything," they said. Some of them planted his crops while others cleaned his home and fixed his meals. When harvest time came, Sammy was well enough to help.

After they harvested everything, Sammy said to those who helped him, "I want you to go get your families and come to dinner at my place this evening."

Several of the squirrels said, "Mr. Sammy, that isn't necessary."

"It most certainly is." Sammy said. "I want to celebrate my recovery with those who God provided to assist me in doing so."

After putting it that way, the younger squirrels accepted the invitation. However, when they returned, they found something they hadn't expected. Sammy had arranged a festival with food and games for everyone to enjoy. He also had gift baskets for every family to take home. He said that God had provided for him so he wanted to share his blessing.

I was the last to leave. Before going, I asked, "What's going on? You're giving even more than usual. What's gotten into you?"

"Susie," he told me. "Being laid up gave me a chance to think about some things. First, I was reminded about how important it is to trust God to provide for your needs. The other thing I learned is that the youngsters I taught how to plant really were listening to what I said and really do care about me! God sent them right when I needed them. I want to remind everyone that God's watching over them, just like He watched over me."

Sammy gave me a hug and told me goodnight. As I walked home under the moon, I had a spring in my step and a warm feeling all over. I felt God looking out for me, too.

Questions:

1. Has anyone ever taught you a special skill?

2. Have you ever taught someone how to do something?

3. Has anyone ever taken care of you when you were sick or hurt?

4. Have you ever taken care of someone when they were sick or hurt?

SALLY AND SARAH:
THE SHARING SHEEP

The crowd kept asking him, "What are we supposed to do?" John told them, "Give food to the hungry, clothe the poor and bless the needy." (Luke 3:10-11 TPT)

Sharing – giving something to someone else without expecting anything in return

Sally and Sarah, Boarder Leicester sheep, two of the many sheep that Tutor Wendy owned, had been sharing with each other since they were born. They shared the same mom. Also, because sheep do not like to be alone, they shared the same pen, bedding, and many other things. While they were used to sharing with each other they never really thought about sharing with others, except Candy the cat who would drink from their water bucket on occasion. However, Sally and Sarah did help Tutor Wendy and her students with an on-going project. You see, Sally and Sarah would grow the wool. Tutor Wendy would have them shorn. Then she and her students would make scarves and donate them to homeless shelters. Like the other ewes that Tutor Wendy owned, they also shared their milk each year after they lambed.

287

Some of the milk was used to feed their lambs while the rest of it was made into soap and cheese which Tutor Wendy and her students would sell. That money was donated to other charities. Without realizing it, Sally and Sarah were helping Tutor Wendy teach her students how to share with others in many different ways.

Questions:

1. Have you ever shared something with someone else? How did that make you feel?

2. Have you ever found out that what you did to help affected more people than you thought it would?

3. Has anyone ever shared something with you? How did that make you feel?

4. Have you ever experienced a time when you or someone else did not want to share something? How did that make you feel? Could you have done something differently?

SMITTY:
THE HELPFUL BLACKSMITH

*If anyone sees a fellow believer in need and has the
means to help him, yet shows no pity and closes his
heart against him, how is it even possible that God's
love lives in him?* (1 John 3:17 TPT)

Helpful – giving or rendering aid or assistance

Smitty Squirrel, who is me and Sammy's brother, was coming
home from a family get-together when he came upon his little
rabbit friend, V.R., sitting on a rock, crying. When he reached the
little bunny, Smitty sat down beside him. "What's wrong, pal?"
he asked. "Why the tears?"

V.R. looked up at Smitty, tears still glistening in his eyes. "It's
my momma's birthday and I don't have a present for her. She's
a really great mom, and I wanted to bless her for her birthday
somehow. She's been wanting some hooks to hang her pots and
pans on. I saved my allowance to buy them for her but I don't
have enough." V.R. burst into tears again.

Gently, Smitty turned the rabbit's sad little face towards him. "Let's go make some hooks."

As they walked to Smitty's shop V.R. asked, "How are we going to make hooks?"

"We're going to heat some iron in my forge and hammer them into shape on my anvil."

V.R.'s eyes grew wide. "You're going to help me make them?" said V.R.

"That's right," said Smitty.

"But Mr. Smitty, if I can't afford the hooks at the store, I know I won't be able to afford yours."

"Don't worry about it, pal. Remember what we're taught in church. We are supposed to help others. You need my help to have a birthday present for your mom. You never know when I might need your help."

When they reached Smitty's shop, he asked, "Where are you planning on hanging these hooks?"

"The ones I looked at could just be hammered into the wall," said V.R.

Smitty knew that hanging them on the wall could be a bit of a problem. He looked at the little rabbit. "Let's go to your house. We're going to plan this project out and do it right.

"But I won't have anything to give her when I get home," said V.R.

"Sure you will," said Smitty. He handed him a hook he had made the day before out of scrap iron. "We'll take this to her as a sneak peek of what's to come."

As they walked to V.R.'s home, V.R. held onto that hook like gold. Smitty had an idea, and he chewed on it for a while. "You know, V.R.," he said. "I sometimes could use some help in my shop. Would you like to come help me after school?"

"Really, Mr. Smitty?" V.R. said. "That'd be great! I'll have to ask my dad first."

V.R.'s dad, Bob, was waiting for him when they got home. "Boy, where have you been?" he asked.

V.R. hung his head. "I was out looking for something for Mom for her birthday. I didn't have anything for her."

"V.R., we told you that you didn't need to get her anything. We said that you could just make her a card," said Bob in a soft voice.

Smitty cleared his throat and said, "Bob, if it's okay with you, V.R. and I have some measurements to take. You see, he and I are going to be working on a project together for his mother's birthday."

"Okay," said Bob. "Come on in."

With everyone else in the living room, Smitty and V.R. quietly made their way to the kitchen. After looking at the space, Smitty whispered, "Okay, here's how we're going to do this." He pointed to the ends of the kitchen. "We're going to make a bar that runs across this ceiling here, and then we'll hang the hooks from the bar. Then your mom can hang her pans from those hooks. How's that sound?" Smitty brought Bob into the conversation and ran the plan by him.

"Oh, Smitty, that's so kind," said Bob. "But we can't afford it."

Smitty held up his hand. "V.R. and I have it all worked out. He's is going to come after school and on Saturday to help me work on it. Also, if he's interested, after we're finished this project, he's more than welcome to come and help me at the shop and I'll teach him how to blacksmith."

V.R. looked up at his dad and said, "May I, Dad? Please, please?"

Bob smiled. "Sure, why not?"

Just then, V.R.'s mother came into the kitchen. V.R. proudly took the hook that Smitty had given him and handed it to her. "Happy birthday, Mom! This is just a little something for you until Mr. Smitty and I finish your real present."

Two weeks later, V.R.'s mom had something to hang her pots on. V.R. is still working with Mr. Smitty in his shop. He not only learned that it is important for people to help each other. He also learned that he had a purpose and was cared about.

Questions:

1. Has anyone ever mentored you? How did they help you?

2. Think of a time when someone came alongside you at just the right moment. How did it make you feel?

SUSIE AND
THE REFRESHING
CONVERSATION

And God-Enthroned spoke to me and said, "Consider this! I am making everything to be new and fresh. Write down at once all that I have told you, because each word is trustworthy and dependable." (Revelation 21:5 TPT)

Refresh – to make fresh again: reinvigorate or cheer (a person, the mind, spirits, etc.)

One day I was traveling through the forest when suddenly I heard a sort of whimpering sound. I looked around and found a young man, about twenty-two years old, sitting under a tree crying. I cautiously approached him. "Hi, I'm Susie," I said softly. "What's your name?" The young man was startled and started to leave. "Please, don't go," I said. "I won't hurt you. I heard you crying and thought I'd see if I could help."

"I don't need any help," he said gruffly. He swiped at his cheeks and sniffed. "Besides, I've never heard a squirrel talk before."

"Okay," I said. "But I'd still like to help you any way I can. What's your name?"

"Stan."

"Well, Stan, may I ask what has you upset?"

"Well, my grandfather died yesterday and he was the only person who ever really understood me. He would always protect me when my dad hit me. My dad told me he doesn't think I'll ever amount to anything. He doesn't understand my dreams." He swiped at his cheeks again.

"What are your dreams, Stan?" I asked.

"I want to help people somehow, but I'm not sure how. Right now, I'm a cashier at a pharmacy, but I help my boss with whatever he needs me to do. My dad thinks I'm wasting my time." He held his head in his hands. "My world just looks so dark."

That's when I said, "I think you need to look at things differently."

"What do you mean?" he asked.

"Tell me, Stan, what color are the trees?"

"Green," he replied.

"What color is the sky?"

"Blue," he said.

"Do you think they're pretty, Stan?"

"Of course," he replied.

"Stan, you've had some rough times. However, do you have some special memories of your grandfather?"

"Yes." He chuckled. "We had a lot of good times on our fishing trips."

"Didn't you say that you have a job?"

"Yes, and my boss has told me I do a good job."

"Then you build on that. Stan, may I tell you something else?"

"Sure."

"Stan, God loves you, and perhaps this is just me, but I find life is a lot brighter when you think of all He's done for you."

Stan sat, deep in thought. Then he said, "I don't know much about God. Grandpa told me He exists but nobody else has really told me a lot about Him. I've never really felt the need to find out for myself."

How was I going to get through to him? I immediately thought of Samuel and Rebecca Hopewell and how they helped their friends over the years, loving them through thick and thin. Perhaps they could help! "Stan, would you like to meet some friends who could help you through this rough time?"

"I'd like that," said Stan.

"Okay, then, follow me."

When we got to the Hopewell farm, we found Rebecca Hopewell putting feed in the birdfeeders. I explained the situation to Rebecca and she suggested that we go talk to Samuel. So, off to the barn we went.

When we entered the barn, Stan's eyes widened as he took in the stacks of hay. "What a cool place!" he said.

"Thank you." Samuel beamed. "Have you ever been on a farm before?"

"No, I'm a town boy." After sharing his story with Samuel, Samuel decided the best thing to do was to call Jacob and ask him to come over.

While they waited, Stan helped Samuel feed calves. When Jacob came over for lunch, Rebecca and Samuel explained that a friend introduced them to Stan and shared his story. They didn't dare tell Jacob their friend was a squirrel. When they had finished, Jacob said, "Stan, the first thing we need to do is call your family to let them know you're safe. Then, you can stay with us until you get back on your feet again. You can come to church with us tomorrow if you like."

By the end of the afternoon, Stan not only had new friends but a church family as well. Because of the Hopewells showing Christ's love, Stan is now a youth pastor with a family of his own.

Questions:

1. Have you ever felt that a situation was hopeless?

2. Have you ever shown anyone that there is always hope?

GLORIA:
THE UNIQUE GOAT

*For I know the plans I have for you, declares the
LORD, plans to prosper you and not to harm you, plans
to give you hope and a future.* (Jeremiah 29:11 NIV)

Unique – having no like or equal; unparalleled;
incomparable

Friends always enjoyed coming to visit Rhoda and her family because they were always doing something out of the ordinary. While most folks bought candy at the store, Rhoda and her family made their own. They made everything from chocolate covered peanuts to homemade taffy, and they often invited their friends to join in on the fun. Rhoda's home was warm and inviting, and everyone who entered the house felt like they could simply be themselves.

Sometimes they would gather around the player piano and sing. Kids who visited loved having a turn at pumping the pedals to make the rolls play. However, the most unique thing at Rhoda's house was a goat. They named her Gloria Excelsis, Gloria for short, because she was born on Christmas Day. Gloria was unique because she liked to wear hats. She had a hat for every occasion, Christmas, New Year's, Groundhog Day, Valentine's Day, you name it. When children who felt down on themselves would visit Rhoda and her family, Rhoda would take them to meet Gloria, who would cheer them right up. Like the day I took Harriet to Rhoda's home. It all started when I found my young friend curled up with Elmer.

"Why, Harriet," I said. "Are you all right?"

"I'll be okay, Susie. I just…" She sighed.

I perched up on one of Elmer's branches. "Want to talk about it?"

"Well," she said. "I'm not like Larry. He's really good at building things, and he seems really strong in his faith. I don't really know what I'm good at sometimes. I wish I were more like him."

I nodded. "I understand. My brother Smitty has this wonderful gift for making things also and I sometimes wish I could do that too. But I know how to be a good friend. Besides, I bet you're good at a lot of things."

Harriet shrugged. "I guess so," she said.

I knew just the thing to cheer her up. "Hey, come with me. I have someone I want you to meet."

I led her up to Rhoda's house, where we found her feeding Gloria. Gloria wore a straw hat embellished with orange and white flowers. I swiftly made introductions, and Rhoda gave Harriet a warm smile.

"Hello, Harriet. It's nice to meet you," she said.

Harriet couldn't help staring at Gloria's hat. "I've never seen a goat wear a hat before," she said.

Rhoda laughed. "That's Gloria for you. She loves her hats." She invited Harriet inside to make some homemade mints. "Have you ever made these before?"

"No," said Harriet.

"Well, you won't be able to say that anymore!"

When they entered the kitchen, Harriet felt comfortable in Rhoda's home. Rhoda kept up a steady stream of funny stories and jokes as she worked at laying candy molds on the table and melting chocolate wafers. When the wafers were melted, Rhoda gave Harriet the job of slowly stirring the chocolate as she added the mint oil. Then Rhoda showed her how to put the mixture into the molds and then into the freezer. While they were waiting for the mints to harden, they both enjoyed a cup of hot chocolate. Once the mints were hardened, the gals emptied them onto cookie sheets. Finally, they placed them in large rectangular containers putting wax paper between each layer of mints.

Rhoda leaned on the counter. "I think you've got a real knack for working in the kitchen. One might even say it's a gift."

Harriet's eyes shone. "You really think so?"

Rhoda nodded. "I know so. Just don't be afraid to share that gift with others."

That's just one example of how Rhoda's home and family became so popular and a second home for kids and adults alike. Folks felt accepted when they were there because they knew they could be themselves.

Questions:

1. Have you ever helped someone feel special for who they are?

2. Has anyone ever done that for you?

PART 5

HUSTLE, BUSTLE,
&
SERENITY

By Eli Hopewell

FRIDAY

The Morland home was a hustling and bustling place. Wes, a dedicated career firefighter never missed a day of work. He was a truck lieutenant at the busiest station in the county. However, as a believer in Christ, Wes thought it was important to use his talents and knowledge to serve his local community. So he volunteered one night a week at his local station. He also attended services and participated in church activities when he wasn't on duty.

Wes was also a husband and father. When he wasn't on duty or volunteering, he spent time with his wife Emily, his high school sweetheart who was an elementary school teacher, and their four children: fourteen-year-old Lily, twelve-year-old Oliver, ten-year-old Victor, and six-year-old Eve.

It was like any other Friday night when Wes had to work. He spent a few minutes with each of his children as they arrived home from school and reminded them that tomorrow was the beginning of a Super Weekend. Wes was coming off a shift and didn't have to return to the firehouse for a few days, so the Morland celebrated these with Super Weekends. These weekends included a huge breakfast on Saturday morning with eggs, bacon, sausage, French toast, fried potatoes, fruit, juice, milk, and coffee. After breakfast the family would do the chores or homework that needed to be done for the day. Then, in the evening, there would be a Super Family Movie Night, complete with make-your-own salads to round out their diets.

Super Weekend Sundays included church followed by carryout pizza for lunch and a board game afternoon. As much as everyone hated to see Wes leave, they wanted him to go and finish his shift so he could come home and have fun with them.

The night continued just like any other when Wes was on duty. Lily, an aspiring photographer, hurried through her algebra problems so she could enjoy part of her weekend snapping pictures. Oliver, an avid reader, as usual, was spending his evening with a good book. Victor, who dreamed of being a firefighter like his dad, was watching rescue show reruns in his room. Eve, who was always concerned about her dad when he was on nightwork, helped her mother bake cookies and sticky buns. Keeping busy seemed to help her worry just a little less.

Following family devotions, the evening proceeded in its usual fashion. Oliver kissed his mom on the cheek, told her good night, and headed off to listen to internet radio as he fell asleep. Victor, who always wanted to be ready to respond to any emergency, gave his mother a good night kiss and went to his room and arranged his pants so he could pull them on both legs at the same time, just like a firefighter. Finally, Emily tucked Eve into bed, with her doll, Patty, next to her. Eve said a short prayer of safety for her dad and his friends before Emily kissed her goodnight and left the room. Lily curled up on the couch next to her mother as she watched the news.

"Lily," her mother said gently. "It's time for bed. You need to rest."

"Oh, come on, Mom, let me watch, please?" She felt, at fourteen, she needed to know what was going on in the world.

Emily stroked Lily's hair. "You're growing up so fast," Emily said. "But even still, a growing girl needs her rest so she can be at her best. And when she's at her best, she'll take her best photos."

Lily sighed. "Okay, Mom." She gave Emily a quick kiss on the cheek and went off to bed, mentally planning her photo shoot for the following day.

Now for a little me time, Emily thought. After a nice, hot shower, she would snuggle under the warm comforter that topped the bed she and Wes shared. She smiled at the thought.

The news reporter said, "Tonight in Hampton Heights, a multi-alarm fire broke out in the Harrison Tire Factory." Emily's hand sprang to her mouth, her peace shattered. Hampton Heights was part of the area her husband covered. "I'm also getting unconfirmed reports of serious injuries," said the reporter.

Wes. Knowing she wouldn't be able to sleep, Emily went downstairs for a cup of tea. She dunked her teabag in the water as her mind filled with worry. Tears flowed as her best friend's number appeared on her caller ID. "Hello?"

The voice on the other end was very hard to understand. Through her tears, she heard her friend Julie say, "Jeff's in the hospital. I've got fire department representatives here to take me to see him, Emily." Julie took a deep breath, as if to gather her courage. "They don't think he's going to make it."

As scared as she was for her husband, Emily's heart broke for her friend. "Oh, Jules, I'm so sorry."

"Is it okay if I bring my boys to stay with you?"

"Of course," Emily said. Julie cried on the other line, relieved. "You know what? I'm coming with you. I'm going to ask my mom and sister to help with the kids."

As soon as Emily hung up the phone, she called her sister Bea and asked her to call her mother, explaining that she needed them to watch the kids for a little while. Emily's phone beeped while she was on the phone with Bea, sparking fear in her heart. Tears started falling from Emily's eyes again. It was her friend Amy, another firefighter's wife.

"I got a call from the department," said Amy. "Alan was injured in a fire."

"Oh, no," Emily sighed.

"I need to go to the hospital right away," Amy said. "May I bring Ally over?"

"Of course. My mom and sister will be watching our kids, since I'm going to be at the hospital with Julie. Her kids will be with us, too. We'll see you soon."

Emily quickly got dressed. Within minutes, Bea and her mom arrived. "Thank God you're here!" she said, rushing to embrace them. "Now, just follow Lily's lead. As long as she's being fair to all the kids, not upsetting anyone, and can handle it, let her do what she wants. She's got this." After Emily waited for what seemed like an eternity, Julie and her children arrived, along with a fire department official.

"Mrs. Morland," he said. "I'm so sorry to inform you that Wes has also been injured." *It will be all right,* a quiet voice said.

Lily had sneaked downstairs dressed and ready to go. "Mom, let me go with you. I can handle it."

Emily turned around and saw her. She reached out and stroked Lily's face. "No, Lily, I need you to stay here to help take care of the kids." Just then Emily saw Eve standing on the stairs, holding Patty and trying to look brave. Emily hurried over to her daughter and gave her a hug.

"Give Daddy a hug for me," Eve whispered. "I'll help Lily take care of the kids, too."

Fighting back her tears and worry, Emily kissed Eve on the cheek and headed for the door. As she walked away, Eve said, "Love you, Mommy."

"Love you too, Sunshine." It was going to be a long night.

As they rode to the hospital, Emily silently prayed for strength and peace. She was scared not only for herself, but also for Julie and Amy.

When they arrived at the hospital, they and one of the department officials were dropped off at the emergency room doors. Immediately, some nurses whisked Julie away to be with Jeff.

Another nurse escorted Emily to a waiting room. "The doctor will speak with you shortly," he said.

When Dr. Weller arrived, he told her that Wes had burns on over thirty-five percent of his body. "He's also sustained a spinal injury, so we're taking him into emergency surgery."

Fear flashed through Emily's body. When she found her voice, Emily asked, "May I see him?"

Emily nervously entered Wes's room. Her ears filled with all sorts of beeping from machines monitoring his heart rate, blood pressure, and other body functions. Once Emily adjusted a bit to the noise, she looked at the bed. It was filled with a body that looked very different from the guy she married. There were tubes and wires going everywhere. Cautiously, Emily walked towards the bed. "Wes, it's Emily. Can you hear me?"

There was no response.

"We have him sedated," said Dr. Weller. "I hate to rush this, but we really need to get him to the OR."

Emily quickly kissed Wes on the forehead. "I love you, Wes." With tears running down her face, she walked toward the door.

She found Amy sitting in the waiting room, holding a cup of coffee. Emily joined her. "How's Alan?"

"He's in surgery, but he's going to make it."

"Why is he having surgery?" asked Emily.

"They tell me he tore both rotator cuffs when he caught himself from falling through the floor. They were amazed he was able to pull himself up enough to keep from falling through. How's Wes?"

"He has a spinal injury. They're taking him to the OR now."

"Oh, Emily," said Amy. She laid a hand on Emily's shoulder.

"It's okay," said Emily. "He's alive. That's a blessing. And even if the worst comes from this, God will still watch over our family."

Emily got a cup of tea and sat with Amy as they both waited for their husbands to come out of surgery. They saw members of Jeff's family entering and exiting his room. Suddenly the door opened and Julie came out.

"He's gone," she said as she approached them. The three women stood, crying together.

After a few minutes, Emily felt a tug at her heart. *You should ask if these ladies want prayer.* She knew their families weren't as involved with the church as she and Wes were, but she wondered if they would be angered by the gesture. After she gathered her courage, Emily asked, "Would you ladies mind if I prayed with you?"

Julie, through her tears, said, "I'd like that."

"I would too," replied Amy.

After they prayed, Julie said, "Emily, would you mind if my kids stayed at your place until this afternoon? I need a little time with my parents and I want to try to get some sleep."

"Not at all, they are welcome to stay with us as for as long as you need. That goes for you, too, Amy."

"Thank you," said Amy.

Julie sighed. "Well, I guess we'd better be going. I'll keep you posted about funeral details. Please, don't say anything to the kids. It's only right that they hear the news from me."

"I understand," said Emily.

As Julie and her parents were leaving, a nurse came and told Emily and Amy it would be several hours before their husbands' surgeries would be finished and informed them they could wait in the lounge opposite the OR. She said it was a little more private and comfortable. As the nurse escorted them to the lounge, she added that the cafeteria was closed but she could bring them some applesauce and other snacks if they wanted. They gratefully accepted what she offered.

As the hours passed, Emily and Amy snacked, watched TV, and talked. Both women received periodic updates on their husbands. Around five o'clock in the morning, Alan's surgeon came to speak with Amy.

"Well, ma'am, your husband got through the surgery well, but he has a long road ahead of him," he said. "You should be able to see him in an hour or so."

Wes's surgeon came by around twenty minutes later. "Okay, ma'am," he said. "I was able to relieve the pressure around your husband's spinal column. Now it's simply a waiting game. I suggest you both get some breakfast." An encouraging smile spread across his face. "You need something other than graham crackers and tea. You won't be able to help anyone if you don't keep yourselves healthy." So, Amy and Emily headed for the cafeteria to see what was being served that Saturday morning.

Meanwhile, at the Morland homestead, Lily had come up with the idea of having a big sleepover in the living room. They all said a prayer for their dads before snuggling in for a couple hours of sleep.

After she tucked the kids in, Lily went to her grandmother and aunt. "Dad was supposed to be off this weekend," she said. "And we were supposed to have what we call a Super Weekend. I would like to have that type of weekend as much as possible. I'll start fixing breakfast at about eight o'clock, if that's okay with you."

"That's fine, sweetie," her grandmother said. "If you need any help, let us know."

"Thank you," said Lily. She was so determined to keep the weekend as normal as possible that she couldn't sleep.

SATURDAY

Lily woke up at about 7:30 and started cooking bacon and sausage for the Super Weekend Breakfast. As she blended the mixture to dip the bread in for French toast, Oliver, Victor and Eve sleepily came into the kitchen. "What are you doing?" they asked.

"I'm fixing breakfast."

"But Dad isn't here to enjoy it with us," Eve protested.

"I know," replied Lily. "But do you think he would want us to just sit around? Besides, we need to keep the others occupied. We all need to focus on something other than what's happened. That's what Dad would say. That's what he said when Lauren's dad got shot last year, so that's what we're going to do. We need to keep life as normal as possible." The four of them worked together on the Super Weekend Breakfast while listening to Broadway show tunes.

The music and the smell of frying bacon woke their friends. Rubbing their eyes, they all walked into the kitchen. "What are you doing?"

"We're cooking a Super Weekend Breakfast."

"It smells good," said Ally.

"It sure does," said Brad and Brock together.

"Well, why don't you guys rub the sleep out of your eyes and

311

brush your teeth. By that time, we'll have everything ready," said Lily.

Their grandmother and Aunt Bea stood in the background, observing the children's progress. Quietly Grandma said to Bea, "Lily is going to make an awesome mom one day."

"She sure will," said Bea. "She knows just what she's doing. At first I thought Emily was nuts when she said to let her take charge but now I understand why she told us to allow her to do so."

After everyone was seated, the Morland kids reached for the hand of the person sitting beside them.

"What are you doing?" asked Ally "We're getting ready to…"

Just then the doorbell rang. Grandma got up to answer it. "Come in, Lauren."

When Lauren and her mom walked into the dining room, her mom said, "I'm sorry if we're interrupting."

"Not at all," said Lily as she got up. "Would you like to join us?"

Lauren looked at her mom, her eyes pleading with her.

"Sure, why not?"

Grandma got up to get two more place settings.

While they waited, Lauren said, "Oh, Lily, I'm so sorry about what happened. We came as soon as we heard."

"It's okay," said Lily. "We're trying to keep things as normal as possible."

Once everyone was ready, Lily said, "Our family prays before each meal, and we do it holding hands. But if you don't feel comfortable holding the hand of the person next to you, that's okay, too."

"What do we do?" asked Brock, looking around at what his neighbors were doing.

"You sit quietly while Lily prays," said Eve.

Lily started in on her prayer. "God, thank You for this food. Thank You also that we can all be together during this hard time. Please be with each and every one of our dads. Also, thank You for giving us friends and family members. Them being here means a lot. Finally, bless this food so that it will give us the strength we need. I pray these things in Jesus's name. Amen."

After breakfast, the group cleared the dishes from the table which was easy since they decided to use paper plates and plasticware. Then they played board games for the rest of the morning. Lily made sure that there was theatre music playing in the background so no one would want to turn the TV on. At lunchtime, she had the kids pack some grapes, nuts, and cheese and they went to the park to play. Grandma stayed at home in case someone would call or come to the house with some news.

At four o' clock, the kids returned to the Morland house. Lily suggested that they take showers and change into some clean clothes before eating dinner and getting ready for Movie Night.

At about six o'clock, everyone had their salad or veggie plate prepared and settled in for a relaxing evening of movie watching when the doorbell rang. Grandma found Julie, Julie's father, and Mr. Don, the fire department chaplain, who was a friend of Jeff's, standing at the door.

"I've come to get my boys," Julie said quietly as she entered the Morland home. Brad and Brock immediately went over to their mom. "How's Dad? When can we see him? When's he coming home?"

Then Brock caught sight of the chaplain. "Brad," Brock said. "Dad's not coming home."

"What do you mean?" asked Brad.

"He always said if Mr. Don came, the news wasn't good."

Brad's bottom lip trembled. "Dad isn't coming home. Is he, Mr. Don?" he asked softly.

"No, Brad," said Mr. Don. "I'm afraid he isn't." Brad fell into his mother's arms, sobbing. Brock buried his face in his mother's shoulder. Mr. Don walked further into the living room to give Julie and her boys a moment. The other kids gathered around Mr. Don, asking for news.

"How's my daddy?" asked Eve.

"He's hurt pretty bad, Eve, but he's still here."

"How about my dad?" asked Ally.

Mr. Don smiled. "He told me that I was to tell you that he won't be able to play tag for a while but that he's going to be okay."

"Mr. Don," said Lily. "How can we help Brad and Brock?"

"Just be there for them," replied Mr. Don. "Just be there."

Emily and Amy arrived at the Morland homestead about nine o'clock. They found their families sleeping as a movie still played on the TV. Emily pointed towards the kitchen and in a low voice

314

she said, "Why don't you go and sleep in the spare bedroom upstairs? You and Ally can go home in the morning."

"Oh, I couldn't do that Emily, you've done so much for me already."

"Amy, I insist. You're tired. You've already called your neighbor to take care of your dog, Ally is already asleep. Now, go upstairs and get some rest."

"Thank you."

SUNDAY

On Sunday morning, the children, who had slept in the family room all night, woke up to the smells of coffee brewing and bacon frying. They simply figured Lily was cooking again, that is until they saw her asleep in her sleeping bag. "Mom!" Eve cried as she ran to the kitchen.

The Morland crew, Emily's mom, Aunt Bea, Amy, and Ally sat at the dining room table and had an enjoyable breakfast.

"When are we going to get to see Dad?" asked Oliver.

"Are we going to go to church today?" asked Lily.

"Wait, one question at a time," said Emily. "Dad's going to be in the burn unit for a while. However, I've made arrangements for you guys to video chat with him on Monday night. Once he gets to rehab and the risk of infection has decreased a bit, I think it'll be okay for you to go and see him."

"What about church?" Lily asked again.

"I talked to Dad before I came home," Emily said. "He wants us to rest this morning and go this evening."

"Miss Amy, would you and Ally like to go with us this evening?" asked Lily.

Amy, looking a little uncomfortable replied, "Oh, I don't know. Maybe Ally and I will just stay home and rest."

"Please, Mommy, I'd like to go with my friends."

"You don't have to dress up or anything," said Emily. "Sunday evening service is casual dress."

"Oh, why not," said Amy. "However, little one, you have to take a nap for me this afternoon. Mom needs a little rest."

"Okay," replied Ally.

Emily said, "I have enough room in the van for two more. We'll pick you up at about six."

Amy smiled, relieved. "Thank you."

Amy and Ally went home right after breakfast and the Morland family spent the day relaxing, reading, and napping. At about two o'clock, Emily made a quick trip to the hospital to see Wes.

"God's going to get us through this, Em," he said. "Now, you go home and spend time with the kids. I'm fine. I'll talk to you tomorrow night."

"Okay," replied Emily. "I do need a little rest."

"Of course you do. Take care of yourself, Em." Emily squeezed his hand, got up, and started for the door.

As she was walking out, Emily saw Amy walking out of Alan's room. "I see we had the same idea," said Emily.

"Say," said Amy shyly, "I really would like some time to myself. Is it all right if just Ally goes to church with you tonight?"

"Sure, that's not a problem. Are you okay?"

Amy looked at Emily and said, "Emily, I haven't been to church for so long... I would feel like a hypocrite if I went now. Alan never seemed very interested in it, anyway."

Emily laid a hand on her friend's shoulder. "It's okay. We're not going to push you to do something you don't feel comfortable doing. Would you like Ally to spend the night so you can have some quiet time? I'll make sure she gets to school in the morning."

"Em, you've done so much already," Amy protested.

"Please, Amy," said Emily. "It's really no trouble."

"Okay, I guess that will be alright. Besides, she already asked if she could." Emily hugged her friend and they walked out of the hospital side by side.

The Morlands and Ally arrived at church at 6:15. The church family eagerly gave hugs and well wishes to them and Ally. During the service, the pastor shared the news about what happened without going into too much detail. The congregation took up a special offering for the families.

Ally especially enjoyed the cheerful music. She looked around and saw people clapping in time, praising the Lord. At one point, she looked up at Lily and whispered, "I didn't know you were allowed to clap in church. My grandparents don't do that at their church."

Lily smiled at her. "Well, we clap here. You can clap too if you want." Ally smiled sheepishly and began to clap, gaining intensity with each motion. She was really enjoying herself.

THE FUNERAL

Jeff's viewing and funeral were held the Thursday and Friday after his death. Eight-year-old Brad was taking his dad's death very hard, and stuck close to his mom for support. Brock, who was very mature for a twelve-year-old, was determined to wear a blue suit, white shirt, and red tie with a 9/11 tie clip on it as his way of honoring his father. Brock was also adamant about speaking at his dad's funeral.

When it was his turn to speak, Brock adjusted the microphone, cleared his throat and read what he and Mr. Don had prepared. He hadn't shared what he was going to say with anyone else.

"Good morning. My name is Brock Bradock. My family and I would like to thank each and every one of you for coming today. My dad was a special guy who loved serving his community. He served in the military before becoming a firefighter. However, he was more than a father and firefighter, he was also a Christian." He took a moment to brush a tear away before continuing.

"One day, when I was about nine, he and I were talking and I asked him, 'Dad, what makes somebody a good person?' He looked at me and said, 'Well Brock, you know I believe we are all sinners and we all need to ask God for forgiveness. However, to answer your question, I believe in order to be a good person, one needs to follow what is written in Luke 10:27.' '...You must love the Lord God with all your heart, all your passion, all your energy, and your every thought. And you must love your neighbor as well as you love yourself [26].'

After having that talk, my dad and I started reading and talking about what the Bible says. We had a great relationship and I will miss him. While I may not ever understand why he was taken so soon, I know he's with Jesus, and that I will see him again. Ladies and gentlemen, if you want to honor my dad's memory, whether you believe in God or not, simply show others that you care about them. He would like that."

By the time Brock was finished, there wasn't a dry eye in the room. Alan, who was in a wheelchair, leaned over and whispered to his wife. "I knew that Wes believed in God by sharing what he and his family do on his days off, but I never knew about Brad. Amy, let's start going to church. I want faith like Brad and Wes."

At the end of the service, Jeff's casket was wheeled from the sanctuary and loaded onto a modified hosebed, the back of a firetruck. The funeral procession walked the short distance from the church to the gravesite, as firefighters in dress uniform, lined the route. Two ladder trucks, with an American flag hanging between them, were parked a short distance away. After Mr. Don finished his remarks, the flag that had been draped over Jeff's casket was

---

26 TPT

folded and at Julie's request, was presented to Brad as Brock returned the salute to the soldier that presented it. Two buglers, in an echoing style, played "Taps" on their bugles after the twenty-one gun salute. A gathering for family and friends was held in the church's fellowship hall after the graveside portion of the service.

ALAN

Wes and Alan had long roads of recovery ahead of them. Though Alan was released from the hospital much earlier than Wes, he still had many challenges to face as well as many hours of physical therapy to complete. However, the road of physical recovery was not the only road that Alan was traveling. After experiencing the warm love of Emily and Wes's church family, Alan, Amy, and Ally started attending their church. He also had Amy take him to see Wes often to discuss scripture. When Wes was well enough, he went to church to hear Alan share his testimony and see him get baptized. Now they were not only fire department brothers, but brothers in Christ.

WES'S CALLING

As they were recovering and studying the Bible together, Wes and Alan would often take time to pray about what God would have them do next. Though Wes was able to walk, which was an answer to prayer, he knew that he could never fight fire again. He wasn't sure what he would do after the fire department. While he was looking forward to spending time with his family, he didn't want to simply stay at home all the time and feel useless.

Then one day, Wes was visited at home by his pastor, Doug Grayson. Sitting in the living room, with his wife at his side, his pastor looked at him and said, "Wes, the church is growing by leaps and bounds. There are so many people I would like to visit, but I simply can't. Our church needs a visitation pastor, and the council and I think you would be perfect for the job. We'd pay you for your services, of course, but we don't want to impact your retirement. However, those details can be worked out later. Will you do it, Wes?"

Wes sat quietly for a moment, holding Emily's hand, then said, "But I'm not trained as a pastor. I'm a firefighter."

"You don't have to be ordained to do this," replied his pastor. "You're good with people. You know your Bible and you have experienced trials. However, if you think taking some classes would help you do a better job, I'll see what I can do about that."

Wes looked at Emily. "What do you think?"

"I think you would be perfect for the job," Emily said.

Wes said to his pastor in a quiet voice, "I'd like to pray about it first."

After praying over it with Emily for a few weeks, Wes called Pastor Doug. "I've been thinking about your offer, and, if you're still interested in taking me on, I'd be glad to do it."

"That's wonderful!" said Pastor Doug. They prayed together before hanging up, and Wes thanked God for presenting this opportunity.

FOLLOWING GOD'S LEAD

While Alan was thrilled to hear about Wes being asked to be the church's visitation pastor, he was still not sure about what God wanted him to do. The fire department had asked him to become an instructor at the fire academy. While he was grateful to be asked to do that, he felt like he was also drawn to another ministry. But he didn't know what.

As they were getting ready for bed one night, Amy asked, "So, are you excited about becoming an instructor?"

Alan took the toothbrush out of his mouth. "Sort of."

"What do you mean, 'sort of'?" she asked.

"I don't know…I feel like I'm supposed to do more than that. But I'm not sure what."

Amy sat on the edge of the bed and looked at her husband. She knew Alan was a good writer. "Have you thought about writing?"

Alan shrugged. "What would I write about?"

"You could write about fire department life," she answered.

Alan considered this. "You might be onto something, Amy. You know something? I've experienced more serenity since my injury than I ever have in my life. We had been so busy before, but all that…it was all unnecessary. I should share what I've discovered since I have been hurt through my book. I could call it *Hustle, Bustle, and Serenity.*"

Amy looked at her husband and said, "If that is what you feel God is telling you to do, then do it."

In the weeks that followed, Alan started his new job as an instructor at the fire academy. However, he also made sure that he took time to worship God, read His Word, write his book, and spend time with his family.

MOVING FORWARD

As one would expect, life was never the same for Jeff's, Wes's or Alan's families after that fateful Friday night. Even so, each family was blessed in many ways. Julie and her boys were showered with love and encouragement from family and friends. Even though it was difficult to go on with life without Jeff, Julie and her boys were successful in moving on with their lives. Julie went back to school to become a nurse. Through Mr. Don's mentoring, Brad was able to wrestle through the unfairness of his father's death and tried to see God working in his life. He and his brother Brock were able to comfort their friends when they went through similar struggles. When he got older, Brad became a social worker and Brock became a firefighter like his dad.

Wes worked to obtain his bachelor's degree in biblical and religious studies as Emily continued being a stay at home mom. She was content with that role. She liked being there for her family. Lily continued taking pictures and eventually started her own photography business. Oliver, after many years of study, became a college professor. Now you probably think that Victor became a firefighter like his dad. That wasn't the case. Victor became a dispatcher for the department. He got to tell his little sister, Eve, where to go because she joined the department and became a truck lieutenant.

With his wife Amy by his side for support, Alan continued his journey as an instructor at the fire academy and as an author. He now shares his story and encourages people to seek a life of serenity. Their daughter Ally is now a youth minister.

The three families see each other at church on Sunday mornings and more often than not throughout the week. All of them now understand how important it is to seek a life of serenity instead of just accepting one filled with hustle and bustle.

PART 6

SPECIAL TIMES

CHAPTER 23

GRADED ASSIGNMENTS

It took Jacob and Mary about two weeks to grade Eli and Elizabeth's work. Both were amazed at what their children had created and decided their accomplishments required some form of recognition. So, they made arrangements for Samuel and Rebecca to come for dinner again when they handed them back.

The six enjoyed a dinner of fried chicken, baked macaroni and cheese, pepper slaw, peaches with cottage cheese, and apple dumplings with vanilla ice cream. After dinner, with tears in her eyes, Mary handed Elizabeth and Eli their assignments and said, "Your father and I are very proud of you. You both did an excellent job!"

Then Jacob asked, "How did you two come up with your ideas? I didn't know either of you could write like that."

Elizabeth answered first. "Mom taught us how to write paragraphs. Besides, this isn't my first story. I've written three others so far. As for my research for this one, I listened to what people were saying at church, read the paper at Grandma and Grandpa's and was given a catalog by Mr. Tom the morning Grandpa took me to his store."

"Okay, but how did you know about Mr. Hersh?" asked Jacob, with a tear in his eye. He hadn't shared any of the information with his children.

Elizabeth hung her head as she answered, "I know we're not supposed to eavesdrop, but one afternoon I was picking flowers for Grandma by the fence and I overheard a conversation you and Grandpa were having. I hid behind the big oak tree and listened. Then I did some research on dementia and discovered animals can actually help dementia patients. That's how I came up with my story. I'm sorry for breaking the rules but ever since I found out about Mr. Hersh, I have been reading about dementia. I have learned that there are 84 different types and that many people with dementia like to listen to music."

As he moved closer to his daughter, Jacob thought, *When did she grow up so much? How am I going to help her keep growing? God, you have to help me with this.* "I'm glad our conversation inspired you to learn more. But it was wrong for you to listen in on our conversation."

"I know," said Elizabeth. "I won't do it again."

"I forgive you, sweetie. Now, how would you like to make your story a reality?"

"How?" asked Elizabeth.

"Well, we offered the Hershes one of the new kittens on the farm. While it would be good for Mr. Hersh to have a buddy when he's in the house, I would hate for him to accidentally fall because of the kitten and have either one get hurt. Would you be willing to take care of Mr. Hersh's buddy when it's here?"

"Yes," said Elizabeth. "I would love to!"

"It's settled then," said Jacob. "I'll speak with Mrs. Hersh in the morning. By the way, what do you mean this wasn't your first book?"

Elizabeth quickly ran upstairs and got the binder that held her other stories. She handed it to her father who began flipping through the pages. "Oh, one more thing," Elizabeth said. "Mr. Tom is opening a market stand and would like for me to help him run it. I would like to do that since it is at the same place where Naomi and Noah have theirs."

"You are full of surprises, Elizabeth! Your mother and I will think about the market. Now Eli, I'm curious about your project. Where'd your inspiration come from?"

"Well, Josh's letter really upset me and I had to find a way to deal with my feelings." Eli said as tears fell from his eyes. "So I decided to write a story about firefighters. As part of my research, I asked Grandpa to continue to take me to the station, because I wanted to understand the life of a firefighter even more. I'd really like to volunteer with the department someday, but I'm still too young to become a junior. However, the guys gave me some fire department history books to read. They told me that a good firefighter knows the history of his occupation. I've read some very cool stories."

"So someone finally found a way to get you to enjoy history," said Mary, raising her eyebrows. "I'm glad. You'll have to tell me about what you've learned." Mary looked at Jacob and said, "When did our children stop being innocent?"

"I'm not sure," replied Jacob. "But I do believe we should allow them to explore their interests."

"You mean it Dad?" said Elizabeth.

"Yes," replied Jacob. "However, I would like to hear the details about the market from Mr. Tom."

Grandpa raised his hand. "May I ask a couple of questions?"

"Of course, what would you like to know?" said Jacob.

"Well, first off, what did these two get on their projects?"

"They both got A's," Mary said. "While I did find a few grammatical errors, they both went so far above and beyond the call of duty that Jacob and I felt they both deserved them."

"Also," said Jacob. "What they learned about their subjects and themselves was amazing."

"Okay," replied Grandpa. "Now, when do Grandma and I get to read these wonderful papers? After all, I chauffeured these two around as they were writing and Grandma cooked for them so they would have enough energy to write these papers," he said smiling.

Eli and Elizabeth scrambled to grab the special autographed copies their mother had made. Elizabeth handed them off to Grandpa. "These copies are for you," she said, beaming.

With that, everyone said goodnight and Grandma and Grandpa went home.

After they climbed into bed, Grandpa looked at his wife and said, "Are you sleepy?"

"Not really," said Grandma. "Why?"

"Would you like to stay up and read a couple of projects?"

Grandma smiled. "Sure, why not?" So, Grandma and Grandpa snuggled beneath their comforter and began reading.

CHAPTER 24
THE KITTEN

At about 6:30 in the morning Mary went to Elizabeth's room and from the doorway said, "Elizabeth, are you awake?"

Still half-asleep, Elizabeth answered, "Yes ma'am, I'm awake. Is something wrong?"

"No, no," said Mary. "Dad wants you to go and help with the kitten at Mr. Hersh's before you go over to see Grandma and Grandpa. You can eat breakfast at Grandma's."

Elizabeth leapt out of bed. "Tell Dad that I'll be right there."

As she walked down the steps, Mary heard Elizabeth scrambling to get dressed and make her bed. Mary smiled at her husband, who waited in the kitchen with a cup of coffee. "She'll be down in a minute."

Mary had hardly gotten the words out before Elizabeth appeared at the bottom of the steps. "Let's go, Dad. I'm ready. We can't be late!"

Jacob shook his head and kissed his wife goodbye. As they walked to the Hershes, Jacob stopped and looked at his daughter and said, "Elizabeth, I am so proud of you. You have learned a great deal, but you still have a great deal more to learn. We all do. Now, follow my lead on this, okay? We're partners in this."

"Yes, sir," said Elizabeth.

"I want to help Mr. Hersh with his illness and you with your dream of helping others. Okay?"

"Okay, Dad," said Elizabeth as she hugged her dad around the middle. "I love you!"

"I love you too," said Jacob. "Tell you what, how about we call ourselves Team Hope."

"I'd like that," said Elizabeth.

"Okay then, it's time for Team Hope to get moving."

A few minutes later, Jacob and Elizabeth stepped onto the back porch of the Hersh's home. Jacob knocked on the backdoor. "Come in," Mr. Hersh said.

"Good morning, Jacob! I was beginning to think we were taking the morning off," said Mr. Hersh. "The Mrs. won't let me out of the house without you being around."

"I'm sorry for being late, but I brought my daughter along with me this morning. We'd like to talk with you and Mrs. Hersh for a few minutes before we go to milk."

Mr. Hersh called for his wife. "Rose, could you come here a minute?"

"On my way," she replied. Next, Jacob told the Hershes about Elizabeth's project and even read the story that she wrote to them.

With tears in his eyes Mr. Hersh said, "Elizabeth, that's very kind of you."

"You're welcome, Mr. Hersh," said Elizabeth. "Why don't we go out and find Candy—I mean, your kitten." She blushed.

Mr. Hersh smiled and said, "Oh and by the way, call us Miss Rose and Mr. Reuben. Mr. and Mrs. Hersh is just too formal for the amount of time you're going to be spending with our buddy."

"Yes, sir," replied Elizabeth. "You don't have to call your kitty Candy if you don't want to. I just did that because it made sense for my book."

"I like the name." Mr. Hersh said. "Besides, the orange striped one happens to be a girl. Why don't you and I go and get my new buddy while your dad starts milking."

After he was finished milking, Jacob came to check on their progress. He knocked on the back door and said. "How are things going?"

"Wonderful," replied Rose. "However, I'm going to have to go to town and get some litter and a pan for when Candy is with us."

With a smile, Jacob held up a shopping bag. "I called Dad, and he and Eli went and picked up two pans and litter while I was milking."

"You seem to think of everything," said Rose.

"We are happy to help," said Jacob. "Now, I will let you get Candy's things set up. Mr. Hersh and I will be feeding the calves if you need anything."

"Thank you," said Rose.

CHAPTER 25

THANKSGIVING

It was a cold morning. The hogs had been shot and hung the night before. Today the rest of the butchering process would be completed. Jacob prepared his children for this day the best he could. Even though they knew where meat came from, Jacob knew it could be overwhelming to watch the process for the first time. The children had never realized the meat that Grandma Hopewell had in her freezer was the result of Mr. Hersh and Grandpa Hopewell's Thanksgiving Eve butchering tradition.

The tradition took place at the Hersh farm. While the men butchered the hogs and put the hams and bacon in the smokehouse to cure, the women, Elizabeth, and Eli wrapped the meat and put it in the freezer. They also worked at fixing a lunch of fried pork tenderloin, green beans, and mashed potatoes.

About halfway through the morning, Mary found Elizabeth sitting cross-legged in the Hersh's living room, her head in her hands. "Are you okay, honey?"

Elizabeth nodded yes.

"Then what's wrong?" asked Mary.

"I feel bad for the pigs," Elizabeth said.

Mary rubbed her back. "I know, sweetie. It's a lot to take in."

Elizabeth looked up at her mother with troubled eyes. "Is it bad that I don't really miss Boston as much? I still love it, but I also love it here, too."

Mary smiled and took Elizabeth into her arms. "I'm glad you like it here. I'm sure you'll never lose your appreciation for the time we spent in Boston, but it's okay to enjoy where you live now." Mary thought about telling her about the other Thanksgiving tradition, but decided to wait till she had Eli with them, too. After another hug, Mary and Elizabeth, once again, joined in wrapping meat, panning scrapple, fixing lunch, and preparing homemade cranberry relish, pumpkin pies and other desserts for the following day.

Thanksgiving dawned cold, gray, and snowy. Jacob and Mary were glad that they didn't have to go far for dinner. Over a breakfast of scrambled eggs, fruit, and toast, they each shared what they were thankful for. Jacob took in the warmth of his family. *Wow, this is nice,* he thought.

As they walked in the door of Grandma and Grandpa Hopewell's house, they were greeted with the smells of juicy ham and turkey. "Find a seat," said Grandma. "Everything's ready."

Grandpa whispered to Jacob, "She has been looking forward to today all week. We are both so glad that you are here to share Thanksgiving with us. We've enjoyed going to the Hershes but it's nice to celebrate with family again."

The family walked into the dining room to find the table covered with an orange tablecloth and ironstone dishes. There was turkey, filling, mashed potatoes, sweet potato casserole, dried corn, green beans with ham and much, much more. Following prayer, and sharing what they were thankful for the family shared a relaxing and leisurely meal. After his third helping of turkey and filling, Grandpa asked Eli and Elizabeth, "Would you two help me feed before we have dessert?"

"Isn't it a little early for that?" asked Elizabeth.

"It is," replied Grandpa. "But I don't want to have to stop in the middle of our fun to go out and feed."

Now what's he up to? thought Mary. Jacob just smiled. He knew what was coming. He hadn't forgotten about that tradition.

When they came back from feeding, Grandma had her dessert smorgasbord which included pumpkin pie, shoofly pie, whoopie pies, apple dumplings and homemade vanilla ice cream.

When they were finished Grandpa said, "Okay, everybody in the kitchen. It's time for another Thanksgiving tradition."

As he walked to the cabinet and got out a saucepan Mary said, "Samuel, we don't need anything else to eat."

"Oh, this isn't for here," Samuel said.

Jacob smiled and put his finger up to his mouth. "It's been a long time since I pulled taffy." Before long the whole family was caught up in pulling, cutting, and wrapping taffy.

While Rebecca packed up some treats for Jacob and his family to take home, Samuel pulled his son aside. "Jacob, do you remember our other Thanksgiving holiday tradition?"

"Of course," said Jacob.

"Would you like to go on Monday morning? Reuben and I are planning on going out about 5:30."

"Sure, why not! It's been a long time since I've gone deer hunting."

So right before they left, Jacob told Elizabeth and Eli about the deer hunting tradition. "It's not right!" Elizabeth said, tears springing to her eyes. "How can you be so cruel to those poor animals?"

Jacob blushed. "I understand you're upset, sweetie," he said. "But we're not doing it to be mean. We do it to keep the deer from ruining the crops. Otherwise, the deer would run amok and eat all of Grandpa's corn. And that would be bad."

Elizabeth while shedding a few tears, sighed and resigned to the deer's fate.

After they got home and put the kids to bed, Mary and Jacob were sitting and talking in the kitchen when Jacob suddenly became quiet.

Mary saw a tear snaking down Jacob's face. "What's wrong?" she asked.

"I know we agreed to spend Christmas with your family," he said softly. "But after today I just wish we would be spending it here."

Mary smiled and said "We will be. We're going to be celebrating Old Christmas with my mom on January 6th since they have continued that tradition after my grandparents moved here from the Midwest."

Jacob hugged her. "Thank you," he whispered.

The following Monday was another time of reminiscence and new adventure for Jacob. He quietly got up at five o'clock to dress and eat an apple before his hunting adventure, but he was too excited to eat. With a spring in his step, he met Mr. Hersh and the two rode over to his dad's place. Once there, he was given a new hunting coat and the .308 Remington he had left there when he moved to Boston. Of course, Grandma Hopewell insisted that the three mighty hunters eat a snack before going on their adventure. So, they each ate a bacon and egg sandwich before heading out.

At about nine, they came back. Jacob and Mr. Hersh had been successful in their hunt. Before taking Mr. Hersh home and heading off to do his morning chores, Jacob asked his dad, "Do you still process your own deer, Dad?"

"No," said Samuel. "It's easier to take them to the butcher. We like him to make deer bologna for us."

"Do you still get it made with pure deer meat or do you have him mix it with beef?"

"We have him mix it. I'll take these two deer to the butcher and then come home and do the morning work."

Just then Eli and Elizabeth came out of the barn.

"What are you two doing here?" asked Samuel.

"We did your morning work for you," said Eli. Jacob and Samuel's eyes widened in disbelief.

"Would you like to check what we've done?" asked Elizabeth.

"Sure," said Samuel.

Jacob smiled at his dad. "Well, I guess I'll go do my work now."

After checking their work, loading the deer in the back of Samuel's truck and eating a quick snack, Grandpa, Eli and Elizabeth took the deer to the butcher for processing. The deer gave the Hopewell family enough deer bologna, roasts and other cuts for the winter.

CHAPTER 26

CHRISTMAS AND NEW YEAR'S

As soon as Thanksgiving was over things kicked into high gear for Christmas at Grandma and Grandpa Hopewell's house. Grandma started baking Christmas cookies. She also taught Elizabeth how to make homemade mints, chocolate covered peanuts, peanut brittle, and many more delightful treats. As usual, Grandma made plenty to share with everyone. On the first Saturday in December, as was always the tradition, Grandpa walked the farm to pick and cut the Christmas tree. Then, that evening, Jacob and his family came to Grandma and Grandpa Hopewell's for supper and helped them decorate the tree. Before they left, Grandma Hopewell gave both children an Advent Calendar. This calendar was covered with little flaps, one to be opened each day before Christmas. Behind each flap was a verse to read.

Eli went with Grandpa to take a large tray of cookies to the fire station. Grandma also sent treats to work with Jacob. However, Grandma and Grandpa's giving didn't stop there. They donated blankets that they had crocheted in the last year to a local charity. They also gave toys to the local toy drive and added to their hat, scarf and mitten collection.

Mary, Elizabeth and Eli's holiday adventures included a get together with the Newcomers on the last day before Christmas break. The group enjoyed a breakfast of scrambled eggs, gluten-free muffins, and fruit. Then, after a brisk walk, they made cranberry holiday salad and gluten-free cookies. Using mincemeat that Grandpa Hopewell had sent, they even made mincemeat cookies, one of Jacob's favorites.

Following a lunch of homemade seafood chowder and salad, the group played board games, sang Christmas carols around the player piano, and read the Christmas story from Matthew and Luke. Mary, Elizabeth and Eli, took some chowder and cookies home for Jacob. They left the rest for Nick to enjoy. They wanted to make sure that their hardworking dads were able to enjoy the treats they had made.

On Christmas Eve, Jacob's family and his parents attended a soup and sandwich supper at the Hershes' before attending a service at church. Following the service, they went to Grandma and Grandpa Hopewell's for hot chocolate, popcorn balls, and a gift exchange. Grandma also read a poem their friend Patricia had written:

CHRISTMAS
C reator
H ealer
R edeemer *of*
I solated
S inners
T otally
M anifested *in the*
A nointed
S avior

The following morning, Jacob and his family spent a quiet time at home before going to Grandma and Grandpa's for a bountiful Christmas dinner. There were so many dishes to choose from: ham, fried chicken, mashed potatoes, filling, green beans, dried corn and much, much more.

New Year's Eve and Day were much more relaxed. On New Year's Eve, Grandma and Grandpa came for a supper of home-made pizza, salad, and ice cream sundaes. After dinner, the family played board games, and around nine o'clock enjoyed a snack of homemade bologna, cheese, crackers, nuts, and fruit. The following day, Jacob, Mary, Elizabeth and Eli went to Grandma and Grandpa's for a pork and sauerkraut lunch, a Pennsylvania Dutch New Year's tradition.

CHAPTER 27
AMISH CHRISTMAS

Early on the morning of January 6th, Jacob and his family left for Mammi Esh's. Eli and Elizabeth thought it was a little weird to be celebrating Christmas after December 25. However, as they drove, their mom and dad explained to them about the 12 days of Christmas as well as Epiphany, Three Kings Day, and Old Amish Christmas.

"Now, kids," Jacob said. "This may come as a surprise to you, but you won't see a Christmas tree at Mammi Esh's."

Eli gasped. "No Christmas tree?"

"Remember," said Elizabeth. "Mom taught us that when we were studying how the different plain communities celebrate Christmas."

Jacob nodded. "Yep. The Amish think they're a bit distracting from the point of the day: celebrating our Savior's birth."

Eli pondered this and shrugged. "I suppose I get it," he said. "But it doesn't seem like Christmas without those decorations."

"That's just how things are in an Amish home," Mary said. "But I think you'll find that you won't notice the lack of decorations too much. You'll be having too much fun eating Mammi Esh's Christmas goodies!"

Mammi Esh's driveway was filled with buggies. But Dad was right: there was no Christmas tree to be seen. But, just as Mom predicted, that all faded into the background when Mammi Esh and their cousins greeted them.

Mammi Esh had several tables set up with chicken, mashed potatoes, filling, salads, and sweet treats. After dinner the group sang songs and played games. They passed baby Esther around and traded stories, overjoyed to be together once again. It was a wonderful family experience for Elizabeth and Eli.

CHAPTER 28
SHROVE TUESDAY

The Monday before Ash Wednesday Rebecca called Mary. "Mary, I'd like to take Elizabeth and Eli to the Mennonite church where they are making fastnachts."

"That would be a wonderful field trip," replied Mary. "Would you mind if I tagged along?"

"Not at all," said Rebecca. "If you'd like, we could go to Ash Wednesday service too."

"That's a great idea," said Mary. "I think it's important for the children to learn about the practices of all the plain denominations."

There was silence for a moment. Then Rebecca asked, "Mary, may I say something?"

"Sure," replied Mary.

"Your response surprises me since Jacob has told me that you didn't attend church when you were living in Boston."

Mary was a little taken back. "Rebecca, it's not that we lost our faith. We both had good jobs and felt that we were serving God. However, we never found a church family in Boston. In fact, Jacob has been a little unsure about committing to a church family here." Mary paused, worried that she had too much. She didn't think Jacob had talked about his struggles with anyone else. "Now," she said, clearing her throat. "What time are we going on this field trip tomorrow?"

"We should leave about seven since they sell out fairly quickly. After we buy our fasnachts, we'll come back here for breakfast."

Mary smiled and thought to herself, *She's always looking for a way feed us and our family.*

The next morning, everyone was up bright and early. When Jacob went to help Mr. Hersh with the milking, Mary and the children headed for Grandma and Grandpa's. They were surprised when Grandpa also came to get in the car.

"Grandpa, don't you have to milk?" asked Elizabeth.

"Already done," said Grandpa, clicking his seatbelt into place. "I wasn't about to miss this."

The church parking lot was packed. The Hopewells quickly got in line. Grandpa had no problem finding someone to talk to. He walked up to the church's pastor and struck up a conversation. Elizabeth and Eli gazed around them, mouths opened. They had never seen so many people gather in one place at one time, especially for donuts.

"Why are there so many people here to make donuts?" Elizabeth asked.

"Well, darling," Grandma said. "Today is Shrove Tuesday. Some people call this Fat Tuesday because it's the day when everyone tries to use up their fat and sugar before Lent."

"Which gives us a day to feast on donuts!" Grandpa cut in before returning to his conversation with the pastor.

"But why do they need to use them up?" asked Eli.

"See, Shrove Tuesday is the day before Lent, and Lent is the period leading up to Easter. Some people celebrate Lent by fasting from things like sugar or fatty foods. Or they may resolve not to use their smartphones until Easter."

"Why?" asked Eli.

"It's a reminder of Christ's sacrifice for us," said Grandma. "He gave up His life for us, and so we give up a little something to remember what He gave." Elizabeth was fascinated by what she was learning. "You never told us all of this," she said to her mother. "But it's kind of cool to see how all these things are connected to Jesus. I wonder what I can give up for Lent."

CHAPTER 29

ELI'S SLEEPOVER

On Wednesday evening the entire Hopewell family attended the Ash Wednesday church service together. They all had ash crosses drawn on their foreheads to symbolize the mourning to come for Christ's death.

Before going to the car, Samuel pulled his son aside. "Jacob, I don't know if I should bring this up now but I've noticed that Eli has become a lot quieter since you handed those writing assignments back."

"Mary and I have noticed that, too," Jacob said. "We've tried talking with him but he won't open up."

"Would you mind if I took a crack at it?"

"Not at all," replied Jacob. "What did you have in mind?"

"I would like for him to spend the night with Mom and me. I was going to get some chicken feed and other supplies in the morning and would like his help lifting things. I thought maybe he could help me milk in the morning and then we'd go out and do something, just the two of us. I'd even take him to lunch."

"That's a wonderful idea and, if it's okay, Elizabeth could come over and spend some time with Mom after you two leave."

"That's fine. It'll be boys' day out."

When they reached the car, Jacob said, "Eli, Grandpa needs some help in the morning. So I'm going to send you home with Grandma and Grandpa this evening."

"You mean I get to spend the night with them by myself?" A glimmer of glee at this new independence stirred in Eli's heart.

"That's right. Then, after breakfast, Elizabeth can go and help Grandma with things."

"But Mom and I were going to work on a special project tomorrow," said Elizabeth. "Can't Eli go tonight and maybe I go by myself tomorrow night? That's only fair."

Jacob looked at Samuel, who gave him an approving shrug. "Yep, that'll work."

As Jacob drove, he stopped first at his home. Mary, Eli, and Elizabeth got out of the car. "Eli, you go in and pack for your night away and I'll be right back for you."

"Okay, Dad!" said Eli as he ran toward the house.

As Jacob was driving his parents home, Grandma spoke up. "Okay, Samuel, what's up? I can tell when you two are working together."

"Rebecca, something's bothering Eli, and I think if I can get him away from Elizabeth for a little while he'll tell me. Look, for the most part, those two are always together. In many ways Elizabeth is much more outgoing, and I think it frustrates him.

I just want to give him the opportunity to be himself and try to find out what is bothering him. Something's been going on ever since they got their projects back."

"Yes, I've noticed a change in him, too," said Rebecca. "I'll help however I can."

Twenty minutes later, Jacob dropped Eli off. "Here's your overnight guest," he said. "Now, Eli, have fun and mind your manners."

"Yes, sir," said Eli.

"We'll be just fine," said Samuel.

With a smile on his face Jacob said, "Night Dad."

"Night Son, go and spend some time with your girls. We'll see you tomorrow."

Once the door closed, Samuel turned to Eli. "How about a snack? Grandma, what do we have around here to munch on?"

"Well, I just baked some molasses cookies. How about those with some vanilla ice cream and milk?"

"That sounds perfect," replied Samuel.

"Grandpa, may we play UNO while we eat?"

"Well sure, let me go get the UNO cards."

Grandma laid their snack out on the table. "I think I'm going to turn in. You two night-owls enjoy yourselves."

Samuel smiled at his wife. "We'll see you in the morning. Sleep tight."

After a few rounds of UNO, Samuel looked Eli in the eye. "So, how have things been going lately? Are you doing okay with your studies?" Tears formed in Eli's eyes. Then one slipped down his cheek.

"What's wrong son?"

Eli took a deep breath, mustering up all his courage. "Grandpa, everyone says that God is a loving god. If that's true, why did He let Josh's dad lose his hand? Josh's dad was a good guy—he didn't deserve that. Also, why does He make people smarter than others? Why do I always have to work harder at things than Elizabeth?" The lump in Eli's throat got bigger and bigger, and the tears kept falling.

Samuel wrapped his arms around his grandson. *God,* he prayed. *Help me comfort this child. Give me the words I need to say.* Eli blew his nose. "Let's go sit on the couch and talk," Samuel said. When they got settled, Samuel put his arm around his grandson. "Eli, you've asked some very grownup questions and I'm going to do my best to help you find some answers. Ok?"

"Okay."

"Eli, do you remember the story of Adam and Eve?" asked Grandpa.

"Yes," said Eli. "Adam and Eve ate the fruit that God told them not to."

"That's right," said Grandpa. "That was the original sin. That's when they knew the difference between good and evil. You see, Eli, God doesn't want us to be like robots. He gave us a choice so we can decide for ourselves if we want to love Him or not. Because

He allows us to make our own decisions, sometimes good things happen to bad people and bad things happen to good people. Does that make sense?"

"Yes, but when is He going to fix that?"

Grandpa smiled. "That'll get fixed when Christ returns on Judgment Day. I know life is hard sometimes, but the best thing we can do is put our trust in God and keep in contact with our church family." Just then, Grandpa knew what he needed to do. "I want to share a couple of scriptures with you." Samuel picked up the Bible from the coffee table and read Psalm 46:

> *God is our refuge and strength,*
>
> *always ready to help in times of trouble.*
>
> *So we will not fear when earthquakes come*
>
> *and mountains crumble into the sea.*
>
> *Let the oceans roar and foam.*
>
> *Let the mountains tremble as the waters surge!*
>
> *Interlude*
>
> *A river brings joy to the city of our God,*
>
> *the sacred home of the Most High*
>
> *God dwells in the city; it cannot be destroyed.*
>
> *From the very break of day, God will protect it.*
>
> *The nations are in chaos,*
>
> *and their kingdoms crumble!*

God's voice thunders,

and the earth melts!

The LORD of Heaven's Armies is here among us;

the God of Israel is our fortress.

Interlude

Come, see the glorious works of the LORD:

See how he brings destruction upon the world.

He causes wars to end throughout the earth.

He breaks the bow and snaps the spear;

he burns the shields with fire.

'Be still, and know that I am God!

I will be honored by every nation.

I will be honored throughout the world.'

The LORD of Heaven's Armies is here among us;

the God of Israel is our fortress.

"Did you connect with anything that was said in that scripture?" Samuel asked.

"Yes," said Eli. "It said God is my refuge."

"Do you know what the word 'refuge' means, Eli?" asked Samuel.

"I think so," Eli said. "It's a place of protection."

"That's exactly what it means," said Samuel. "One of my favorite pieces of scripture is Psalm 91:4, 'He will cover you with his feathers. He will shelter you with his wings. His faithful promises are your armor and protection'."

Eli considered the verse. "He really does care, Grandpa," he said softly, like the words were sinking in.

"Yes, He does," replied Samuel. "He didn't say it would be easy. He's just asking you to trust Him."

"I might need your help with this," said Eli.

"Of course," Samuel said. "We all need to lean on each other to walk this path. However, I would like for you to also tell your Mom and Dad what's been bothering you. You can lean on them, too, you know."

"If I do that, Grandpa, I'm afraid Dad will want me to talk to somebody I don't know."

"Eli, your dad is a reasonable man. He knows how helpful counseling can be. However, if you bring up that concern, I don't think he'll make you do that. How about you and I work through this by studying the Psalms together?"

"Okay," Eli said.

"Now, before we turn in for the night you asked me about Elizabeth being a better student than you. Let me ask you something, can Elizabeth chop or stack wood as well as you? Is she able to mow a lawn like you can? Who is better at raking leaves?"

"She does okay at all of those things, but I think I do a better job."

"That's right. Elizabeth has a gift for what I call brain work and you have a gift for physical work. Eli, let me read Romans 12:6-8 to you: 'In his grace, God has given us different gifts for doing certain things well. So if God has given you the ability to prophesy, speak out with as much faith as God has given you. If your gift is serving others, serve them well. If you are a teacher, teach well. If your gift is to encourage others, be encouraging. If it is giving, give generously. If God has given you leadership ability, take the responsibility seriously. And if you have a gift for showing kindness to others, do it gladly.' Eli, it's simple. Elizabeth needs to be who God made her to be and you need to be who He made you to be. Does what I'm saying make sense?"

"Yes, sir"

"Do you feel better?"

"A little."

"Good, now let's get to bed. We need to get up early tomorrow."

Early the next morning, Eli and Grandpa ate some cereal and drank some orange juice before heading out to milk. Once they were finished, they went and told Grandma they would see her later. "Do you need anything while we're in town?" asked Grandpa.

"No, no, I'll make out with what I have." Grandpa remembered how she raved about Ed's hot fudge sundaes. *Oh, I'm definitely bringing her one of those*, he thought.

After visiting the local farm supply store, Eli and Grandpa had lunch at the local diner. On the way home, they quickly picked up some coffee, tea, ice cream, butter, rolls, cereal, and cheese from the local market. They stopped at the General Store and picked up a hot fudge sundae. Once they were home, they carried the groceries in and put them away as Grandma sat and enjoyed her treat and thought to herself, *My husband is so considerate!*

Grandpa took Eli home and went to find Jacob before he did the evening milking. He shared what he and Eli talked about and asked if it would be okay for him to do a Bible study with Eli once a week.

"I think that's a wonderful idea" Jacob said. "He obviously trusts you. Sometimes children simply can't talk with their parents. I'm just thankful that he's willing to talk to you. See you later."

CHAPTER 30
ELIZABETH'S TURN

At 8:15, Elizabeth came downstairs with her overnight bag. "I'm ready to go, Dad," she said.

"Go?" replied Jacob. "Are you supposed to go somewhere tonight?" asked Jacob with a smile.

"You know that I'm supposed to go and spend the night with Grandma and Grandpa."

"Oh, that's right. We better get going then."

A few minutes later, Jacob dropped Elizabeth off at Grandma and Grandpa Hopewell's backdoor. "Here's your overnight guest," he said.

With a mischievous smile on his face, Samuel looked at Rebecca and asked, "Were we supposed to have a guest this evening?"

"Oh Samuel," replied Grandma. "You knew she was coming."

With that, Grandpa walked over, put his arm around her and said, "Yes, I knew you were coming."

"Well, I'm heading home." Jacob said. "Be good Elizabeth. I'll see you tomorrow."

Elizabeth replied as he closed the door behind him, "Yes, Dad. See you tomorrow."

"So, what should we do first?" asked Grandpa.

"Whatever you and Eli did first," Elizabeth said. "I don't want to miss out on anything he got to do."

Grandma smiled. "You might not want to do what Eli did."

"Why's that?" asked Elizabeth.

"Well, for one, you don't like molasses cookies," replied Grandma. "And that's what they snacked on last night."

"Oh," said Elizabeth. "Well, may we have some cheese, crackers, and fruit, then?"

"Of course," said Grandma

As Grandma fixed their snack, Grandpa said, "I'll go get the UNO cards."

"UNO?" said Elizabeth. "You know I don't like to play UNO."

"But you said you wanted to do what Eli did."

Elizabeth blushed and studied the floor. "May we play Authors instead?"

"Of course," said Grandpa. "I'll go get the cards."

After playing a few hands Grandpa said, "You know, Eli and I had a Bible study last night, just us."

Once again, Elizabeth looked down and said, "I would like to read the Bible, but can all three of us do it? I don't think it's fair not to include Grandma."

"Sure."

After cleaning up the kitchen, the three of them went into the living room. Grandpa had Elizabeth sit between him and his wife. Then he looked at Elizabeth and said, "Sweetheart, all evening you have said that you wanted to do what Eli did last night but I think you've realized that you are not like Eli because you don't like the things he likes. Am I correct?"

"Yes, sir," replied Elizabeth.

"Well, then, let's take a look at the scriptures." He then read 1 Corinthians 12 to her. When he finished, he asked her, "What is this saying to you, Elizabeth?"

With understanding in her eyes, Elizabeth replied, "We all have a special talent and we all have a purpose, and God made me the way He did for a reason."

"That's right," Grandpa said. "Don't try to be someone you're not. God made you who you are because He has a special job for you. Do you understand?"

"Yes," replied Elizabeth. "However, I do have a question. May we take Grandma with us tomorrow?"

"I think that'll be just fine," said Grandpa, smiling at Grandma. "By the way, what are we going to do while we're in town tomorrow?"

"We're going to take a copy of my book to Mr. Tom, silly," said Elizabeth. "And we're going to pick up a notebook for my Bible study with Grandma. I can't wait to see what I learn!"

CHAPTER 31
MAUNDY THURSDAY

At about 6:30 p.m. on Maundy Thursday, all the Hopewells left for the love feast at the Brethren church. "What's a love feast?" asked Elizabeth.

"Well, you see," said Jacob. "The night before Jesus died, He and His disciples celebrated a Jewish holiday called Passover together by sharing a meal. To show his love for them, Jesus knelt down and washed all His disciples' feet. It was a lowly task, usually done by servants, but it had to be done because at the time everyone walked everywhere in sandals, and their feet would get really dirty."

Elizabeth shuddered. "Yuck!"

Jacob continued with the story. "So Grandma and Grandpa's church, the Brethren church, gathers for a meal on the night before Good Friday. They call it a 'love feast' because it's supposed to remind us of Christ's love for us. After everyone's eaten, we read the story of the Last Supper and everyone washes each other's feet. Then we take communion."

"Wait," Eli said. "What's communion?"

"It's sort of a recreation of the Last Supper," said Grandma. "We take some bread and drink some grape juice as symbols of the bread and wine Jesus drank with His disciples."

"It's a reminder that we are part of Christ's family," Grandpa added. "The bread and juice represent His body and blood. When we eat the bread and drink the juice, we remember what He did for us on the cross."

When they arrived, Elizabeth and Eli quietly followed their parents and grandparents into the building and enjoyed the soup and sandwich supper the church served before the sermon. During the service, the pastor read the story of the Last Supper from John 13 before the women all gathered on the left side of the sanctuary and the men gathered on the right side. Elizabeth and Eli followed. On each table was a basin of water and a towel. The women washed each other's feet, and the men did the same for each other. Jacob washed Eli's feet, and Mary washed Elizabeth's feet.

As they observed church members participating in communion, they both thought about what Christ had done for the world. Their minds whirred with all they took in. Once they were back in the car, Eli gave his sister the look that said, "We need to talk." Elizabeth nodded.

When they returned home, the family prepared for bed. Eli and Elizabeth said goodnight to their parents and then went to their rooms. But once they were changed, they slipped into Elizabeth's closet for a secret meeting. Candy, who usually slept on the bottom of Elizabeth's bed, joined them.

When they were settled on the floor, Eli asked, "Elizabeth, what do you think about what we learned in the service today?"

It took Elizabeth a minute to answer his question, "Well, I think and believe that we need to take Christ's death seriously. It is hard to believe that He chose to die on the cross for us. He loves us so much. It makes me want to understand what is in the Bible even more."

Eli nodded silently. "I don't think I want to do normal school work tomorrow. I want to learn more about what happened to Jesus and His death on the cross."

Elizabeth looked at her brother and saw tears coming from his eyes. "Let's go talk to Mom and Dad." Eli nodded.

Quietly, Eli and Elizabeth walked to their parent's room. Elizabeth knocked on the door. "Mom, Dad, may we talk to you?"

"Of course," said Jacob. "Come on in."

As they walked in the door, Mary noticed a tear track on Eli's cheek. "Eli, what's wrong?" asked Mary as she started walking towards him.

Eli fell into her arms and sobbed. Mary held him as he wept. Just then, Jacob noticed a tear traveling down Elizabeth's cheek.

"Guys, what's wrong?" asked Jacob.

Eli, still crying, said, "Elizabeth, you tell them. I can't."

Again, Jacob looked at his daughter, his eyebrows raised in concern. "Elizabeth, what's wrong?"

Elizabeth took a deep breath. "Eli and I are amazed by Jesus and what He did." She went on to tell him about their conversation in her closet. "We want to learn about what actually took place on Good Friday and why."

"Of course," said Mary as she stroked Eli's hair. "We would love to teach you more about what is in the Bible and who Jesus is."

Jacob leaned closer to his family. "God is clearly moving in all of our hearts," he said. "I love that we can talk and grow together as a family. Since we're all sharing, your mother and I have some news we need to talk with you kids about." He took a deep breath. "We're going to purchase Mr. Hersh's farm."

"What!" said Elizabeth.

Jacob held up his hand. "Let me explain. None of his other family members are interested in it, so he asked me if I would like to buy it, and after talking it over with Mom, I said yes. I have a meeting next week with Mr. Hersh's son, Amos, at his office to finalize the details and sign all the paperwork."

"Are we going to move from this house?" asked Eli.

"Not right away," replied Jacob. "But we will eventually be moving and Mom is going to use this house for a business."

"A business?" said Elizabeth. "What kind of business?"

"Well," said Mary. "I thought I would do some tutoring. I've had some young ladies, not from our congregation, ask me if I would teach them how to cook. They also asked if I would help them teach their youngsters to read. I'm even considering putting a garden in."

"Will you still help us with our schoolwork?" asked Eli.

"Of course," she said putting her arms around her children. "You and your sister will always be my most important students.

Besides, I was hoping you would be willing to help me with this as part of your schooling."

"I'd love to!" cried Elizabeth.

"Well, I think it's time for this family to get some sleep," said Jacob.

"I agree," said Mary. Eli and Elizabeth slipped off to their rooms, ready to turn in for the night. Knowing their children were at peace after their discussion, Jacob and Mary returned to their room prepared for a good night's sleep.

CHAPTER 32
GOOD FRIDAY

Early the next morning Mary called Rebecca and said, "I need your support. We had a wonderful conversation with the children last night." Mary proceeded to go into the details of last night.

After hearing about what happened Grandma said, "Why don't you bring the kids over for breakfast. We'll make hot cross buns and scrambled eggs. Then we can read and talk about Matthew 26 - 27 with them. Samuel has a wonderful exercise he can show the kids, where he makes a cross out of a piece of paper with just one tear."

"Rebecca, that would be wonderful. Thank you!"

"No problem, you know that I love to talk about Jesus."

Mary smiled to herself and said, "We'll see you around eight."

As Mary, Eli and Elizabeth walked up the lane to Grandma and Grandpa Hopewell's house, Grandpa drove out toward them.

"Where you headed, Grandpa?" asked Eli.

"I'm running to the store for a few things. I won't be long."

"May I go along?" asked Eli.

"Not this time, Grandma is expecting you. She's working on some breakfast goodies for you. I'll be right back. See you soon."

They waved as Grandpa pulled away. When they arrived, they knocked and walked in the door. They were greeted by the smell of bacon and sausage on the stove. "Come on in," said Grandma. "Once you're done eating, I'll need your help."

"Okay," said Eli. "What do you need help with?"

"Setting up for an indoor picnic. We're having lunch guests later. Now, I have hot cross buns baking in the oven and bacon and sausage cooking on the stove. When Grandpa gets back, we'll have breakfast. Then we'll talk about Good Friday. Right now, though, I need your help. Mary, would you keep an eye on the bacon and sausage while Eli and Elizabeth help me in the dining room?"

"Sure," replied Mary. "I'd be happy to."

After walking into the dining room, Grandma said, "The first thing we need to do is make the table bigger. So, Eli, you take one end and Elizabeth will take the other, and you both will pull."

Both children stared at her. Who ever heard of pulling on a table?

"I'm serious," said Grandma. "Pull. I need to put the leaves in to make the table bigger." Eli and Elizabeth pulled on either end and, to their amazement, the table got longer.

"Now, bring those leaves over there and we'll fill in the space with them," said Grandma. Both children brought the straight pieces of wood over. Grandma showed them how to line them up so they would fit properly into the expanded space. "Now," she said, dusting off her hands. "All we need is my checkered red and white tablecloth."

As the three worked on getting it straight, Mary called from the kitchen. "The bacon and sausage are finished. Would you like for me to start cracking some eggs?"

"Sure," Grandma said. "Is Samuel back yet?"

"Yes, he just pulled in."

"What about the buns?"

"A few more minutes and they should be ready."

"Fine, fine," said Grandma. "I'll be right out to make the icing for the buns." Then she turned to Eli and Elizabeth. "You two go and help Grandpa carry groceries in. Put the meat and cheese in the refrigerator and leave the rest in the bags. We'll finish putting everything away after we eat."

After a breakfast of scrambled eggs, bacon, sausage, fruit salad, and freshly iced hot cross buns, everyone helped to put the groceries away and then went into the living room to read about Christ's crucifixion.

As Grandma read about the thieves on either side of the cross, Elizabeth started crying.

"What's wrong?" asked Mary.

"I just never realized how much God loves us," Elizabeth said as she snuggled against her mom. "Even for the thief who mocked Him, Jesus was so compassionate."

"Eli, are you okay. You've been awfully quiet," said Grandpa. "There's something bothering you. What is it?"

Eli blushed, his eyes downcast. "You're going to think it's silly," said Eli.

"No we won't." said Mary.

"Well," said Eli. "After I read Psalm 91 with Grandpa, I was really amazed at how God was talked about like a bird that protects its children under the shelter of its wings. It made me feel so safe knowing that God was covering me and protecting me. I saw a hen puppet at Mr. Tom's store and he had a little chick puppet beside it. I'd really like to have those puppets to remind me of how God cares for me. But I don't know if he still has them."

"Why don't you call and check?" said Grandma.

"Really?" asked Eli.

"Sure," replied Grandma. "In fact, to remind you of God's love for us, I'm willing to pay for it."

"Rebecca..." said Mary.

"No, no, I insist," said Grandma Hopewell. "Now Eli, you and Grandpa go to the kitchen and call Mr. Tom."

Following Grandma's orders, Samuel and Eli went into the kitchen. Suddenly, she heard Eli say, "Thank you! Thank you, Mr. Tom. Would you stay and have lunch with us?"

As they walked back into the living room, Samuel smiled while Mary dropped her jaw. She couldn't believe that her son had invited someone to lunch without asking first. "Eli...."

"Now, don't you say a word," Samuel said. "The boy did a very respectful thing."

"What happened?" asked Elizabeth.

"Well, Mr. Tom said that he still had the hen and chick puppets and because he's had them for a while, he's willing to sell them for half-price. He also wants to talk to Mom and Dad about Elizabeth working at his market stand on the weekends."

"Well," said Grandma. "It appears we're going to have an interesting business picnic."

"It sure does," replied Grandpa. "Eli and I will go start the grill. Jacob and the Hershes will be here shortly."

As Grandpa and Eli grilled hot dogs and hamburgers, Mary, Elizabeth, and Grandma filled bowls with macaroni salad, potato salad, pepper slaw, broccoli salad, and fruit salad. As she worked, Mary wondered what was going on. Everything was just about ready when Jacob, Mr. and Mrs. Hersh, and their son, Reuben Jr. came in the door. Before long there was a knock at the door and Eli, quickly answered it.

"I heard that I can get something good to eat here," said Mr. Tom as he walked in.

"Yes, sir," replied Eli.

He handed Eli the bag in his hand and said, "I think this is yours."

"Thank you, Mr. Tom!" said Eli. Grandma drew her wallet out of her purse.

Mr. Tom held up his hand and said, "Rebecca, you and I will straighten up later. For right now let's enjoy this occasion."

Once everyone was seated Grandpa said, "Let's pray." With everyone holding hands, Grandpa thanked God for the food He had provided and for the gift of His son.

As they passed around the hamburgers, Mr. Tom said, "Jacob and Mary, Elizabeth mentioned she was interested in helping me on Saturday mornings at the market."

Elizabeth looked at her mom and dad.

Jacob looked at his wife and said, "It's okay with me if it's okay with you."

Mary said, "Well, she will be going on a two-week field trip this summer. Other than that, I don't see any conflict. What time do I need to have her there?"

"You don't," replied Mr. Tom. "My wife will pick her up and bring her home. We'll even buy her lunch. We simply appreciate her willingness to help us out. We tried running the stand with just one person and while it's doable, it's a challenge."

"Well, it sounds like Elizabeth will be a great help!" Mary said. "We appreciate you giving her this opportunity."

After everyone finished the delicious meal, Grandpa showed the kids how to make a cross with a piece of paper and only one tear and challenged them to try it. As Eli and Elizabeth tore out their crosses, they thought of the sacrifice Jesus made on the cross for them.

CHAPTER 33
EASTER SUNDAY

After a quiet and reflective Saturday, Jacob and Grandpa were up early on Easter Sunday to milk their cows. Then everyone prepared to go to the sunrise service. Before the service, Jacob and his family went to Grandma and Grandpa Hopewell's for breakfast.

When Jacob and his family entered the house, the smell of coffee brewing welcomed them. While everyone waited for the breakfast casserole to bake, the grownups enjoyed hot coffee while Elizabeth and Eli lingered over a mug of hot chocolate. Though it was spring, there was still a chill in the air. When the casserole came out of the oven, the family ate the hot dish with some fresh fruit.

After breakfast, both Hopewell families headed to Sunday School and church. Following church, they headed to the Hersh farm for dinner. Mr. and Mrs. Hersh had invited Jacob and his family and Grandma and Grandpa to Easter dinner because Jacob was purchasing their farm. However, as you might guess, Mary and Grandma Hopewell didn't go empty-handed. Mary took the candy that Elizabeth and Eli had helped her make while Grandma provided whoopie pies, asparagus casserole, and fruit salad.

After an afternoon filled with fellowship, good food, and fun, Mr. Hersh's children prepared to go home as Jacob and Grandpa went home to get ready for the evening milking.

As Jacob walked home, Eli called after him, "Dad, may I go along this evening to help?"

Jacob raised his eyebrows in surprise. Eli had never asked that before.

"Sure," he said. "Hurry up and get changed." In no time, Eli caught up with his dad and headed to the barn.

"May I help Grandpa tonight, too, Mom?" Elizabeth asked, not to be outdone.

"Sure, why not? Just be careful." Elizabeth took off running.

"Those kids really love these farms," said Mrs. Hersh.

"They sure do, Rose." replied Mary. "They sure do."

CHAPTER 34
ASCENSION DAY

Since Jacob's family spent Easter with his family, he and Mary agreed that she should take Elizabeth and Eli to Mammi Esh's for Ascension Day. Ascension Day takes place forty days after Easter. It is observed in recognition of the day when Christ ascended into Heaven. Since Mary never joined the Amish church, neither she or her family followed the custom of fasting, reading, and reflecting. Instead, they got up early and ate breakfast with Jacob, Grandpa, and Grandma Hopewell before heading to Lancaster County.

Elizabeth and Eli were amazed at the number of people who came to visit Mammi Esh. Mary had told them that it was a day for visiting but they weren't prepared for this type of experience. They met scores of relatives they didn't know existed. They spent the day eating and playing volleyball and softball.

As they traveled home the following day Elizabeth asked, "May we go again next year, Mom?"

Mary smiled as she replied, "If you insist."

* * * * * * * * * * * * * * * *

As the weather turned warmer, Jacob and Grandpa Hopewell plowed the fields and tilled up the gardens. Grandma Hopewell, who always had a large home garden, had a little help this year from Elizabeth and Eli. Mary started a vegetable garden and an herb garden at their newly purchased farm. She also marked off two smaller sections, away from the main garden, where Eli and Elizabeth would make butterfly and moon gardens with her guidance. As the Hershes looked at how the Hopewells transformed it, they were thankful they had sold their farm to someone who would appreciate and take care of it.

CHAPTER 35
FIRST ANNIVERSARY/ MOVING DAY

Exactly one year to the day they had moved to Pennsylvania, Jacob and his family were moving again—this time to the Hersh's house. While Mr. Hersh loved being on the farm, he and Rose realized he could no longer live safely in the farmhouse. So, they and Candy had moved into an in-law suite at one of their son's home. While they would no longer be living at the farm, they would be nearby and would visit often.

Jacob was up early to milk and came home to eat one last meal in the house that he and his family had called home for the past year. Before eating their breakfast, Jacob prayed, "Father, thank you for the many blessings you have given my family this past year. You have blessed us with health, wealth, and special relationships. We're so thankful that You led Mary and me back to our roots. Thank You for allowing us to share these special times with our children. May they continue to enjoy the life we have introduced them to. Finally, thank You for the new chapter that we will be starting today, another new beginning."

Around ten o'clock Jacob's driveway was filled with cars and people. Grandma and Grandpa Hopewell, Mr. Nick, Miss Noelle, Naomi, Noah as well as Mr. Hersh's sons were there to help Jacob and his family move to their new home. However, there was one other special person there that Jacob never expected to see on that special day. Mr. Bob, from Boston, also came to assist.

After receiving an affectionate greeting from Eli and Elizabeth, Mr. Bob looked at Jacob. "Did you really think I'd let you move without coming to help?"

Tears welled up in Jacob's eyes. "Thank you, my friend."

While they moved furniture and boxes from one house to the other, a group of church members busily set up tables for a community lunch. There was a choice of ham and cheese or chicken salad sandwiches. Eli decided to have one of each. The members also brought homemade potato chips, watermelon, iced tea, lemonade, and, of course, cookies and homemade ice cream.

Jacob was so overwhelmed by their kindness that he made a special announcement just before the pastor gave the blessing. With tears in his eyes, he said, "Folks, I can't tell you all how thankful I am for how you have blessed us this past year. You have welcomed me and my family with open arms. I am grateful for you and your friendship while we have worshiped with you during this past year. You know that I have been thinking about becoming an official member of the congregation. Well, after the love you have shown me and my family over this past year, I can't think of attending any place else. Pastor David, let me know when the next membership class is and I will be there." He looked over at Mary and saw tears streaming down her face nodding her head up and down. "Actually Pastor, make that two."

The members of the church cheered and clapped. Nick and Mr. Bob gave their friend a thumbs-up. Jacob looked over and saw his parents beaming because of the relief they felt. They were glad to have their son back home, back in the fold, with his faith intact.

After Jacob finished, Pastor David replied, "Jacob, we'd be more than happy to have you as part of our church family. The congregation also has a housewarming gift we would like to give you. One of our members, Patricia Lewis, is an author of meaningful acrostics as well as a composer. I believe you have already been blessed by some of her work on your rocking chairs."

Jacob looked over at his father and smiled.

"Well," said Pastor David, "we would like to present you a collection of Patricia's works. May you enjoy what she has blessed our congregation with through her gift of music and poetry." Jacob and his family accepted the gift with warm gratitude.

"May I see the book?" Elizabeth said.

Jacob handed Elizabeth the book. She ran her fingers over the leather cover and started flipping through the pages. "I am very excited to read through these," Elizabeth said. "And look, Mom," she said as she held a page up in front of Mary. "The lyrics are so beautiful. I would love to learn how to play the piano that Mr. Hersh left in the house for us."

"I think that's a great idea," said Mary.

"I know someone who offers piano lessons," said Grandma. "I can give you their phone number, if you like, Mary."

"Wonderful," said Mary. "Elizabeth, dear, give that book back to your father so he can put it up while we finish eating."

Elizabeth handed the book back to Jacob and took a bite of her chicken salad sandwich, bouncing in her seat with excitement.

"Mom is it okay if I go take some pictures of the farm?" asked Eli. "I think it would be neat to hang some up in my room."

"Have you unpacked your camera yet?"

"Yes, it's on the desk in my room!" Eli said.

"Well then, after you clean up your plate, you may go take a few pictures. But we still have a lot of unpacking to do, so not too long. Okay?"

"Okay!" Eli whipped up from his chair and ran into the house to grab his camera.

After the meal and a good hour of conversation, the group offered to help Mary unpack. Mary politely declined, and said they all have done enough and invited them over on Saturday for dinner to show her appreciation.

As everyone trickled out, Mr. Bob was the last one with the Hopewells. "Are you sure you don't need anything else?" he asked.

"I think we've got it from here," Jacob said. "We still can't believe you came all this way! We appreciate you so much, and know you have a long way back to Boston."

"It was my pleasure," said Mr. Bob grabbing Jacob's hand.

"Kids come say bye to Mr. Bob."

Eli, camera still around his neck, and Elizabeth both hugged Mr. Bob, and said their goodbyes. As they watched him walk away, they both looked at each other.

"Saying goodbye to Mr. Bob feels different now than when we first moved here," Eli said.

"It does," said Elizabeth. "I miss Mr. Bob and Boston, but I am so happy we have our life here in Pennsylvania now. I love living close to Grandma and Grandpa, and we have some great adventures awaiting us on this farm!"

"Speaking of great adventures," Jacob said behind them. "Eli, want to help me do the milking?"

"Yes!" Eli said as he followed his dad toward the barn.

It was a beautiful afternoon. Jacob and Eli worked on the farm, and Mary could hear them laughing through the open windows in the house. She and Elizabeth worked organizing and decorating their new home. It was the ending of one season and the beginning of another, and the Hopewells were ready for the next journey ahead.

MEET PATRICIA A. LEWIS:
THE PRAISING LYRICIST

I met Patricia A. Lewis when our hairdresser brought us together in 2006. At the time of our meeting, I was running my own tutoring business in Taneytown, Maryland, and Pat had recently resigned from a small Christian school where she had served in teacher and administrative positions since its inception. After my first meeting with Pat, I wasn't sure what to think. I was leery about starting a new friendship because I had been burned so many times. I had experienced, more often than I care to remember, someone wanting to befriend me simply to get something they wanted or needed. Yet, God created a path of friendship for us. I sensed that Pat was different, that she truly

389

did want to be friends. She also had a real relationship with Jesus and didn't simply play church on Sunday. God reassured me that I could trust Pat and as a result, we quickly became friends.

But Pat became more than a friend. I adopted her as my Spiritual Mom. Even though I had grown up in the church and graduated from a Christian college. I had never met a woman, or anyone for that matter, so in love with God and so filled with the Holy Spirit.

When I opened my present business, Wendi's Works & Writings, Pat became my personal assistant after agreeing to work for food. We ran my market stand on Saturday mornings. After my first book was published, she started helping me with book signings. We even worked Kids' Night at a local restaurant once a month. I would make balloon creations and she would do face and hand painting. We, with God's help, became a well-oiled working team.

As I wrote my fourth book, I kept sensing that our relationship was to grow into something even more special. I felt we were to link our ministries to win more souls for the Kingdom. God nudged me to release Pat as my assistant and team with her as a ministry partner. So I asked Pat if I could include her songs and acrostics in this book.

Pat started using acrostics when she was teaching first grade. Eventually they became something that she used to encourage adults as well as children. Sometimes she would use them to emphasize a particular topic or season. For example, GRACE (God Reaching Across Circumstances and Events) was given to her by the Holy Spirit when her church body had an evening of prayer and the word "grace" came up. When she was ministering at senior citizen homes, she would ask the Lord for a word. He would give it to her and the program would evolve around that word with hymns and scripture.

When Pat started writing songs many years ago, the Holy Spirit would speak to her as she played her autoharp. Now she usually receives the melody in her heart, and then she goes to the piano to work it out. After she has the melody basics, the words follow. For example, the song "For the Joy" came as a result of being asked to sing a special number for a Christmas program. The Advent theme for the day was joy. She received the phrase for the joy set before Him in the form of a chorus and the melody and the words followed. She has told me that she tries every day to listen for directions from the Holy Spirit because she believes what is stated in John, "my sheep hear my voice." It is because of her personal relationship with God that she gives Him the glory in all that she does.

I am very grateful that God put Pat in my life and I look forward to seeing what He has planned for us in the future.

ACROSTICS

Written by Patricia A. Lewis

BLESSING

B ig *or*
L ittle
E xpressions *for those*
S uffering
S ilently
I n
N eed of
G race

BRAVE

B oldly
R esist
A dvances *of a*
V icious
E nemy

CHANGE

C ircumstances
H appening
A llowing
N ew
G od
E ncounters

CHRISTMAS
C reator
H ealer
R edeemer *of*
I solated
S inners
T otally
M anifested *in the*
A nointed
S avior

DNA
D ivine
N ature
A ttributes

FAITH
F earless
A ttitude
I n
T rusting
H im

FORGIVE
F reeing
O thers *of*
R esentments
G rudges *with*
I ndications *of*
V alidation *and*
E steem

FRIEND

F orgiver

R esponder

I nspirer

E difier

N otifier

D efender

GRACE

G od

R eaching

A cross

C ircumstances *and*

E vents

HEAL

H e

E liminates

A ll

L ies

HOPE

H elping

O thers

P ursue

E ternity

HUGS

H elp

U ndergird

G od's

S aints

JUSTIFY

J esus'
U nconditional
S acrifice
T otally
I nsuring
F reedom *for*
Y ou

KINGDOM

K now
I ndeed
N ow
G od *has come*
D own *into*
O ur
M idst

LEADER

L iving
E xample
A ccepting
D irection *by*
E liciting
R esponsibility

LOVE

L istening
O beying
V aluing
E ach *other*

MARRIAGE

M agnificent

A rrangement *of a*

R ighteous

R elationship

I n

A greement *with*

G od's

E dict

MERCY

M agnificent

E ternal

R iches *of*

C hrist *in*

Y ou

MY GIFTS

from   **M** e *to*

      Y ou

      G od's

      I nfused

      F avor

      T alents

And   **S** ongs

PEACE

P owerful

E ntrance *of*

A llowing

C hrist *into your*

E xperience

PEACE

P resence *of God that*

E nters

A midst *the*

C lamor *of*

E vents

POWER

P entecostal

O utpouring

W orking

E ternal

R esults

PRAY

P urposefully

R espond *to the*

A uthority *of*

Y ahweh

PRAYER

P etition

R epent

A sk

Y ield

E xpect

R ejoice

PRECIOUS

P ure

R are

E xceptional

C ostly

I ndividual

O utstanding

U nique

S pecial

PROMISE

P ersonal

R evelation

O vercoming

M essage *when*

I ntroducing *the*

S avior *into the*

E vent

RISEN

R esurrected

I nto *our*

S avior's

E ternal

N ature

SAFE

S heltered *in the*

A rms *of the*

F ather's

E ternal *love*

SALVATION

S avior *is*
A live
L oving
V aluable *and*
A ctive *Who gives a*
T imeless *offer by*
I nvitation
O nly
N ow *is the day*

SHELTER

S ecurely
H eld *in the*
E ternal
L ove *of our*
T ender *and*
E verlasting
R edeemer

SHEPHERD

S avior
H elps
E liminate
P roblems *and*
H eads *His*
E rrant *ones in*
R ight
D irection

STRONG

S teadily
T rusting *and*
R elying *on the*
O mnipotence *of our*
N ever-changing
G od

SUSTAIN

S upernatural
U ndergirding *of*
S trength *in*
T imes *of*
A ffliction
I ndecision *and*
N eed

TRUST

T otally
R elying
U pon *the*
S aviour
T oday
(For the tomorrows will take care of themselves)

WAIT

W atchful
A nticipation *for the*
I ntent *of God's*
T iming

WALK

W omen
A ligned *and*
L iving *for the*
K ing(dom)

WORSHIP

W ondrous
O utpouring *of*
R everence *by*
S howing
H umility
I n *God's*
P resence

SONGS

Written by Patricia A. Lewis

Come, Let Us Go Up to Jerusalem

Verse 1

Come, let us go up to Jerusalem. Let us go to the city of our God.

Chorus

For He is our Rock, He is our Strength, He is the Author of Salvation.

He is the King, The Lord of All the Earth, He is God of All Creation!

Verse 2

Enter His gates with thanksgiving, and into His courts with praise.

Chorus

For He is our Rock, He is our Strength, He is the Author of Salvation.

He is the King, The Lord of All the Earth, He is God of All Creation!

Verse 3

We offer up to You our hearts of worship,

We give to You our lives in living praise.

Chorus for Verse 3

For You are our Rock. You are our Strength. You are the Author of Salvation.

For You are the Lord, the King of All the Earth, He is God of All Creation.

Reprise

Come, Let us go up to Jerusalem.

Comfort

I see you in your deepest darkness, when you think you're all
alone.

My Child, know I am with you. You are never on your own.

There are seasons in your lifetime, of sorrow and of pain.

When you know you're in a valley that is filled with storms and rain.

I am waiting in the shadows for you to come to Me.

If only you will ask Me, I will come to set you free.

You feel trapped and so abandoned, I am waiting as your friend.

Know my Child as you yield to Me, it will all come to an end.

Give Me all your disappointments, your brokenness, your tears.

I'll take the ashes of your mourning and redeem you from your
fears.

Give Me all your tears and heartache, all your pain and all your loss.

Lay them at My feet, remembering I paid for them on My cross.

Know I love you oh so deeply, when things don't go as they
should,

But when you surrender completely, I use them all for My good.

So, Child, come to Me in submission, let Me guide you every day.

Know that I will never leave you, I'll stay close in every way.

My Holy Spirit will refresh you as we meet as friend to friend.

I will heal, comfort, console you as on Me you now depend.

Share your story of forgiveness, share the song of soul release,

Share the goodness of My mercy and the greatness of My peace.

Let us now walk together, hand in hand as dearest friends.

I will always love and protect you, till your journey of life ends.

Draw Me Deeper, LORD

Chorus

Draw me deeper, LORD. Draw me deeper, LORD.

Draw me deeper, LORD, into Your Presence, I pray.

Let me seek Your face in the secret place.

Draw me deeper, LORD, into Your Presence to stay.

Verse 1

You are the Savior of my soul.

It's by Your blood that I am made whole.

The sacrifice You paid for my sin

Now make me holy, pure, and clean within.

Chorus

Draw me deeper, LORD. Draw me deeper, LORD.

Draw me deeper, LORD, into Your Presence, I pray.

Let me seek Your face in the secret place.

Draw me deeper, LORD, into Your Presence to stay.

Verse 2

You are the lover of my soul.

It's in Your Presence I am made whole.

Help me to yield to You all that I am

For my life is in Your loving hand.

Chorus

Draw me deeper, LORD. Draw me deeper, LORD.

Draw me deeper, LORD, into Your Presence, I pray.

Let me seek Your face in the secret place.

Draw me deeper, LORD, into Your Presence to stay.

Verse 3

You are supplying all my needs.

It's by Your grace that I can receive

The Word You've planted in my heart

That Your love I may now impart.

Final Chorus

Draw me deeper, LORD. Draw me deeper, LORD.

Draw me deeper, LORD, into Your Presence, I pray.

Let me seek Your face in the secret place.

Draw me deeper, LORD, into Your Presence today.

My Passionate Twenty-third Psalm

The Lord My God watches over me,

He's my Pastor and Fierce Protector.

He offers me a resting place in His luxurious love.

His tracks lead to an oasis of peace, and the brook of quiet bliss

Where He restores and revives my life

And opens before me His pathways.

The footsteps of His righteousness reveal to me His pleasure.

So as I follow what He's prepared, I can bring honor to His Name.

Lord, when Your pathways take me through the valley of deepest darkness,

Fear will never conquer me for You already have!

In those times You remain close to me and lead me all the way.

The authority you use over me become my strength and peace.

The comfort of Your endless love takes away my fear.

Loneliness is now removed for You assure me You are near.

You become my delicious feast when enemies dare to fight me.

You anoint me with the Holy Ghost and my heart with love o'erflows.

So why should the future cause me fear, for You pursue me only?

You shower me with Your goodness and Your unfailing love.

Then afterwards, when my life is through, I'll return to Your glorious Presence.

Where I will be eternally forever with You. Forever with You.

The Lord is My Strength and My Song

The Lord is my strength and my song

To Him my praises belong.

He is my Lord and King so to Him I humbly sing.

The Lord is my strength and my song;

The Lord is my strength and my song.

The Lord is my joy and my peace.

He makes my sorrows cease.

As I cast on Him my care,

For me He is always there.

The Lord is my joy and my peace.

He gives me sweet release.

The Lord is my Comfort and Guide.

In Him all my needs are supplied.

He walks with me each day

As we travel down life's way.

The Lord is my Comfort and Guide.

In Him I daily abide.

The Lord is my Savior and Friend.

His love for me does not end.

He redeemed me from my sin,

Now He reigns and dwells within.

The Lord is my Savior and Friend.

His love for me does not end.

Do you know the Savior today?

He is the Truth, Life, the Way.

Jesus died upon the cross

So that you would not be lost.

Do you know the Savior today?

He is the Truth, Life, The Way.

The Lord is my strength and my song.

To Him my praises belong.

He is my Lord and King

So for Him I humbly sing.

The Lord is my strength and my song.

The Lord is my strength and my song.

We Come Into Your Presence Lord

We come into Your Presence, Lord

With grateful hearts of praise.

Give us ears to hear Your voice, oh God,

To grow in love and grace

As we gather in this place.

Empower us with Your Spirit, Lord,

Because our lives You've changed.

Help us be examples of Your love

As salvation we proclaim.

We go in Jesus Name.

His Word is True (To God Be the Glory)

I have times when no one cares, but Lord, You are there,

To God be the glory.

Then You take my broken parts and heal them in Your heart,

To God be the glory.

As You trade my shattered schemes and replace them with Your dreams,

To God be the glory.

For when I turn to You, I find Your Word is true,

To God be the glory.

When my circumstances fail and my soul is in travail,

To God be the glory.

You hear my desperate cry and say, "Give it one more try,"

To God be the glory.

Then You place Your hand in mine and whisper "You are mine,"

To God be the glory.

For when I turn You, I find Your Word is true,

To God be the glory.

Because You suffered on the cross, You understand my loss,

To God be the glory.

As You agonized for me, You died to set me free,

To God be the glory.

You give me all I need to help me succeed,

To God be the glory.

For when I turn to You, I find Your Word is true,

To God be the glory.

So I give to you my life with its brokenness and strife,

To God be the glory.

In You I find release as You fill me with Your peace,

To God be the glory.

I will come to You in prayer, believing You are there,

To God be the glory.

For when I turn to You, You prove Your Word is true,

To God be the glory.

As I worship at Your feet in You I am complete,

To God be the glory.

I pursue Your perfect will for your plans to be fulfilled,

To God be the glory.

Let me be a witness true as I live each day for You,

To God be the glory.

Help me in Your spirit flow everywhere I go,

To God be the glory.

For You prove Your Word is true, so I will follow You,

To God be the glory.

A Song of Repentance

Holy Father, we come to worship You;

We come to praise Your Name.

Holy Spirit, refine and remold us

So we will not be the same.

Remove stony hearts of irreverence,

Selfishness, greed and pride.

Let us look to the Savior for forgiveness

So in fullness we can abide.

Help us see the truth of Your holiness

As we pursue Your heart

To bring others into Your Kingdom, God,

Enable us to do our part.

Convict us of our petty grievances,

Our prejudices and our lies.

Gracious Lord, lovingly transform us

So in Your grace we may hide.

Let us see with Your heart and eyes of love

Those who have gone astray.

Help them find the salvation of Jesus Christ

Who is the Truth, Life, the Way.

We come, Holy God, to worship You;

To praise Your holy name.

Please refine and remold us in Your image

And we will forever be changed.

We will be changed.

For the Joy

Long ago in past eternity, Father God spoke with the Son.

"We need to plan redemption before the world's begun."

"For the joy set before Me," Jesus said, "I'll go and pay the price.

I'll willingly lay down My life, I will be the sacrifice."

So He set aside divinity and took on human form,

Came to men as a baby boy and in this sinful world was born.

For the joy set before Him, He came to live on earth.

He showed all how to live and die and to have a second birth.

He became a pure example to show us how to live.

He reflected Father's heart of love and taught us to forgive.

For the joy set before Him, Jesus came to live on earth.

He showed us how to live and die and to have a second birth.

He became the perfect sacrifice to cleanse the world of sin.

He was killed for our transgressions, but in three days rose again.

For the joy set before Him, Jesus died on Calvary.

He willingly gave up His life to set all of us free.

And so, my friend, I ask You this, "What will you do today?"

Will you reject Him as your Savior or turn to Him and say,

"For the joy set before me I accept your gift for me.

Show me how to live and die for You. For You have set me free-

For all eternity."

My Security

The LORD is my refuge and my strength; He is the theme of my song.

I trust in Him as my Savior so to Him I now belong.

He is my shelter and my wings; 'neath His feathers I will hide.

I choose each day to belong to Him, so now in Him I abide.

He sets me safely on His Rock and protects me from alarm.

He guards me with His very love and keeps me safe from harm.

He is my truth when the enemy comes to cast on me his fear.

He gently whispers to my heart, "My Child, rest, I am here."

He puts His angels all around to keep me in all my ways.

I will not fall in the enemy's traps that cause me to stray.

I am the victor over things that come by day or night;

Trusting in His Holy Word defeats what causes fright.

And so, I praise Him with my voice, my life, my very be-ing.

I call, He answers, protects, and saves because He truly knows me.

He's with me in my troubles and He rescues me from strife.

He promises to favor me and be with me all my life.

MORE FROM PATRICIA

Patricia A. Lewis's album "My Gifts" is available for download at egen.co

Physical copies of her album are available for purchase at wendiwrites.com

CONNECT

Patricia Lewis - The Praising Lyricist

 facebook.com/encouragingduo

RECIPES

These first two recipes came out of a cookbook from Fetterhoff Chapel United Methodist Church Children's Department. The church is midway between Waynesboro and Greencastle, PA. Grandma Hopewell had a friend who attended the church at the time and purchased her a copy of the book as a Christmas gift. The author and publisher wish to thank Fetterhoff Chapel United Methodist Church for allowing us to reprint these recipes.

Zucchini Bread

3 eggs

2 c. sugar

1 cup oil

1 tsp. vanilla

1 tsp cinnamon

1 tsp. nutmeg

1 tsp. baking powder

1 tsp. soda

½ tsp. salt

½ tsp. ginger

3 c. flour

3 c. zucchini

1 c. raisins

1 c. nuts

1 c. cooking oil

Mix all ingredients except flour, raisins, and zucchini in a large bowl. Beat at low speed 1 to 2 minutes, until smooth. Squeeze zucchini to remove excess juice and add to the mixture. Add flour and raisins, and stir until smooth. Bake at 350 degrees for 55 to 65 minutes.

Shirley Helman

Zucchini Nut Bread

3 c. sifted flour

1 tsp. baking soda

¼ tsp. baking powder

2 c. sugar

1 Tbsp. vanilla

1 tsp. flour

1 ½ tsp. ground cinnamon

1 tsp. salt

3 eggs

1 c. cooking oil

½ c. chopped walnuts

2 c. grated, un-pared or pared zucchini squash

Sift together 3 cups of flour, cinnamon, baking soda, salt and baking powder. Beat eggs well in a bowl. Gradually add sugar and oil, mixing well. Add vanilla and dry ingredients, blend well. Stir in zucchini. Combine walnuts with 1 teaspoon flour; stir into batter. Pour into 2 greased 8 ½ x 4 ½ x 2 ½ inch loaf pans. Bake at 350 degrees for 1 hour or until bread feels firm. Cool in pans on racks for 10 minutes. Remove from pans, cool on racks. Makes two loaves.

Sharon Sheffler

Alice, a family friend, gave this recipe to Grandma Hopewell several years ago. It has since become a family favorite.

Grandma's Molasses Cookies

½ cup butter

½ cup sugar

1 egg

½ cup molasses

½ cup buttermilk

2½ cups cake flour

1 tsp. baking soda

1 tsp. cinnamon

1 tsp. ginger

¼ tsp. cloves

¼ tsp. salt

½ cup raisins (optional)

Beat butter until soft and gradually add sugar and molasses until light and creamy. Beat in egg. Sift together dry ingredients. Add sifted ingredients in 3 parts to sugar and buttermilk, alternating each. Beat until smooth after each addition. Drop batter onto greased cookie sheet. Bake at 350 degrees for 8–12 minutes.

Another family friend, David, gave this recipe to Grandma Hopewell. The whole Hopewell family has enjoyed it many times over the years.

Frozen Banana S'more Dessert

2 cups graham crackers, crushed

1/3 cup butter, melted

2 to 3 bananas

13 oz. jar marshmallow fluff

2 qts. Neapolitan ice cream

1 cup heavy cream

½ tsp. freeze dried espresso

2 cups chocolate chips

1 tsp. vanilla

1 tub of whipped topping

1 cup graham crackers, crushed

1 cup nuts, chopped

15 maraschino cherries, placed evenly on top

Prepare graham cracker crust by pouring 1/3 cup melted butter over 2 cups graham crackers. Mix well. Spoon this mixture into the bottom of a 9 x 13 pan. Press down with a spoon. Slice bananas and lay over crust. Freeze until firm. Warm marshmallow fluff in microwave for 1 minute, then spread over frozen crust. Slice ice cream, ½ inch thick, and lay on top of marshmallow fluff. Return to freezer and freeze until firm. Next, pour heavy cream into a saucepan, add espresso and simmer for 20 minutes. Remove from heat. Add chocolate chips and vanilla. Allow mixture to cool enough not to melt the ice cream, but still be warm enough to spread. Freeze until ready to serve. Before serving, spread whipped topping over top. Sprinkle with 1 cup graham cracker crumbs over all. Sprinkle chopped nuts over all. Evenly place cherries on top. Cut and serve.

Serves 15

CONNECT WITH THE AUTHORS

Wendi's Works and Writings - The Encouraging Duo

 facebook.com/wendisworkswritings

Wendi Hartman - The Renaissance Writer

 facebook.com/wendiwrites8

Patricia Lewis - The Praising Lyricist

 facebook.com/encouragingduo

Website: wendiwrites.com

eGenCo

Generation Culture Transformation
Specializing in publishing for generation culture change

Visit us Online at:
www.egen.co

Email us at:
info@egen.co

 facebook.com/egenbooks

 twitter.com/egen_co

 youtube.com/egenpub

 pinterest.com/eGenDMP

 instagram.com/egen.co